Hyacinthus

L.Alarcón Miguel

Hyacinthus

First edition: December, 2024.

ISBN: 9798301834318

Text ©:

L. Alarcón Miguel.

© of the design of the cover of this edition:

Monika Alarcón Miguel.

Special acknowledgement to Nerea Díaz Martos and Ybernia SC.

And I will cry a thousand times when I write it, and countless times when I read it because this is my gratitude for when you saved me, turning me into the best person I could be, someone who manages to see through the dirt... I hope for a thousand more years where you find yourself by my side, so I can learn from you. Because I will follow you, Phoebus, I will follow you... I know you would do the same for me:

To the kind son of Leto, to Phoebus Apollo who wounds from afar.

Playlist

I listened to the following songs during the writing and editing process of this book. Every time they play, my mind flies to this little work you now hold in your hands.

Please note that this is an addition to the English edition, and exclusive to the second edition of this work.

Achilles Heel — J.Maya.

Apollo—Timebelle.

A thousand years — Christina Perri.

Back to you — Selena Gomez.

Born to Die – Lana del Rey.

Bring me to life — Evanescence.

Carry me — Eurielle.

City of the Dead—Eurielle.

Ego - Indila.

Euphoria—Loreen.

Fairytale — Alexander Rybak.

Gloomy Sunday — Billie Holiday.

Hate me — Eurielle.

Hold me closer — Cornelia Jakobs.

How to save a life — The Fray.

I am yours — Jason Mraz.

I tuoi particolari — Último.

If I die young — The Band Perry.

Impossible - James Arthur.

Je t'adore — Eurielle.

La stella piu fragile Dell' Universo — Último.

Mini world — Indila.

My immortal — Evanescence.

Pourquoi la mort te fait peur — Pomme.

Sad Song — We The Kings ft. Elena Coats.

Safe and sound — Taylor Swift.

Second Delphic Hymn to Apollo (the one from epiharmos on YouTube).

See you again — Carrie Underwood.

Skyfall - Adele.

SOS—Indila.

A year without seeing rain — Selena Gomez.

War of Hearts—Ruelle.

Wide Awake — Katy Perry.

Young and beautiful — Lana del Rey.

Dear reader,

I am writing to you to comment on a few notations of this work of mine. As you may have already figured out, the main idea behind this story is not my invention, but based on a myth that various classical writers wrote about in the past.

Thus, this work is based on the myth of Apollo and Hyacinth. Because of the many variants of this story, none of which can be asserted to be the correct one, there are different ways of telling the myth. I have tried to adapt everything from the works of all these writers, also following what my own soul and the beloved muses sang.

Hesiod, for example, talked about Hyacinth being prince of one of the two areas into which Sparta was divided. I agree wholeheartedly with this approach. Other writers are of the opinion that he was the son of Piero, king of Macedonia, and Clio, muse of history. Likewise, nothing is known about the first meeting between Apollo and the young Hyacinth, just as there are a thousand doubts about the true nature of his death.

Some argue that it was Apollo himself who, without the intervention of any creature, murdered Hyacinth, because while playing the discus, Phoebus threw it, and Hyacinth ran for it. As it fell it hit him on the head. Other variants say that it was the god Zephyrus, the west wind, who, jealous of the love between them, diverted the trajectory of the discus to kill Hyacinth. A few authors adopt this last version but changing Zephyr to Boreas. And a classic one states that Hyacinth killed himself due to his own clumsiness when throwing the discus, since apparently the young man caught well, but threw poorly.

So, because of so many variants, my Hyacinthus will be the son of a king, and the possibility is also open for the reader to decide if Clio is or is not his mother.

As one of the secondary characters, I selected Tamyris, who in some versions loved Hyacinthus. I also chose Polyboea, who was the prince's sister.

Regarding the gods of the winds, they will also be part of the work. However, I wanted to add something about these, thus avoiding misunderstandings:

Neither Zephyrus nor Boreas are vile creatures. If the present version of the story is true —something I do not doubt — both would act in such a way because of a force which is not in the hands of either of them: 'fate', controlled by the Moirai, who weave the destinies of beings. If the Moirai dictate that someone must do something, even when this is not typical of their personality, it will happen for some peculiar reason.

I warn of this, since, as it is the case with others — there is no better example than my beloved Hela, the Norse goddess upon whom Helya of Rhindanos is based — these gods have a much deeper history behind them, and their behaviours were modified throughout time either to justify mortal acts or to fulfil the wishes of destiny, as possibly happened with the story of Hyacinth.

Having explained this about the deities who, far from being horrendous, are the greatest wise men, I shall explain the etymology used in certain parts of the manuscript:

Although it would have been ideal to adopt Latinisms and various words of Greek origin to designate certain gifts or statuses, this has been an impossible mission. We are dealing with the area of Sparta, and little or nothing is preserved of the language apart from the Classical Greek spoken in Athens — the one that is usually taught at schools, which I myself have learnt — so whatever little vocabulary I have transcribed directly comes mostly from the language spoken in that region and not in the area where the events actually take place. Although some words could coincide in various parts of Ancient Greece, it is difficult to say for certain.

This work not only tells the myth of Hyacinth and Apollo, but at the end of the book you will find prose and verses dedicated to Phoebus Apollo, who wounds from afar.

And this ends my little letter. Enjoy, reader!

Sincerely,

Liam Alarcón Miguel.

PS: Forgive me for the small cover mistakes. I still don't understand everything to do with KDP and it is still giving us some mistakes we have fixed, but continue to fail.

.

I am not the one who writes, it is a powerful being that takes over my body, that moves my fingers, thus giving birth to words that very few could pronounce, much less write. I am a servant of the muses and of Apollo. They use my body as a medium to spread their melodies.

— *L. Alarcón Miguel.*

'Know yourself and you will know the gods and the universe.'

Sing to me, then, Muses, of when Gaia was young, and the gods united in matter with mortals!

Sing to me, then, Muses, the enormous unhappy love of Phoebus Apollo, who wounds from afar!

Sing to me, Oh Muses, with the purple flower between your lips and you will have given me everything I need!

Sing to me, O Calliope, Clio, Erato, Euterpe, Melpomene, Polyhymnia, Thalia, Terpsichore, Urania! Sing to me like on that day when we met by the sea! Sing to me too, Sappho of Mytilene, tenth muse and once most wise mortal; sing to me, then, the story of Hyacinthus and his beautiful immortal lover.

Foreword

Blood decorated the grounds, forming red rivers never created before.

This blood flowed down the slope of that singular hill, bathing everything in that bitter liquid that dragged the words and wishes of a short life that deserved to be eternal. The sounds of the voice could be heard, conversing in agonizing wait, so his beloved would not escape from his hands.

Had he been able to walk with him, the story would have changed, but could an immortal being be destined to die? Could an immortal being fall into the strong arms of Thanatos? If perhaps he had been able to board the boat with the soul of his beloved.... If the slightest possibility existed, he would have tried, but he understood it was in vain. That was not his fate. He would never know death, and true love would slip through his fingers with the breath of a light west wind.

Between his strong arms lay the body of a being whose last breaths escaped his lips. He stared into his eyes and understood that he could not look away from that other gaze, which read his soul, when not even the gods were capable of doing so. He looked into his eyes, he could not turn away, they read his soul that not even the gods themselves could comprehend.

His brown eyes resembled two puddles of honey, now that the sun's rays were shining fully on him. His smile would not leave his face, and Phoebus told himself that there was no curse as cruel and hostile as that one. There was no misfortune as great as the one he was experiencing in those moments.

And his body fell to the ground, without letting go of the future corpse of his lover. He touched the earth with his warm hands, and the river of blood gradually became larger, making furrows between his fingers. He avoided them, although despite this, they still caressed his skin. He would thus understand that the fates are already woven and that no one can discover them, not even the one who was and still is the god of prophecies.

He had neglected his divine tasks, due to the desire and longing to be next to such a fragile creature. Now that he saw him clearly, in his hands, attached to his bare chest, observing his soul bidding farewell to that life with bitter joy, he realized how weak the human being was. After all, they had been moulded from clay, and clay melts if water embraces it.

His curly hair created, from moonless nights, was soaked in reddish fluid. The life of the one who should have lived forever escaped through this thread.

He was crushed against his face with its noble and graceful features. The corner of his lips was still slightly bent. His last thoughts were still part of his mind, and his tears ran down his beautiful face. However, he was wrong, they were not simple tears, they were golden, and they came from other eyes that would never forget the being that waited in his arms, the being to whom he sang his verses, the creature to whom he dedicated the sound of his lyre.

The west wind continued to roar behind them. It seemed as though he was celebrating such a horrendous accident. Phoebus was certain that this was the case. He celebrated, he cheered, he probably laughed. If Hyacinthus was dead, it was his fault.

Blood of life, sleepy lover, the soul he had loved escaped from his hands. He did not deserve to be forgotten, to be lost in Hades, he deserved to live remembered for all eternity. Mortals had to pray to him, because a god had found true divinity in that fragile being.

If the world were fair, it would have changed its course. If the world were as Phoebus wished, Hyacinthus would never die, for the most beautiful things should never perish. Music would never die, nor would poetry. And if Hyacinthus was anything, he was the purest art found on Earth.

And the blood that flowed from his body reminded Apollo that he should hurry, because soon his soul would be lost in the place to which they were all heading. He could not deify him, even if he wanted to, since his slow heartbeat threatened to stop completely. He held, therefore, the future corpse of art. He was holding, then, the future skeleton of Hyacinthus, whose soul would soon descend into the kingdoms of his uncle. A memory of the eternal love that he thought he had, and the fact is that the gods, being immortal, do not realize that death exists for some.

From the blood that ran through the hillside, from the soul that escaped from that set of skin and bones, he would create something that flourished every second, something to look at and remember. Humans would not forget it either.

From his essence, he made a flower with purple petals spring up. The most beautiful of them all. A plant that represented Hyacinthus, the one that would never be forgotten.

And creating this new species he repeatedly murmured the winged words that lie here:

'Remember our beginnings. Listen to the singing of the music. It's still there. From when you were just a child, and I was a god who looked out over the cornice. Hyacinthus, remember the songs of spring if you still appreciate them, don't let them leave your side! Feel the sun caressing your naked skin, in the knowledge that it shines and will shine for you when your heart cannot resist. Feel the warm breeze of the seas that surround us at the end of the day in those summers of immense mastery. Listen to the wind. It blows slowly, tearing off the leaves when summer ends, and autumn approaches with clandestine lights. Think of the cold winters in front of the brazier, where the fire crackled on the wood.

'And now look into my eyes, and remember our strange beginning, my prince. Remember the paths we travelled side by side, you holding my hand. Were they not the best moments we could have ever experienced? And I have lived too much. If I could give you a few more years, a few more days, a few more minutes, or simply some moments in which to say goodbye, I would do so in a heartbeat. Sprout on the slopes, display your purple petals, and make no one forget you. Make them remember you as I will every dawn when I wake up. Paint the world purple, may the vile Zephyr regret having diminished you. You who shine by yourself, may not even the coldest of years keep you silent!'

In that moment, he caressed his face looking for the last time through those windows surrounded by a thousand flowers that represented him, immortalizing his legacy.

His vision was going out of focus, lost forever, and Apollo cried like he had never done before.

'Remember that I love you, and I will never stop doing so. Nor will I forget your life, your smile, or your thousands of joys, for you were once the reason why the sun rose every day.'

Tears soaked the nascent flower, and these would remain engraved in it until the end of time.

I

'Hyacinthus!'

He looked up from the parchment that lay in front of him. He had tried to write a hymn praising the beauty of Gaia, in an attempt to go unnoticed among his relatives, but it was clear that it had been in vain.

His father watched him, clenching his jaw tightly. He seemed to want to yell at him, but at the same time he wished to remain calm. A thousand diverse emotions and feelings were written in his eyes, in that dark look that he himself had inherited. A thousand and one different emotions that he could have name if he had wished. Human emotions were so simple that they just seemed to have their feelings engraved with signs of bitterness.

In the middle of that semi-detached patio, with the firm rays of the rising sun illuminating their faces, his father's crown, which seemed to be made of laurel, shone like it had never done before.

His skin, polished from the time exposed to daylight, gave even more seriousness to his already regal face. His hard features were forced to look even harsher, and the shine of his tunic fabric gave no other noun to the wind than that of king. King of a small place, not of an important place, but king, nonetheless.

And that young man, who was his son, seemed little more than a child. A child who did not obey even when he was reprimanded. But what could he do if the conversations his father had in the yard were never interesting? Much worse were those that usually took place in the *andron*, which Hyacinthus was forced to attend. Sometimes he wished he was his sister. She had little to worry about. Although he also understood that her life could be complex, even though she was a princess.

His gaze, immersed in the starless, moonless nights, examined Hyacinthus, and silently, without saying a word, begged him to behave. Both in front of the rest of his family, as well as the members of his army. But he was behaving in the only way he knew how to.

The father did not want him to only listen and not participate in the small conversation that had started just a couple of minutes before. His duty was to speak in such talk. He had to be the military strategist that the son of a king had to be. He must have looked like the son of Athena, but the young man was not even an Athenian, and he was sure that not even a hint of her golden blood ran through his veins. So, in order not to disappoint his father, his sister, or the slaves who were either working or waiting for the next orders that would escape his lips, he had decided to do something that he was not at all bad at. But of course, it was not enough for his father.

What was the point of having a male child if he was to dedicate himself to the arts, sports, and had no notion of politics or even the art of the military? Perhaps if he had not come from a family with royal blood, it would have been enough, it would have been sufficient, but nothing was. And he was not going to waste his time on things he could not control.

So, his reaction was nothing other than to shrug his shoulders and lower his eyes. He returned his attention to his verses, to his writing, to the beautiful calligraphy he possessed. He returned to the world he created through words. He returned to the enormous praise he dedicated to Gaia.

And the sigh that escaped from the implacable figure of his father confirmed the thoughts that were in his mind. Those which claimed that the king must be disgusted by the offspring he had fathered.

'Hyacinthus.' His voice unfocused him again.

'What do you want, Father?' He asked without even taking his eyes off the parchment. The pen was still in his hand and, until the ink ran out, he would not stop.

Upon hearing this, the father continued speaking using winged words that went like this:

'I was telling you and the rest of the house that someone important is coming for lunch. A person who wishes to meet you, my son.' Hyacinthus rolled his eyes. It was the last thing he wanted to hear.

He understood that the person who wanted to see him was either a woman who wanted to be a princess with the slightest possibility of becoming a queen if her brothers died after the father of the family did, or a teacher who would truly instruct him in the art of the military, something that he certainly did not find very interesting.

'I'm glad,' he said, because it seemed like his father was praying to all the gods for him to respond. And he knew well that they would ignore him. After all, along with enjoying misfortunes, that was all gods did.

His sister tried hard to hide the smile that had appeared on her face when she heard those two words, said with as much bitterness as irony.

Polyboea was her name. And she was endowed with immense beauty. She had a clear and clean look, which denoted intelligence, one that Hyacinthus believed he lacked. Her eyes were two blue pearls, like two cavities that overlook a pair of inland lakes where everything was clear, the waters of the Aegean Sea caressed by the winter breeze. Her straight hair was a brown similar to that of falling leaves in autumn. And the features of her face were not extremely soft, but hard like those of her brothers, though it was a beautiful, beautiful harshness, as if it hid something else. It seemed as though the young girl had been caressed by mystery itself. The light that her eyes transmitted... A thousand times they had asked the king if she was the daughter of a goddess. If perhaps she was the daughter of a daughter of Zeus, and the good father always responded the same: 'She is my daughter and her mother's.'

That answer, said by the powerful and deep voice of a king, was usually enough to silence the gossip. However, Hyacinthus was not surprised that people asked. He doubted he was half as beautiful, or even half as virtuous, as she was. He seriously thought that it should have been her soul that inherited the entire paternal fortune.

The man looked at her with a hard expression, but he immediately softened. She generated that type of reaction in souls. Without realizing it, the corners of their lips seemed to want to smile.

'I think Hyacinthus is quite fed up with these visits he is forced to attend, right?' she asked suddenly.

'That's right, my sister.'

'Well, I'm afraid you can't escape,' the father told him seriously. 'Maybe it would be good for you to go out and exercise. That way you will keep your mind busy.'

After that and without waiting for a response, he prepared to leave. However, his daughter's voice stopped him:

'Father, where are you going?' His gaze seemed empty. If anyone should disconnect, it was the father of the family.

'I have to meet with several people. Excuse me, my children.' Again, he did not wait. He just left.

The young woman's eyes locked onto her brother's.

'Rejoice!' She said with a wide smile on his face.

'Why should I?' He asked while his sister took his hands and caressed them lovingly.

'Because I have seen the man who wants to see you.'

'You've *seen* him? Can you explain that to me?'

'No, I haven't had any vision. Those kinds of things never happen to me. I guess Apollo didn't choose me for it. I have actually seen that man with my own eyes.'

'Where?'

'A couple of weeks ago. He came with the excuse of meeting our father.'

'You're talking about a man, right?' She nodded. 'So that means I don't have any suitors yet. Unless that man wants to talk to me so that I can unite with his daughter under Hera's penetrating gaze.'

'I don't know what he wanted, since he and Father spoke privately. But I would risk saying that it was not about marriages. I can tell you that that man was very young, apart from being incredibly beautiful.'

'If it was a couple of weeks ago... Why are you telling me now? Why didn't Father tell me anything? And where was I? Could it possibly be that that individual you speak of passed by me and I did not even notice?'

'Why so many questions, Hyacinthus?' Her brother looked at her quite seriously. She simply laughed, amused. 'I don't think it's something very worrying, so get that wrinkled expression off your face, because in the end you're going to look like Father!' The sweet and pleasant tone she had used caused Hyacinthus's features to relax.

'Alright. I will smile more if you explain to me what you know.'

'I'm telling you now because it's clear that the visitor that Father is talking about must be him. Besides, it seemed very silly to tell you when I didn't even know if it was going to turn out well... Do you remember when Tamyris invited you to that horse ride where you discovered that, despite being a great musician, he was an inexperienced rider?' He nodded. 'Well, it was during that shameful day for poor Tamyris that it happened.' Polyboea was able to project every little detail of the encounter in her mind. 'And that man was so epic that it would have been impossible to separate him from your being... What radiant and powerful energy he transmitted! If he seemed anything but human! I was here in the patio, talking with some of our slaves about the new tragedies that will be represented in the warm months, when suddenly he appeared walking between the columns with an immensely gifted smile, like a thousand diamonds drawn on his face.

'He had golden hair. It gave the impression that it was bathed in gold, so much so that the sun's rays seemed like simple dust. His eyes were light, although I couldn't tell you the exact color. His skin was tanned as if he were a warrior, or perhaps a hunter, but I swear to you that he was endowed with the beauty of the most beautiful of kings. So, when he burst into our patio, accompanied by the loyal Adelphos, I knew that this man had great goals in mind, because he walked with enormous confidence and determination, as if he knew he would achieve whatever he set out to do.

'Honestly, at first, when he walked towards me, I thought he was going to ask for Father, whether it was about a matter of kings, or a matter of marriage. But to my surprise he didn't say anything about Father, not in the first place at least. He introduced himself with a huge smile and told us without even saying his name and with some beautiful, winged words: "I hope you are enjoying this wonderful morning. If you are wondering why I am here, I will tell you: I wish to meet the one I know to be your brother, Hyacinthus." After that, he added the following: "Could you tell me where your father is, dear Polyboea?" You don't know how surprised I was that he knew my name. It was as if he knew me perfectly, as if he had always seen me. With that in mind, I got to thinking. We never knew mother well, maybe he was her younger brother. I don't know, but I think I'm mistaken. Be that as it may, I told him that Father was on his way, and that at that time you were not at home, so the young man waited. He didn't have to do much, since a few minutes later, Father entered the yard. The slaves had told him that there was a young, unknown man looking for him. They both greeted each other and went to chat somewhere alone. I haven't dared to ask Father, nor do I think it's any of my business, but I suppose the visit will be this man's.'

'Why are you so sure, Polyboea?' He asked, looking up completely from the parchment. The pen rested on it, and the ink it still contained fell softly without making a sound.

'Because I saw it, Hyacinthus,' she replied. Her eyes shone with immense intensity. 'I saw it. And I know that man is today's visitor. I know, because I looked right into his soul when he came here two weeks ago. He had determination in that look of his, and he looked so handsome.'

'Have you fallen in love with him?'

The young woman crossed her arms upon hearing these words, thus quickly removing her hands from her brother's. Her face, previously immersed in joy, became serious.

'No,' she snapped. 'Falling in love is not as simple as watching a beautiful man walk through the halls of one's home. Falling in love goes much further than that, and I am sure that neither you nor I will know that feeling, at least not in its entirety. So, no. That's my answer. I'm not in love with him. I'm just saying what people say, what my being dictated the first time I saw him. That man, Hyacinthus, is someone great. I saw it in his eyes. And if I make a mistake and it's not someone important, it's because he's not important yet, but he will be. You don't see a person like that every day, and Hyacinthus, he was looking for you. I'm sure he's not from these lands. Perhaps he has travelled for long days to get here, so that he could speak to Father about you, even though he might not have been able to receive him. That man waited a short time, because the king whom he came to visit rushed to appear, but if that had not been the case, I am aware that he would have spent the night outdoors just to see you and talk to Father.'

'Alright. I trust your words. You haven't fallen in love with him, ergo you don't want him to trust you so that he can be closer to us, being in turn closer to you in the hope that he feels something for you.'

'Of course not. Besides, he was looking for you. Even if I had been interested beyond how curious I was because of his presence, he wouldn't have even seen me, much less spoken to me if I weren't your sister.'

The young man with curly hair looked at her for a few moments in complete silence. After that, he raised his eyebrow slightly and concern suddenly took centre stage on his face.

'And tell me, Polyboea, you who are usually right and see the objectives of others with immense clarity, why do you think he was looking for me?'

His sister looked down. She remained thoughtful for a time which seemed eternal to Hyacinthus. Although he already knew the answer.

Polyboea was, therefore, one of the most intelligent girls in those parts, since she was a very studious person. She read a lot about history and had come to understand at a very early age that history always repeats itself. The knowledge acquired based on her studies in this field had also helped her analyse the situations she experienced on a daily basis. Thus, she could imagine in great detail the next movements of the people around her. Like history, the human mind, despite being different in each individual, always remained attached to the same things, resulting in a repetition of events.

'I think he must be a former student of one of those schools that exist now. Those that educate in different subjects.'

'But that's nonsense. I already have my teachers for the vast majority of disciplines, and I don't need one to teach me even more things. If I want to learn, I will be the one who goes to the teachers, and not the teachers to me.'

'I know, Hyacinthus. I would also think the same but think about Father... Think about our home. The people need leaders who not only know how to play sports, write poetry, compose music, history and philosophy. The people need real leaders. Ones that flow through all disciplines and never fail in any.'

'That's what our older brothers are for! You tell me to think about Father!' The words were formulated by his lips in a soft, almost inaudible whisper. 'Are you telling me, Polyboea, that you think that father has contacted some kind of school focused, possibly, on militancy, to that I learn to be like him? Are you telling me that this man I will meet today is a former student or perhaps even a teacher whom Father has paid?'

'It's simply a hypothesis. It would be very possible. Perhaps they exchanged heralds, since our messenger has been going out very often for quite a few months now. This would prove why he knew my name, and yours. If this hypothesis is false, how would he know our names?'

41

'We are princes, everyone knows our names.'

Polyboea rolled her eyes.

'Do you think the common people care what our names are? They may have heard our names, but they don't know them.'

He looked away from his sister's clear eyes, focusing on the plants growing around the various columns as if they could tell him something interesting.

He could simply not understand the concern that his father had regarding his strategic gifts. Could he not, then, entrust that part of his reign to someone who was really qualified? For example, one of his brothers. He firmly thought that the military arts had to come naturally, and that they could not be learned. He was not a strategist. It was the only requirement of being king that he did not meet. And despite being the only one, he felt ashamed and angry with himself. His father could not have given up on him so quickly.

'Do you have any other hypotheses?'

'Yeah, do you want to hear it?' The young man nodded.

'Please.'

'Maybe he came on his own,' she began to say. 'Perhaps he does not belong to any institution, but is another prince, or perhaps a young king or member of an important family who wants to help you in some way. Maybe he wants you as his personal ward. It wouldn't be completely strange, nor would it be the first time it happened.' She paused. 'Hyacinthus, if something is talked about in our lands, perhaps even beyond these, it is that you are very handsome. Maybe he wanted to confirm it with his own eyes. Maybe he's simply an orphan and his sister needs a husband.' By now she had got the attention of her brother, who was looking at her resting his head on his hand. 'Perhaps he wants to marry you to her so that his kingdom will see that he is not weak. A pretty good strategy… Look, Hyacinthus, sometimes my hypotheses make a lot of sense, but then they turn out to be false. Other times, they are far-fetched, and then they are in fact not far from reality. With this I want to tell you that I really don't know what that man wants from you, but I know that Father loves us. He would never do anything to put us in danger. And if that guest is the man I'm telling you about, he won't cause us any kind of problem. I promise you.'

The young prince smiled tenderly upon hearing such winged words.

'Thank you, Polyboea.'

43

II

He walked through that kind of forest, feeling the wet earth under the sole of his shoes.

His face had a brief reddish hue, because of the effort he had been making. Despite this, he did not want to return home. After all, a stranger was waiting for him who could change the course of his destiny. If he was honest, he would have admitted out loud that he was afraid. He felt fear even though his good and talented sister had told him not to, that the presence of that spirit he had not yet seen would bring nothing bad. But her words mattered little if he continued being scared.

He knew that fear was not a bad thing, quite the opposite. It told a person that they were on the right path, that they had courage, because without it no one would ever face situations that would bring them a certain amount of dread. Instead, he didn't know how to feel. He still held tightly between his fingers the wood of his javelin, with which he had practiced for a couple of hours, among other sports disciplines. He would have preferred for today's activity to be riding. At the very least, he would have forced himself to swallow his own nervousness so as not to affect his horse. But it was not to be and, in a way, he understood it.

Beads of sweat fell down his face, but it was still just as beautiful. His dark hair endowed with curls, coloured by the very gathering darkness, lay somewhat flattened. His tanned face was tense, but the beauty that he was said to possess remained. His brown eyes were illuminated by the sun's rays and gave the impression of being made of copper.

He sighed lightly, as he tried to calm his mind. His gaze was lost in what lay in front of him. He told himself that this was the only way he could breathe again. The only way to return home calmly to face whatever the uncertain fate had in store for him.

The north air seemed to blow. He said to himself that Boreas might be watching him:

'Poor little boy,' he would say, or maybe he would just laugh at him.

Perhaps Artemis was in that mountain, hunting with her entourage of oceanic girls. If they exchanged a glance, she might kill him to spare him suffering.

Hyacinthus was sure that the gods existed. He felt them under his feet, in the air, and in every creature, tree or rock. He knew they were real, but he also understood that they didn't listen to mortals, and who would, if not even mortals were able to listen to each

45

other? Thus, any help or warning from the gods beyond the various oracles was null and void in his reality, and he was certain that it was also null and void in that of others.

To him, Apollo seemed to be, due to the fact that he had a pythoness as a fortune teller for the world, one of the more acceptable gods, but despite this he did not know why the god committed certain acts. He didn't care about the answer either.

The icy breeze seemed to surround him, and the clarity of the sky that filtered between branches turned the firmament into something similar to a sea, which instead of below was above the world, covering it with its mantle. The leaves of the trees, which never changed, shook, generating the sensation that they would fall, but the young man knew well that that would not happen. And the sounds of wildlife conveyed messages to his soul. None of them seemed dangerous.

He would not have been surprised if, in the midst of that restorative silence, he had heard a flute rising through all the territories of the known world and the one yet to be discovered. He would not have been surprised if he had been able to hear the nymphs singing endless ballads or, perhaps, odes to the infinite beauty of the place they lived in. Nor if he had seen a dryad escape from its leaves or trunk, in order to dance the dance of the end of times, which would not even stop when the end of the world would come.

His body felt so tired! Not so much because of the exercise performed, but because of the tension that the nerves produced. As a result, he couldn't resist lying down among the soft grass:

He put his javelin aside. He knew that no one was around those parts, and he trusted that the animals had not yet learned to use an instrument like that in the correct way. He untied the strings of the sandals he had decided to wear that morning. He left these next to the javelin. And finally, he removed the clothes that covered this body.

He felt free without the constraints of clothing. Without having to support the weight of his athletic body, simply focusing on the energy that emanated from the ground, on the earth that caressed him, on the birds that did not want to extinguish their perfect melody... And on the rays of the sun that touched his body, passing through his skin and reaching his naked soul.

He would have been an easy target if there had been a war, but it mattered little. Immense joy invaded him because of such audaciousness.

He closed his eyes to immerse himself in the memories:

He travelled back, remembering everything he could have lost. It wasn't blood that ran through his veins, but joy. A joy so immense that the world would have never stopped laughing had it drank from it.

He was seven years old and was naked on a plain whose limits he could not see with his own eyes. He played with the other children, and for once, everything seemed strangely natural. They played ball games which, without their understanding, would help them mould their physical form until they reached what was required.

From time to time, he looked up, searching with his eyes for his other siblings, especially Polyboea. He used to find her right away in front of him, with that smile plastered on her face, illuminating the lives of those who knew her. She grabbed the ball in her hands with agility when it was her turn, but also with gentleness.

He admired Sparta for that very reason. There, women could also do things that were not allowed in other places. He remembered having met a girl in those days who turned out to be the best of all those her age, she was even better than older boys. He would have liked to have known more about her, about how the years had treated her, but he had never seen her again. He perfectly remembered her dark hair, vaguely the features of her face, and that eagle look that many before had commented was impossible to find in a woman, but she had it.

Nothing was impossible. Every day, every hour, every minute, every second that passed made him more aware of that.

At times, he felt like he had lost a lot by having the father he had, although on the other hand he preferred him. Otherwise, everything would have been completely different. And different could have been synonymous with good, or perhaps its antonym. He would never know. In his opinion, it wasn't worth thinking about either, since it would never come to be.

Suddenly, while he continued thinking with his eyes closed, he noticed how the direction of the wind changed. Boreas had stopped blowing. The leaves no longer whispered his call, nor did the trunks creak because of him. For a moment, he thought the birds had stopped singing his praises.

Carefully, he began to move his arm away from his body, trying blindly to find the javelin. He felt a presence above him, watching him. It seemed to examine him. He thought about praying to Ares to protect him, but soon put that out of his mind. Ares didn't care what happened to him. Of that, he was sure. If he had to fight, it would be he who would save himself, not any deity.

As his fingers closed around the hard wood, he stood up abruptly and opened his eyes. Without even thinking, he attacked.

A strong hand stopped his assault. The gentle west breeze blew, replacing the icy north wind. A greyish gaze with a slight silver tinge was staring at him steadily.

'You're fast, but you haven't used enough force.' He told him with a mocking smile that didn't please Hyacinthus at all.

'Do you know who I am?'

'Do *you* know who I am?'

The young man looked at him hard for a few moments, examining him in depth.

He looked like a full-grown adult already. He estimated that he was about thirty-four years old. His hair was very dark blonde, if that could still be considered blonde. It got darker until reaching brown at the tips. He had a very short and well-groomed beard. His gaze was sometimes silver, other times it was endowed with a simple storm grey.

The features of his face denoted seriousness. He gave the impression of being someone important. This, added to the question the man had just asked him, made it very likely that this was the case.

Despite being dressed, you could see at a glance that he was in shape. He had muscular arms, and the veins in them were marked, since he had not yet released the javelin. Hyacinthus knew right away that he could have taken it away from him in the blink of an eye. If he wanted him dead, it was taking him a long time to do so.

The prince snorted.

Words were about to leave his lips, until he realized the way the opponent was looking at him. So, he simply turned around, and quickly got dressed.

'I wonder what the prince is doing naked under the sun's rays in this mediocre place with a simple javelin as an escort.'

Hyacinthus had his back to him, and was fixing his clothes in order to put on his shoes.

'I will be more direct than you. What's a man like you doing walking around here and stopping to watch a young man?'

'It's rare to see people with your lineage naked.'

'Please, address me the right way.' He snapped as he turned around, looking at him in the eyes.

Coldness was reflected in the young man's gaze, and the other man seemed to understand it.

'Please accept my apologies' he said. He wasn't used to saying that kind of thing. 'We've got off to a bad start. I approached you, sir, because I honestly believed something catastrophic had happened to you.'

'It still seems peculiar to me that I did not hear you arrive, but nevertheless, I sincerely thank you for your concern. However, as you have already seen, I feel perfectly fine. I was just resting from a short, yet hard, training session.'

He looked up at the sun, and seeing that it was approaching its highest point, he let go of his side of the javelin, beginning to walk. Hyacinthus was struck by the fact that the gentle movement of the west wind remained behind him.

The stranger, none other than the god Zephyrus, who, fascinated by the prince, had decided to meet him in person, walked behind him.

'Hyacinthus, your javelin,'he said.

The young man stopped with enormous skill. The god did not understand how someone was capable of doing something so simple in such a hypnotizing way.

'You can keep it if you want,' he replied. 'I have more.'

Zephyrus walked until he was at his level.

'I insist. Take your javelin, it's yours for a reason.'

'I'm not stupid, sir.'

'I did not say otherwise.'

'Of course you did not say it, but I look into your eyes and I know your intentions. Keep it. Maybe instead of spying on me, the next time you want to see me you can use it as an excuse.'

'Are you sure of what you're saying?' He nodded.

'I am. Have a good day! Maybe we'll see each other sooner than expected.'

And with those words, the handsome Hyacinthus resumed his way home. Zephyrus did not insist, he simply turned into a wind, which caressed the prince's body with his warm hands, now turned into a breeze. He, who was just as intelligent as his sister, felt the hair on his neck stand on end due to the breath. He turned around suddenly, and he could no longer see the stranger who had dared to look at him naked as he dozed under the morning sun.

He assumed that he had gone off along some path that led through the quiet forest. He wanted to believe that Polyboea had not exaggerated when describing him, and that this handsome man would turn out to be the one they had talked about after Eos, the pink-fingered one, had cut the morning Uranus.

III

That young man with a splendid look walked on earth. He understood humans, and also the creatures that dared to look at him. He understood the beauty of the world, although he had a certain contempt for the gods. But he didn't care much.

He watched every movement Hyacinthus made. He watched over him as he crossed the sky with his golden chariot. He transformed into wind when night came, simply to listen to his words. Those same ones that he recited under the immense full moon whenever there was a Selene day.

He slept next to him, even when he didn't know it. There was so much beauty, so much intelligence, so many virtues that reigned in him, that from the first moment Apollo, who hurts from afar, felt attracted to his person.

He was so young, but so wise. He was so beautiful! Because that was the true word to define it: He was art. The same art that Apollo represented for mortals.

It seemed incredible that a god like him had been able to find such emotions at the expense of a simple mortal who would die in minutes. A fragile creature made of clay.

Even rain could kill that creature, Apollo didn't even need a pandemic. Just simple rain. Cold storms that could penetrate through his flesh and reach his bones, turning them into ice.

He didn't need anything more than a simple fall. One hit on the head with a rock, and it would be over.

They were simple and weak by nature, that's how Prometheus had made them. But now Apollo understood what the latter had managed to see in them. He saw all those positive qualities that defined the human being in a young man who sometimes even doubted his existence. A young man who, despite having the opportunity, refused to receive Delphic verses. A young man who was just that: a young man, who yesterday was a baby, and tomorrow would be an old man.

He knew very well the evil that could harbour the heart and soul of human beings, since he was often in charge of punishing them. All the diseases, all the epidemics that they suffered had been launched from his bow. But all that seemed to fade from his mind every time he saw that boy. Every time he smiled, he couldn't help but be cheerful. Every time Hyacinthus was happy about some achievement, Apollo felt that happiness twofold.

There was so much love gradually growing inside him that he was unable to imagine a life in which Hyacinthus no longer walked through Gaia's rocky body. Although he knew well that a mortal's life was a simple sigh in his own existence, an instant, a blink of an eye, a sneeze, or perhaps a sketch.

He did not care. That was the truth. He didn't care that it was an instant, and that the next second he would no longer find him. He didn't care about his fragility, nor his stubbornness. He didn't care that Hyacinthus didn't trust him. He didn't care that he didn't understand his decisions... Hyacinthus could have provoked him, and he wouldn't have hurt him, he wouldn't even ruffle his hair. As a prophetic god, he was the one who best understood that we had to live in the present, because the past was no longer there and the future sometimes turned out to be dark verses narrated by his beloved fortune teller. It wasn't worth asking about it, especially with respect to a mortal. He wasn't blinded enough yet to ignore the fact that he would die.

But there he was, and there he had been since he discovered the existence of that life that bloomed like the most beautiful of roses.

He had seen how people looked at him, including that musician who was trying to seduce him. Personally, Apollo had to control himself so as not to stick a poisoned arrow into his heart. Love was eating him up inside. He was incapable of not sharing it, of not making Hyacinthus see how many mixed feelings his presence caused in him. He could not stop, much less when he discovered Zephyr, the west wind, hovering around the young prince.

He had not spoken with him, but he would not allow his young man—whom he already considered his lover —to be corrupted by someone like that. He knew that it would hurt him, because Apollo understood that the love he felt towards Hyacinthus was nothing but true love; however, neither Aphrodite nor her son, Eros, used to make it easy. And Apollo, even in that archaic time, had a long list of romantic misfortunes.

With Hyacinthus, it would be different. He knew it. He wouldn't force him to fall in love with him, nor would he kidnap him. He would make the young man give him his heart, and if he wanted it firmly, he would turn him into a constellation as a divinity, or simply grant him immortality so they could be together forever.

If the gods, who are simply pure soul, had hearts, Apollo was sure that the prince of Sparta would have his in his hands.

The words he found to define what he felt did not do justice to what was really happening inside him. It was the dance of the leaves in autumn, the snows in the highlands of winter, the rebirth of flowers in spring, the storms of summer, and it also brought a certain instability and growing insecurity. That same thing that humans must have felt when one of their poisoned arrows hit their cities with funereal diseases. It was a lump in his throat, as well as butterflies fluttering nervously in his stomach.

He knew he was walking a tightrope devoid of all his powers and abilities, but when he looked at him, it no longer mattered.

He could have stayed in the known safety of the heights, on Olympus watching the one he loved from afar and imagining him close. He could have transformed into a star or looked down from his golden chariot and stop in the arc it made. He could have turned into a warm morning breeze and could have caressed his soft skin, or perhaps simply found himself at his side in a way that mortal eyes are not usually able to see, hear, much less feel... he could have descended, in this way, imagining a life in which Hyacinthus could see him, touch him, feel him, while he composed a thousand verses dedicated to the young man.

But no. It seemed unfair to him, and unfair to himself. Why imagine if you could do it in real life? Why imagine if he was just a snap of the fingers away from making it a reality? Why imagine if he was a god and for these there were no defined limits!

Why imagine if Zephyr surpassed him in this romantic game that no one else apart from Apollo should win? Why imagine if you could make it happen?

And with these unsettling questions gradually running through his mind, he decided that he would do it.

He would have to meet him. He would give him the love he felt, and he would fall in love with him in return, like the stars were with the moon. He knew that their feelings would soon be mutual. He sensed it in all its essence. He also noticed a disturbing tragedy that surrounded him, a misfortune that hovered around him, a misfortune like many before! However, the love was so strong, the romance so strong, the emotion so immense, that it overwhelmed his senses. It blinded him like his presence blinded mortals. He didn't want to listen to it, so he didn't.

And the day before visiting the boy's home, he approached his muses for advice.

They all looked at him very surprised when he confessed what he felt, when Apollo opened his entire being to them, showing them what he had found in a simple mortal.

None of them recommended it:

'You know what happens with this type of events, Apollo, sir.'

'Just consult the endings of your tragic loves. If they know you as *Apollo, unhappy in love*, it's for a reason.'

Apollo told them in response that, with Hyacinthus, history would change.

'It won't change, and you know it as well as we do,'they said then.

They all spoke expressing their disagreement. They did not want to ruin their companion's hopes, but they wanted to make him see that it was not worth spending time with a mortal, that in the best of cases he would reject him, and in the worst... They left that to the imagination of Leto's son. All of them except Clio, muse of history.

She kept her lips sealed at all times, and when Apollo noticed her, he approached her with care and immense stealth.

'Clio, you are the only one who has not given your opinion, do you think the same as them?' The god of the arts and a thousand other spheres of influence, had listened carefully to the words of his friends and colleagues, who often acted as advisors, and he had really come to consider that perhaps they were right, since his plan was a very far-fetched one; however, he wanted to listen to all of them, Clio included.

'Come with me, Phoebus, please.'

So, the god cast a farewell look at his other companions and began to walk alongside Clio.

He considered her a very important part of his team, since history always ended up repeating itself. It contained great knowledge about the past, and unintentionally, also about the future.

'You're talking about Hyacinthus,'she said, using the informality that the muses were accustomed to when they spoke privately with Apollo. You speak of Hyacinthus, son of war, prince of Sparta. Do you know what he's facing? He's a great thinker, and he's interested in history, so I know him pretty well. However, he does not seem to want to risk his life in his name, or mine, or for any of us. He wouldn't even risk his life in his father's name. Maybe for his homeland.'

'I know. I live in that knowledge. I have been watching him for a while too.'

'We've all realized it, but we honestly believed you wouldn't cross the line. Descending to the world of mortals to spy on a very handsome young man disguised as a wind or a bird, I'll accept it, but descending as a human or possessing human appearance... Making him fall in love with you... Where could that lead? And who gave you that disastrous idea?'

'I'll be honest with you, Clio, I'm not the only one who is after Hyacinthus,' he responded.

'I imagine. He is endowed with great attractiveness, mortals cannot...'

'I mean, I'm not the only deity interested.' He interrupted her in a terribly polite and delicate way. It was as though Clio was a crystal and Apollo a hammer that threatened to destroy her walls.

The muse's eyes shone with a fury that Apollo could not explain, since it barely lasted a moment. Maybe it hadn't even been visible. If he hadn't paid attention, it would have gone amiss.

'Who? It's not Zeus, is it? Because if that's the case, you don't have to be Athena or have half of her wisdom to be able to see that it is better to turn away.'

'No. It is not my father,' he replied. His gaze was lost in the horizon. 'It is Zephyr. At first, I believed that Boreas had something to do with it, assuming he is not also interested. I do not want my Hyacinthus to be courted by a mere mortal musician like Tamyris, but I wish much less for a minor deity to think themselves powerful enough to win the heart of art itself. Zephyr knows that I watch him with great enthusiasm. He knows that sometimes a part of me haunts him, lost in his soul. He also does it and only the Moiras know how long he's been doing it for, but he wants to get ahead of me. Soon he will make Hyacinthus notice him. If he can, so can I, and rightly so.'

'Zephyr does not have a long list of loves that ended in tragedy. Apollo, would you risk that?'

'The worst thing that ever happened to me was that Daphne rejected me, running away from me, but I won't make the same mistake this time, Clio,' he answered with complete sincerity. 'I had a vision about him a while ago. That's why I know that our love is mutual, or at least it will be if time is true, if it didn't end when Cronus was banished.'

'What was happening in that vision, Apollo? What did you see?'

A wide smile was drawn on the face of the most beautiful god of all:

'I didn't feel the wind or even the breeze surrounding us under the beautiful firmament that was still dark and illuminated with the

64

light of its stars, creating a sombre night without a moon, yet endowed with the same mystery that all of them possess.

'Hyacinthus was in front of me, with that beautiful face of his, his smile was splendid. And I swear to you, Clio, I swear to you by all my spheres of influence, and even by my mere existence, that he shone brighter than all the stars. His eyes, made of blackness, had a slight purple hue, although it is impossible, but that's how I saw it and I am telling you exactly what I saw. We were talking. Don't ask me what we said because if I could hear him, I didn't give it any importance, because I had him before my eyes and he was looking at me, returning my gaze. He saw me and even caressed me. His icy hands touched mine in an instant that seemed eternal, and then they became warm.

'Suddenly, the scene became different: We were kissing in a golden dawn. I felt his fragile body close to mine, and his hair was messy and lost between my hands. There was a soft breeze coming from the west, and tears between cries of misfortune... It was Zephyr, who realized that he had lost. He had lost the mortal he loved, and immersed in bitterness, he forcefully lashed our clothed bodies, although our souls were naked and lacked any mystery that the other one ignored. I noticed it, Clio. I noticed that our love was the purest. Not a romantic one, nor a sexual one, but all kinds of love united in two completely different beings. One destined to live forever and the other to die, and isn't that the most twisted thing that fate and the Moiras themselves have woven?

'Suddenly, we found ourselves in the vast field in the late light of day. I spoke to him and told him the truth. I told him what my true identity was. He didn't go crazy, he wasn't even surprised, and when I asked him he responded with immense confidence and wisdom: "I already knew."

'This image, this memory of the future, because that is what it is, my future, his, ours, faded very easily, and as soon as I could imagine we were on a plain, varnishing our bodies. Now yes, without any ties, just showered in vine oils. We had a disc in our hands, like those mortals use. We were talking about playing and after his harmonious voice accompanied by a look bathed in the green grass, everything became dark. I heard a voice whose words I did not understand. It looked familiar to me, but I couldn't decipher it. However, it was not his, since it was feminine, nor was it my sister's. If I'm honest, I don't know whose it was, but it doesn't matter because he saw me, looked at me, talked to me, touched me, understood me. Because he knew me. It is the only thing of great weight in this story that I am telling you.

'Clio, if this were a mistake... Why else would my own prophetic gift send me these visions? You know, dear friend, that I give verses to mortals so that they can discover things for themselves rather than it being so simple, but in reality, I see everything, because I observe everything. After all, every day I illuminate even the most hidden places of the Earth and the Universe.'

The muse of history had listened to him attentively, and in those moments, she looked at him curiously as they walked along Mount Olympus.

'Do you love him that much, Apollo?' Her question was not what he expected as an answer, but he smiled sweetly at her.

'Yes, Clio, I really love him. It is not a whim, nor an obsession. I feel connected to that creature. I feel like a lump in my throat when I separate myself from him. I feel nervous flutters inside me when I look at him... However, once I am next to him, all emotion fades away, except for the broadest and most diverse of all: Love. Honestly, if it hadn't been for those visions, I wouldn't risk descending into earth. He might go crazy if I told him who I am, and I wouldn't like someone like him to suffer, especially if it's my fault. So, Clio, and after this talk to which I have subjected you, what is your judgment? Tell me honestly what you think. If you think it's crazy, tell me. I wish for you to be honest.'

'Apollo,'she said, 'it is not my duty to tell you what you should do or not do, but if you think this is the right thing to do, go ahead. I was afraid that you wouldn't really like him, that you would just see him as one more on your list of loves, but now that I have you in front of me, face to face, I look into your eyes, and I know that your love is real. I hope your visions become true. You're good, Phoebus. You deserve someone equal or better, and Hyacinthus... Hyacinthus also deserves someone like you.'

IV

When he arrived at his abode, he found all his slaves moving around. It seemed like something incredible was happening.

Several of them, whom Hyacinthus had known for as long as he could remember, looked at him smiling. However, there was something in their eyes that he didn't quite like. It was as if they were afraid of something. Perhaps they had heard the rumours that the visit had something to do with him, but like the prince they did not know about it, and despite not wanting to imagine the worst, deep down they did.

But what was the worst? That it was a teacher who would take him to another place? Maybe to Athens, or maybe even further away, to Lesbos for example? Hyacinthus, in his good sense, assumed that this would not be so horrible, although of course he was not eager to know. But truly, there were more horrible things. Events that happened to just and good people. So, if that was what the Moiras had woven for him, so be it!

The bald old man, with a dry and polished complexion, with dark, slanted eyes like the eagle that watches attentively from the heavens, approached him in complete silence. He bowed slightly, paying his respects, and kept his lips sealed until Hyacinthus gave him his turn to speak.

'Adelphos, what's going on?'he asked with great kindness.

It was not necessary, since their social differences were more than obvious. He was a prince, a warrior, and the other was just a helot. A very good, noble, and loyal one, but one that despite all those pleasant qualities remained what he was, a slave. Still, it seemed fair to Hyacinthus. If you wanted to be treated kindly, you had to treat others the same way.

'Hyacinthus, sir,' he replied, 'you have a visitor, but it would be good if you changed and cleaned up, since you don't...'

'Don't I smell good?' The old man nodded. 'You know, Adelphos, that you have the blessings of our family, because it is also yours, and that you have complete freedom to make these kinds of comments.' He reminded him as he walked slowly, so as not to overwhelm the helot who was somewhat unbalanced. 'So, tell me, has the man I am to meet arrived yet?'

'Yes, sir.'

Hyacinthus smiled amusedly.

'Well, he is fast.'

'How come, sir?'

'I've encountered him before.' He responded with immense confidence.

So much so that Adelphos did not object, even though Polyboea had clearly told him that they did not know each other.

'Continue without me, Hyacinthus. I have to do other things.'

'Alright. Have a good day, Adelphos.' Before leaving he examined him with his eyes. The man was having trouble breathing. Perhaps because of the asthma that the arrival of spring usually provoked, or maybe, he was simply too old. 'Try to rest. If you see that you can't do something, tell my father, and he will send someone younger.'

'Thank you, sir... Although it is not necessary.'

'Adelphos, please consider my words.'

And with that the good prince continued walking down the hallway, until he entered one of the rooms.

Adelphos, who had stood still for a few moments, smiled broadly, pursuing his master with his gaze. Possibly, he was a good warrior, and not a good strategist as rumours claimed. However, he possessed something that very few had: a heart full of compassion.

And Apollo, whose essence was there, decided that what he had in mind was the best thing he would do throughout his entire eternal existence.

When he left the room with the aim of going to meet his father, he found his sister, who was leaning against a wall waiting for him.

'Hyacinthus, they are in the *andron*. Women can't go in there as you know, but I wanted to see you before you went.'

'Why, Polyboea? Don't tell me that you are also worried like everyone else. Even the horses seemed to look at me uneasily!'

'No. I'm not worried, I just wanted to see you.' With those few words, she turned on her heels and prepared to leave, but then Hyacinthus grabbed her arm. As a result, she stopped and fixed her clear gaze on his.

'Polyboea…'

They understood each other just with the name leaving the boy's lips, accompanied by a simple look. The complicity they shared was enormous!

'I fear, Hyacinthus. Everything is talked about. Nobody is silent and I don't know anything. I find it unfair that I am not allowed to participate in the meeting.'

'You've done it before, why not today?'

'Father has not allowed me, because he is a foreigner and he is not used to this... But listen, Hyacinthus, if that man offers you to go far away, do not dare to refuse, accept it! It might be an incredible opportunity.'

'I know. I have already met him.' An expression of surprise appeared on his sister's face.

'Are you talking seriously?'

'I think so,' he replied. 'And now, I have to go, otherwise they will send me far away, but not the attractive stranger, but father.'

'It's okay.' Polyboea stood on tiptoe and kissed him on the cheek. If he proposes it to you, accept it.' Those were her last words before disappearing down the hallway.

Hyacinthus, seeing that he was alone, took a deep breath, closed his eyes and when he was ready, he began to walk towards his destination. He did not know what was happening to him, but there was something inside him that dictated that this peculiar meeting would mark a before and after in his life. As if his entire destiny depended on whoever was within those four walls talking to his father. And maybe that was the case.

His steps took him to the *andron*, and without hesitation, without even thinking about it, he entered.

He expected a completely different, yet similar, situation. Such a strange feeling surrounded him when he saw his father with an unexpected person, that it could be said that it was not the man from the forest... It must not be.

His presence there caused both of them to be silent, both of them to look at him, and even to examine him. His father had said something that had made the stranger smile, and there he was with a wide smile on his face. He said to himself that his sister could never have described him better.

He wasn't the man of the forest, no, not at all. They didn't look alike. They did not possess even a similar trait. They were completely different. Although they both radiated something powerful, it was not the same.

Silence seemed more necessary than any clumsy words. Stillness wanted to be that moment, and it was wrapped in a thousand different emotions that opened immense horizons to the young Hyacinthus, who for the first time looked in the eyes of a god who loved him with all his being. He saw it in his eyes. That shine endowed with golden lightning, as if perhaps the sun's rays, manufactured with solid gold, had drawn it. His blonde hair, somewhat wavy, fell in a typical hairstyle, though the prince told himself that no one had ever worn it the way he did. In an instant, he thought he saw moisture emanating from his eyes. It was not sadness in a liquid state, but joy in its purest splendour.

He saw himself reflected in that look, and he knew deep down that his suspicions had been true. His world, his entire life had changed because of a simple second where he had found that other soul.

The young man stood up, and the king of Sparta did the same, although the latter remained in the rear watching his guest and his son. He approached the prince with a determined step, and when he was within arm's length he looked at him even more deeply before speaking.

'You are looking at my soul.' Hyacinthus longed to say, 'You are looking at my soul, as no one has ever done before. You look at my soul as if you knew it. Maybe you do. Maybe you even know it better than I do. But you're not looking into my eyes, you're looking into my soul, the depth of my being. You are seeing me naked, even when I wear these clothes that are of little use in front of you.'

Apollo, in his mortal form, also wanted to speak, but what could he say? He wanted to answer him, understanding how his mind worked. He comprehended everything he was, and those thoughts reached him even when they had not been spoken aloud.

There were so many things he wanted to do, to say, so many that he wouldn't have had time even if he had a lifetime. Finally, he had him there: The lover whom he had been observing for so long, the same one whom he created verses for. The silence of his eternal vow, and the punishment that the world could grant him.

A part of him told him that he couldn't fail. Hyacinthus must not stray away. He had to be at his side, next to him, leaning on his chest. He needed it to be that way. Who figured? Him, one of the favourite gods of mortals, needed a being who would soon cease to exist.

So great were the ironies of the twisted fate!

Seeing that none of them opened their mouths, the king, with an amused grimace on his face, proceeded to make the introductions:

'Hyacinthus, my son, this is Phoebus. Phoebus, my son, Hyacinthus.'

'Nice to finally meet you.'

The voice he possessed. The sweetness with which he pronounced the words... Was there a mortal in the world who could match his perfection? If indeed he was a mortal. Honestly, Hyacinthus had already seen and heard too much to suspect his true identity. And if he was, he was sure that no one could possess even half of his beauty.

'Likewise,' he murmured in a low voice, although he knew he was perfectly heard because of the smile that his counterpart gave him. It seemed like he couldn't stop smiling. 'Phoebus, my father said your name was, right?'

'That's right, or at least that's what they call me around this neck of the woods.'

'Around this neck of the woods?' He asked curiously, so absorbed in the man that he was not able to see that his father was signalling him to start eating.

'Yes, around this neck of the woods. I am not from here.'

'Are you perhaps a slave?' He laughed, amused. 'Why are you laughing?'

'Because of the smirk that has made its way onto your youthful face. Would you be so surprised if I was a slave?'

Hyacinthus remained silent for a few moments, contemplating his possible responses.

'You don't seem one.'

'I'm not.'

'Are you from Attica?'

'I'm not even sure where I'm from.'

That answer could have generated great dilemmas, but for Hyacinthus it turned out to be as common an answer as any other.

'Why…?' He wanted to ask him. He longed to know the answer, but quickly realized that being too direct might not be appropriate.

'What do you mean, Hyacinthus?'

The false mortal knew very well what he wanted to say, but he wanted to know how far he would go. The prince, however, looked down as his cheeks turned somewhat reddish.

'Nonsense,' he replied.

'There is no such thing. Everything has value and importance. Even the smallest, most useless things can be the key to the prophecy we stumble upon around the next corner.'

The teenager nodded slightly, although he didn't say a word. He didn't even try.

'Now that my son has arrived, we can begin our little banquet,' the king commented, breaking the frost that threatened to turn into ice in that room. 'Mr. Phoebus, please make yourself at home.'

'Phoebus, Phoebus…' That name sounded so familiar to him. He could have sworn he had heard it before. *Even the smallest and most useless things can be the key*. The stranger's words sailed in the turbulent ocean of his thoughts. *They may be the key*. He had

79

the impression that he wanted that, for him to give free rein to his mind, and thus discover the true reason why that foreigner had made a trip, who knows how long it had been, just to see him.

'I will do so. Thank you for your hospitality.'

The three sat around the stone table. Sometimes his family ate while lying down, but especially after the baths. Over time, this would become a tradition in some ancient civilizations.

Hyacinthus began to eat silently. His father and the stranger resumed a conversation from which the prince instantly disconnected. Despite this, from time to time he felt a gaze on him as if he were being examined. Again, that feeling that he was being seen through his clothes, his skin, and even his soul as if it did not represent any mystery to the eyes of someone who truly knew how to see. That feeling bothered him and attracted him in equal measure, in a way that he would never be able to explain. He supposed that this was how the waters must feel when they saw the moon appear in the immense sky. Its force causing the tide to rise. Or perhaps, herbivorous animals felt something similar when day broke night in the dangerous dawn, when the mares of the herds surrounded their young, prepared to kick if necessary. Both the ocean and the horses were waiting for that moment. They were worried, immersed in immense anxiety, but they wanted it to happened. Perhaps because of the mystical sensation, or perhaps, so that it would pass as quickly as possible.

However, he did not know why he felt like that, but he thought that this was the best way to explain the emotion that threatened to take over his entire life.

'Right, my son?'

His father's voice was a knife blow that shattered the walls of his daydreaming, snatching the wood with the ease with which the strong wind drifted a sapling.

'Excuse me, Father, what were you talking about?'

'You should be paying attention, Hyacinthus.' His tone was very hard and serious. 'We have guests, and that means that you have to be present, and really be present, you understand?' The young man nodded.

'Yes, father.'

'Well, if you understand it, don't try so hard to do it.'

That conversation reminded Apollo in a certain way of those he shared with Zeus, although the difference was the concern reflected in Hyacinthus's father'sgaze.

81

He had told him that he had heard people talk in Greece about his son's slenderness. Which was not entirely false, since the musician Tamyris praised Hyacinthus in all his compositions. Phoebus claimed that he was there because of that gossip. He wanted to see with his own eyes if it was true, in order to be closer to him. His father swore that what Apollo sought was to be his teacher, also to adopt him as a lover. Only one of those things was true.

The king of that place was worried, as he did not want Phoebus to back down because of his son's stubbornness. Of course,he didn't know they would never be separated. That same feeling was what told Apollo that Hyacinthus was quite lucky to have a father like that. He was hard, but because he cared about his children.

'You don't need to do that,' the disguised god had to comment. He knew, therefore, that in this way he would gain some of the prince's trust. It is normal that he was absent-minded.

'Don't you find it horrifying?' He asked.

'It really doesn't bother me.'

The king of Sparta spoke again, quite surprised:

'Hyacinthus, I was telling our guest that you are a person who likes to acquire knowledge. Apart from being quite good at sports or physical activity, in general. I was telling Phoebus that you are possibly the best rider in the region. Maybe even in the whole of Greece.'

'Thank you for that compliment, Father, but I do not believe I am worthy of receiving that title.' He then addressed Apollo. 'I'm telling you honestly, I'm not that good.'

'Nonsense, Hyacinthus!'

'Well, that's not what the gossip says,' Phoebus told him.

'I don't know what gossip says, but you know... It's just that: gossip. At the end of the day, they mean nothing.'

'Sometimes, gossip tells the truth.'

'And others, disastrous lies.' Hyacinthus completed.

His father watched them both with interest. He firmly believed, he risked swearing by all the gods, that his son was making a good impression, even when he seemed to have put his foot in it.

'Why do you think they mean nothing?'

'Gossip, you mean?' He nodded. 'Just ask yourself, who dictates it? Who takes them to all corners of Gaia? Who sings them? Who verifies them? It is usually done by people who have nothing more interesting to do. There are two authors of gossip: Those who hate or are envious of the protagonist, or those who love them. The former will bring out all the bad qualities of the individual and exaggerate him so that he turns out to be a monster, even when he is not such a monster. However, because of their greed and envy, that is how they feel. The latter will exalt all the positive qualities, but they will adorn them so much that they will contain very little truth. But they are guiltless, they are in love or, in the best of cases, they idolize the subject in question.'

'So, what do you think?'

'Gossip is similar to legends. They start from a real basis; however, the other foundations that the gossip itself stands on... They are all disastrous lies.'

Another smile appeared on that beautiful and intimidating face. Not because of its features, but because of what it conveyed. A force so archaic, Hyacinthus wondered if his father felt it too.

'Don't you know what to answer me, Phoebus?' He asked with a slight hint of mischief.

'What am I going to answer if I completely agree with you?' After that it was the prince who smiled. 'What branches of knowledge interest you?'

'I have a special affection for history. It is peculiar, but it is as if its very essence were part of me.'

'It makes sense to me, since as long as one lives, one is part of history.'

'I understand your point, but what I feel is so deep... Sometimes I have the feeling that history runs through my veins.'

Apollo then glanced at the king out of the corner of his eye, and then returned his gaze to Hyacinthus.

'The muse Clio will be proud of you, then.' The god noticed a slight shine full of longing in the eyes of the father of whom he already considered his beloved.

'I don't know,' Hyacinthus commented sincerely. 'I'd love to...'

'Hyacinthus, please behave.' Piero almost begged him again. 'Tell Phoebus what other branches interest you.'

'I don't dislike the arts, and I like astronomy, and also philosophy.'

'It's interesting to know.'

They ate for long minutes where eternal silence reigned, which would not have ceased if a slave had not called out the king's name, letting it escape from his lips. Thus, the two young men proceeded to remain alone.

The prince ate from his plate, losing his gaze on it, feeling strange in that room that no longer reminded him of his home.

He felt in a dwelling whose name no longer resonated in his being. He was alien to everything around him. And the walls were no longer those walls, nor was the furniture that furniture, nor were the floors the floors on which he used to dance in the cold early mornings. His house was no longer home, and home was not his house. It was an unknown hole, which instead of being gloomy, was equipped with a thousand clandestine lights, which illuminated the place with the force of the fire that burns in the brazier during the winters. However, a sad feeling of eternal melancholy accompanied by longing walked inside him. A thousand words could have described the situation, but what it required were millions of verses that would never satisfy such bitter emotion.

He saw himself in his own head, being so weak, acting so timid in front of a stranger he didn't even know where he came from. He was, therefore, faced with a simple human who was not at all capable of challenging him, prince and perhaps next king. But that sensation that increased inside him in a growing curve screamed at him to be careful. Infinite men better than him would have fallen into better planned traps than that and had died because of having remained silent. And he was silent, and couldn't even come up with an appropriate word, much less would he be able to pronounce a sentence possessing a certain logic. The glare that that man gave off extinguished his senses. It silenced them like strong winds sometimes managed to silence voices.

But he didn't hate him. He could feel it in the air. Despite the tension in it, despite the imminent danger that his body warned him about. Despite those deep and primitive emotions that invaded him. He didn't hate him. Phoebus didn't hate him… He would never hate him. He noticed it. He noticed it without even having to look him in the eyes, without exchanging words. He was endowed with that mystical archaic strength that seemed capable of reducing the prince's athletic body to simple ashes, but he would not do so. He wouldn't hurt him. He felt it in his heart.

The advice that the mind gave him were simple sighs of rotten breaths whose efforts would not serve the intended purpose. The palpitations of his heart, which, first calm, became stronger and faster every moment, told him, narrated to him a story that he never thought he was capable of knowing. They told him the myth of life, the myth of the sun, of the arts, of the future, talking to him and assuring him that everything was real. Then he stopped believing and began to know.

He was a simple human being, who despite possessing gold, land, who despite wearing delicate clothing made with the best silks and fabrics, remained a fragile creature naked and lost in the face of the powers that ruled the world. So, he was in a desert. One in his own home or in the one he believed to be such, because he knew from that moment that that was no longer his home.

He was a naive warrior who had become separated from his troops. A warrior wounded and lost in the impending ocean of the earth. And neither strong winds nor cruel tides could shrink him like that growing sensation, assuring him that he was nothing more than a small piece in the imagined world. In those moments, the warrior had found the strength that he had always been told about. The one that everyone heard about, but that no one ever knew about. So few people did, that they did not know, but rather believed, and believing was not enough. However, he was knowing in those moments, without even being fully aware. Without even being able to name what surrounded him. That thing that grabbed him and attracted him to the person in front of him. If that was a person, and not a mask.

If he kept quiet, he would regret it. If he spoke, he would discover it, but his mind, his soul and his heart said different things!

'Run away while you can!' The mind screamed, blocking its ears.

'Shut up and watch.' The always wise soul told him.

'Speak and praise. Love and die.' The heart assured that this was the answer that would make sense of the riddle.

The mind was moving away, lost in an imperfect melancholy dressed in greens and greys.

The soul observed the heart and analysed the situation. Yes, love was still the driving force, and the love of learning was the pillar of why the soul was wise. Without love of knowledge, it would never have achieved anything. And the being in front of his dark eyes was someone archaic endowed with infinite experiences that a mortal human could never have imagined.

While the mind locked itself in and began to remain silent, the heart and soul united, giving way to an eternal symphony.

A symphony composed for lyres, power peeking out from the cornice. He heard an unknown voice, the most beautiful he would ever hear.

He wanted to get closer to the singer whose hands dominated the instrument in a graceful and fantastic way. He should not get up, nor even run to look for him, because he lay before his eyes.

Soft sunlight carrying warmth, encouraging look. Could someone be saved from the shadows? He was that light personified. The drawn arts were in his gaze with golden hues, and the energy that surrounded him, so archaic, so royal, confirmed the suspicion that had been born in his soul.

He didn't say anything about this, he just played along. How far could a god like that go? How far could the legendary Phoebus who strikes from afar go? The most revered after his father. The favourite of a great deal of mortals. The one who owned a temple in distant Delphi, who was born in Delos.

He gathered enough courage, and fixing his gaze on the other, he asked:

'Why are you here?'

Apollo knew, from the confidence with which he said it, that the young man knew more than he would let on, but he preferred it that way. If the topic came up, he would deny it, but he would also appreciate it.

The mortal's eyes shone with immense determination. He liked that. It was the strength that existed in his spirit being reflected in its windows. He was a serene soul, but he was still young, and he suspected that unpleasant curiosity would soon return.

'I want to show you everything I can.'

Those were the words that escaped his lips, after looking up from the plate he was eating from.

'Where will you take me?'

Apollo found in his words the nuance of the adventurer, of one who wants to get away to live the story of his life, and also the growing concern of a young man who deeply loved his family.

'Do you want to go somewhere?' he risked asking.

The more he asked, the more answers he would get, ergo, the more he would know. He could see everything if he wanted to, know every little detail that passed through his thoughts, but he didn't see it as fair. So he preferred to discover it, as if his future love was built by mortal bricks.

'If you wanted to, and my father allowed me...'.

'Hyacinthus, I will not force you to do anything you don't want to do,' he said, wanting to assure him. 'And no, I wasn't planning on taking you anywhere. This place pleases me.' *It is the most beautiful in all of Greece, because you live in it*, Apollo wanted to add, but he knew that would be too much. After all, in theory it was the first time he had seen him. 'And you are happy here, right?'

The prince looked deeper into his counterpart's gaze before answering the question, and he waited long seconds to give his judgment.

'I am. Has father offered you a room? If we stay, you'll have to live somewhere, right?'

'That's right, but I already have a home here.'

'Where?'

'Does it matter?' he said, amused. Hyacinthus smiled back.

'If you are going to be my teacher, it would be good to know.'

92

'Somewhere in this neck of the woods. Is that answer enough?'

'Not at all.'

'What is enough for you?'

The prince prepared to respond, but he did not have time, as his father burst into the room at that moment.

He opened the door and looked through it. What his eyes found was not his son with a stranger, but two friends who were smiling at each other with amusement. Happiness crept into his eyes.

'Have you told him the news, Phoebus?'

'That's right, your majesty.'

The king turned to Hyacinthus expecting a response, consent on his part, because despite thinking that Phoebus was the best option for his son, he did not want him to suffer.

'Honestly, Father, I think Phoebus and I will manage to understand each other.'

'Are you sure?'

'Totally.' He responded.

The king of Sparta managed to see sincerity and honesty in his son, because he was speaking from his own heart. And he was not wrong, he spoke from the depths of his being.

He was at the beginning of his adventure, of the learning that the man who ate in his home would bring him; however, he already heard the instruments echoing, approaching his person. If his suspicions were true, this would not be a nightmare, but a dream too interesting to be true.

V

Polyboea was waiting for him in the hallway that led to the room they were in. When the men left the *andron,* she walked with her head down towards the patio, trying to make them see that she was simply passing through. Both the handsome young man and his father ignored her, as they were both walking together and chatting excitedly. Perhaps it was simply Phoebus's strategy to gain the king's sympathy, and thus be allowed to spend even more time with the prince.

However, her brother Hyacinthus did see her. He noticed her clearly. He stayed behind with some excuse prepared, and instead of going after his father, he changed course and chased after his sister.

The sunlight was shining that afternoon, and Polyboea's hair had regained a very light tone, which Hyacinthus found quite beautiful and interesting, but he did not even have time to praise her for that, since the questions did not take long to come out from her lips:

'What is he like? What is it? Where are you going? Because you must have said that you are leaving, right?'

'Polyboea, please breathe.'

'Before you said *I don't know what you saw before*, was it the same one? Why not? Why is this one more perfect? My Gods! He looks like a statue because of how perfect he is! If I were you, Hyacinthus, I wouldn't even think about it for a second, I would be in his arms right now for the eons that must pass!'

'Polyboea, stop.'

'Stop me? By Aphrodite, Hyacinthus! You've seen him? Have you seen his intentions? Have you felt them? That man emanates power, harmony! If he is beautiful in essence, in presence and seems to be nice! He is perfect!'

'Polyboea, please. Let me at least speak.'

Concern appeared on her face.

'Have I talked much?' His brother nodded and smiled sweetly.

'Quite. You have asked many questions, but do not despair, I will tell you everything I know, everything we have talked about.' *But I will not tell you about my suspicions.* He was about to add, but not even he fully understood what these were about.

'I'm sorry, Hyacinthus... But I fear and at the same time I feel an immense joy that takes over my body from the depth of my soul, passing through my organs and my skin...'

'Maybe that's your subconscious telling you that everything will be fine.'

'Let's start at the beginning, then, Hyacinthus, what is his name?'

'He says his name is Phoebus.'

'Why "says" and not "is called"?'

'Because it's not a very typical name, don't you think?'

'I don't know what you're referring to, and I don't really know how to interpret that shine that lies in your eyes... Is it good? Is it, perhaps, bad?'

'Nothing is bad, and at the same time everything is; the same thing happens with kindness. I don't know him or at least not yet, but I feel this growing sense that this won't degenerate into anything vile.'

'So, you mean to say that you liked this Phoebus guy?'

'Quite.'

'And what did he want?'

'He wanted to work with me. He wants to be my teacher.'

'But, you already have a teacher.'

'Yes, but he wanted to go teach at an institution in Athens, don't you remember? Maybe I forgot to tell you, but Father forced him to stay until someone came who could replace him. Looks like we've found it. Furthermore, even though he is young, I don't have to do without him alone either. I was talking to father about what he wanted to teach me, so possibly my old teacher will have to reject the dream of going to another region.'

'Isn't that somewhat unfair?'

Hyacinthus shrugged.

'I don't think a king knows what it means to be fair. After all, his people are dying, while he eats delicacies several times a day.'

'I guess you're right... So, you're not leaving?'

'No. He told me he would never make me leave here if that's not what I want. He has assured me that he would not do anything that I did not allow.'

Polyboea embraced him in her arms.

'I'm so glad you're not leaving!'

'But, you didn't want me to leave?' He asked strangely, separating himself from the affectionate gesture.

'No, silly, I didn't want you to leave. I wanted you to stay, but I also wish the best for you. Look, you and I are like branches of the same tree. Wherever you go, I will go. That's why it would be so hard to see you leave... However, if that man had wanted it that way, I'm no one to stand in the way, and even more so when leaving means seeing the world and learning, do you know what I mean, Hyacinthus? You may not be able to understand it, but from an early age I have wanted to travel throughout Greece, visit every region and every town in it... But I soon forgot the idea. It's something impossible for me. Not only for carrying the weight of being part of a family with this caste on our shoulders, but also for the fact that in many places I would not be respected. On the other hand, you could have taken advantage of the opportunity if it had presented itself to you... There are so many young people from good families who travel with their teachers! You would go unnoticed, Hyacinthus, and you could leave these four walls that not only represent this house, but also our home, and the only known world...'

'Why would you risk being caressed by loneliness so that I would leave?'

'It's not just you and me, Hyacinthus. There are more people in this abode, there are more branches on the tree.'

'Is it me or are you avoiding the question?'

'It's not you, it's me. I have avoided it, because I consider the answer so extremely simple that I firmly believe you already know it.'

'Polyboea, you already know that I consider you charming, but I find you quite complicated: At first, you are euphoric, and the next you are lost, and you want to cut your words... If you want to answer, answer me, if you don't, it'll be alright, but please, don't make me feel like I'm stupid.' He told her sincerely. She smiled sweetly.

'You are smarter than you think, Hyacinthus. And the answer is really simple.'

'You know what, sister?'

'What?'

'There will soon come a time where men, in some cases, will try to silence women, and do you know why that will happen? Because when you open your mouth, a clever phrase coming from male lips is worth less than a simple word coming from yours. By this I mean, if either of us is intelligent, it's you. There is a reason the goddess of wisdom is a goddess and not a god. Furthermore, your mind works much faster and more efficiently... What you understand in a second may take me centuries.'

'You are exaggerating about the last thing!' she paused slightly. 'I would even risk years without seeing you so that you could enjoy the well-being, experiences and knowledge that you deserve. You deserve to be happy, Hyacinthus.'

'You too.'

Misfortune appeared slightly in the girl's crystalline eyes, but it soon faded, giving way to the enthusiasm of the beginning.

'Where does that affable man come from?'

'Don't know.'

'Hasn't he told you?'

'No, he just said he came from somewhere far away.'

'Do you have any idea?'

'Honestly no,' he lied.

'It wasn't the person you saw, right? By the way, why did you think it was him?'

'No, of course not. They are quite different, although it is true that they seem to have the same blood, a similar air, as if they came from the same place.'

'Didn't I give a good description?'

'There is no better description, of course. All the words you used define him perfectly, however in the forest with the sun's rays caressing my eyes, that other man was quite close to the idea I had.'

'Didn't you go out this morning to exercise? What were you doing in the forest?'

'That's how it had been, but I finished and didn't want to go back. I was afraid too, you know? I too am afraid even when I hide it, but despite this, the fear remains inside me, and sometimes those wolves that surround me end up brushing up against me. In those moments, I just want to be alone, disconnect.... That's why I went to the forest. I had to put my priorities in order before returning here and facing the unknown that might change my entire life.'

'How was he? He must have been very handsome to look like Phoebus.'

'At first, I thought it was him, although there were things, I have to admit, that didn't fit your description. This man seemed a little older. He did not have that hair that you spoke of, nor the same look... However, he was endowed with that same strength that you told me about. So, I just thought you exaggerated a little. But Phoebus seems much more refined in some ways. If anything, that's the right word to define what I'm thinking.'

'What exactly do you think, Hyacinthus?'

'There are so many things running through my mind right now, Polyboea, I don't know that I won't go crazy.'

'It shouldn't be that bad either!'

'Possibly it's not, but you know me, something gets into my head, and I don't stop thinking about it until I find the answer.'

'And you never let yourself be helped.'

The prince smiled sideways at her.

'How well you know me, Polyboea!'

'I know, I'm your favourite sister for a reason.' They laughed amused. 'However, despite having a hypnotizing physique, has he been kind to you?'

'A lot.'

'What have been your thoughts?'

'I'm not going to be completely honest, Polyboea, but I'll risk saying that he is a person that I will like very much.'

'In what sense?'

'I don't know that yet.'

Silence surrounded them. Polyboea watched him clearly interested. On the other hand, he didn't realize it. He kept his eyes on the clear sky.

He felt eclipsed by the beauty of the world, and suddenly everything made sense. There would always be something that human minds couldn't figure out, and that was clearly the spiritual. In the spiritual there were also beings more developed than others, and perhaps those entities were the gods. Perhaps, they were not true gods, but creatures of nature, much more connected to it than any other being. They were the gods because they represented something unattainable that human glory could not even caress.

'I have been blinded for so long! I was so sure I knew everything! I now lie in the knowledge that there is still much to learn.'

'What are you looking at so closely, Hyacinthus? What's going on in that prodigious mind of yours? Have you woken up?'

'I had never realized it, Polyboea. I am simpler than you think. Look at that patch of sky,' he said as he pointed out the area, with a look that seemed capable of crossing any limit imposed by time and space. 'It's always been there, but I've never noticed it. I had never seen how much beauty it possesses. Everything has something beautiful, Polyboea, even the most horrible of things. Now I'm realizing it. The world that the poets talk about is completely true. It is in front of us, but we do not want to see it. It is easier to say that the world is ugly, and therefore we are wrong, than to admit that the world is beautiful, ergo, saying that we have no reason to be unhappy. Even the most unfortunate soul could see the harmony of this place if he really saw, but we don't see, Polyboea, we don't see! We think we do it, but the truth is that we don't. We don't see it, my sister... We don't see it. Oh, if I could! If I could travel back in time, I would tell myself to stop and see this! If I could change the course of things... Oh, oh if I could! I would build a thousand temples for every year of my life!'

'They say that love changes your perspective, has that man deceived you so much?'

'No, no, Polyboea, you are wrong for once in your life... What I feel at the moment is not love, and the beauty that I am able to contemplate is certainly not due to it. What I see is reality. the one that nobody sees. I am waking up, Polyboea, waking up at a banquet with a stranger who has made me think. When you look outside you dream, when you look inside you wake up, and when you wake up the world turns upside down. It's completely different, I understand it now.'

'What do you understand, Hyacinthus? Your words seem so strange to me!'

'Don't you see it? Look at the light. Watch how the sun lights up the skies. See how much beauty the firmament houses.'

'I don't understand what you're saying, Hyacinthus... I really try. It remains for me what it always was, heaven, which some believe is in love with the earth, but that does not seem entirely true to me.'

'I know it's true,' he said. 'I know it's true. Who wouldn't fall in love with the earth if they saw it from above? If you saw it in its entirety, how long is it? I think I would faint, Polyboea.' Then, he looked her in the eyes. His gaze shone like never before. Polyboea did not understand it. For a few moments, she thought he had gone crazy. 'Gaia, this place, whatever you want to call it, has perfect harmony. It is very beautiful even immersed in darkness, even watered by the blood of humans who are killed by their brothers... Even with all the suffering it suffers at our expense, this place we inhabit is beautiful. Someday you will see it, Polyboea. Some day. I don't know what that stranger will bring into my life, but his mission has been accomplished if he wanted to show me how much beauty there is here. I have been blind for a long time, now I understand.... I understand everything, everything makes sense inside me. Polyboea, I'm awake. I have never been before.'

'Hyacinthus, how did you do it?'

'I completely ignore it.'

'What do you feel?'

'The world is then a perfect symphony. The strings, the keys, the breezes, the rocks, the leaves... Everything has an improvised score that fate composes without haste, losing itself in the misfortunes that surround the world... It is a song that will never be written. Never recited by mortal lips, never touched by simple hands. A melody as long as life itself. It started millennia ago, it will never end. If one could listen to what I am hearing, if one could do it, we would find joy... You don't need anything more than the earth to be happy, Polyboea. We only require eyes to see it.'

'What you define is so beautiful, but I am unable to understand it. It's as if you lived in a different place than the one I live in, yet you say you live in the same place. Same reality, same world... So, how do I achieve that glory that is found in the labyrinthine streets of your soul?'

'Learn. Learn to observe, to really see; learn to feel; Learn to listen, and you will be able to find the truth. Reason, live from your intellectual strength, and you will understand that that little piece of firmament houses the same beauty that is talked about in books.'

'When did you become a wise man?'

'I guess I've looked into the sun's eyes for too long. When the rays cleanse the layer of sand that exists in your eyes, one sees with singular clarity.'

Polyboea watched him without recognizing him, but at the same time she did. She didn't understand how he could start saying those things when not long ago it was said that it didn't exist. But now, despite being another, he was more himself than he had ever been before. She could see it in his eyes and felt it in his vibrations. She understood, then, that he had not gone mad, but that he was right: he was waking up.

VI

The icy cold of the nights seeped through his skin and bones. Lying on his bed, he looked at the ceiling in pure silence. He felt watched, as if someone was at his side. However, that feeling that invaded him was not negative, quite the opposite. The presence wanted to protect him; he knew it. He did not wish him any harm, and was at his side in case something went wrong.

It was like the moon. An archaic look that was there, on that singular night, in which he questioned himself. He asked himself everything a thinker could ask. Many of those questions lacked answers. Not because he didn't know them, but because he didn't know how to express them in words. However, even so, that essence preceded him which embraced him with golden lights, assuring him that what he felt was true, what his wise soul said. He had found a world to love, not separated from his reality, inhabiting the same one to which he belonged. He had reached the stellar mantle that houses the truth, just by looking through two stars that seemed to love him even when they were strangers... If only he knew! If only he understood! However, he did not do so, and everything he found was false or at least resembled it.

He was afraid of what an uncertain fate would bring him, but that figure was next to him and assured him that everything would

110

work out. That being that was watching him was looking out for his good. He understood it. It was thanks to his presence that he decided to close his eyes, this time for real, thus returning to the recesses of his mind.

In this he only found clarity. An immense white light that surrounded him, even caressed him, with a warm breeze that could not be false, because being in bed, he felt it.

It was a path, all infused in that white eclipse that did not want to disappear. That morning wind that did not want to fade, and some silver lights that he observed in the distance. He knew what it was about. He understood what it was, having found himself there before at an early age. His dreams always guided him to that place when he was scared. Those lights warned him, accompanied by the songs of a lady he had never seen. However, deep down he knew that she was someone who cared more for him than life itself.

He walked. Walked without direction, since although the place was familiar, he did not know it at all. Honestly, his feet did not respond to him, nor did the other parts of his body respond. He tried to speak, and his tongue did not obey him. He tried to laugh and fell asleep. He tried to change direction, but his legs wouldn't obey him. His being knew where to go, even when he wasn't fully aware. He knew in the depths of his soul which direction to take, which corner to turn, which rock to pass, and which tree to reach.

He listened to the songs in the distance, so far away, but at the same time so close, that home was written in his soul. He never remembered the notes when he woke up, much less the tone of voice, nor the place... He only knew that he had been there before once he returned.

There was no sun, no moon, not even the stars in that perfect world built by white lights. Only the strange notes mattered, the chants of immense battles, and the voice that was silent one moment, and spoke the next. It overwhelmed him. He was overwhelmed because he couldn't hear the voice or distinguish it like he had done other times.

Everything was the same. However, there was something changing, destined for eternal future... And that same something that didn't feel right made its way onto his path. And the light vanished, swirling in the same place, giving shape to something that he could not see. His steps stopped, and the orders of conscience asked him to wake up, but he did not obey them. He had to see that. It was the right thing. Despite the uncertainty that surrounded him, he was not afraid. He knew that whatever would emerge from the fog that was now foam would be known. He wasn't wrong. In the world of dreams, he never was.

So, in the arms of Morpheus, Hypnos the sinister, the foam turned into mist again. A mist that had a human shape, and from it emanated the figure of a woman.

Her dark hair was styled in an updo typical of her time, leaving her face unobstructed, except for a couple of wavy strands that fell on both sides of her face like little snails. Her smile was sincere and wide, from ear to ear, one could say. Her slightly tanned complexion was painted with red hues on her cheeks. Her thin lips were also the tone of blood, but Hyacinthus knew immediately that they were not painted... Nothing on her face was painted. She was like that, and in a way, she looked like a sculpture, or maybe a painting. It depended on how one looked at her. The eyes, dark like moonless nights, reminded him so much of his own that he felt terrified in a certain way. And it was not the colour, but the way of looking, which he also shared with some of his brothers and sisters. In her eyes, the young prince saw thousands of battles, facts and events that he knew of through books.

It was no surprise that she spoke, and he recognized her voice as that of the one who always told him stories, trying to reassure him:

'Yes, it always came from me. I am the beginning. From my lips came that voice that encouraged you when you were afraid, dearest Hyacinthus. And my voice will forever continue to be the one that calms you, that helps you if you need it. Nothing bad happens. You'll be fine. You always have been, so don't fear.'

'I can't help doing it.'

'Why can't you?'

'I don't know.'

'Do you really not know, or you wish to not know?'

'Because an immense presence surrounds me.'

'Are the misfortunes that surround that very deity what you fear? Are you afraid, my son, that this misfortune may come to touch you?'

'It's not that I'm afraid of that. It's just that I feel a hole in my stomach. I have never felt this. This immensity, this archaic form... The closest thing I have are these contacts between you and me, which are possibly uncertain, created by my mind.'

'What seems created by our mind, in the end it turns out to be the truest thing we have. But why do you fear if you don't fear that?'

114

'It is Apollo, Phoebus who hurts from afar. I can't refuse a god. I don't want to, either.'

He surprised himself when his voice spoke those words, words that with his eyes open would have been taboo. However, he was not master of his actions in the world of dreams, just a guest, who had to obey the master of the house. And the master was his subconscious and everything that lay in it, both good and bad.

'You can refuse, you just don't want to. I not only have that knowledge because of your words, but also because of your gaze. You have a special glow, Hyacinthus. You envision a future, perhaps near, perhaps distant, in which you are happy by his side.'

The young prince looked at the woman who stood before him sceptically. He didn't understand how she could know every single thing that crossed his mind. Although, after thinking about it carefully, it did not surprise him.

'Do you believe that? Would you allow it?'

'I am not the one who rides the horse of your decisions, much less the one who sews the thread of your destiny. It is you who makes the choices, even if fate is already sewn.'

'What would you do if you were me? What would you do?' Desperation emanated from his being.

The mist that formed her body became more solid, causing the figure to become more and more real. The woman who brought the arts and light to Hyacinthus approached him, staying mere centimetres away. So, he smelled the aroma that filled the air in those moments. A smell like old papyrus, freshly used ink... An ink that had written, thanks to expert hands, the history of the world.

'I would do what my heart told me.' She responded with tremendous sincerity. The greatest honesty that he had ever heard. Hyacinthus, do not refuse to open yourself to Apollo for fear of the tragedies that precede him. There is a good chance it will repeat itself, but it doesn't have to be so. And the ending doesn't matter, son. The path, the feelings and the learning you obtain during the time you travel, that is what matters.'

'Do you mean I will die?'

'I mean that I don't know, but if human beings stopped doing things out of fear, they would never leave the house.'

'Fear is the predator of man, right?'

'Fear, Hyacinthus, leads to worry, hatred, and a thousand different emotions in which humans can lose themselves, but you are strong and intelligent. You will not fall into those traps that the gods have placed in your paths. The being that lives, feels, and the one that feels, suffers. You cannot spare yourself suffering because it is part of the path of life. Instead, you can fight for what you believe will make you happy. I look down, Hyacinthus, now that I don't set foot on those lands and all I see is a horrible sadness:

'People don't love what they do, and they get lost taking simpler shortcuts that won't get them anywhere. However, there is a more complex path that cuts through the forests and, with them, beauty. This path full of stones leads to joy and happiness for humans and all sentient beings who dare to feel it. So, Hyacinthus, take risks for what you want, for those you love... It does not matter if you face eternal punishment, as for example Prometheus had to do, if it is for something that you believe is right, for someone you love, for something that you love. Fear blocks, fear slows down, fear destroys more lives than war.'

'What if I'm just a game, good soul? I fear more being a game, a piece on his board, than leaving in a tragic way like every mortal whom he cares about seems to do. At the end of the day, tragic death or not; I was born with the goal of dying at some point in my life.'

'Ask yourself. You have the answers. Each and every one you want. Do you think he considers you a game?'

The question left him thinking for a few moments. In his mind, fragments of the conversation he had had with Phoebus at that banquet returned as memories in a very vivid way. He could see it reflected in part of the fog that had separated from the one he believed to be his mother. She also looked, in a sweet, warm way.

He saw himself, then, that lunchtime. They talked together with a wide smile etched on their faces. How his eyes shone! Now that he could see himself, he was ashamed. From the first moment, they both looked at each other as if they had known one another for a long time. Apollo had a countenance that could not be faked. He conveyed a joy that could not be performative either. He seemed so interested in him! So much so that Hyacinthus's heart skipped a beat.

It began to throb harder. He listened to it following the rhythm of the god's words. He saw himself later, with his sister in their patio, watching the sun, feeling its warm rays on his skin. It seemed like the sun was following him. He didn't want to stay away from him.

'Is the way he smiles to you the way you smile to a toy? Or the way you look at a chess piece? Is it possible to feel that love he gifts you with for a toy?'

'That's not love, Mother. That's all the positive feeling I can find on Earth... After all, gods are not supposed to love like humans. They love differently, I see it. No, no, love is a very simple word. Uranian, divine love is greater. So much so that I notice him surrounding me, hugging me, kissing me even when he is not present, or at least without seeing him. It's not just love, it's a feast...'

'I was afraid too, Hyacinthus, so I understand you, but he loves you. He really loves you. Maybe you are the creature he has loved the most throughout his existence, which is not short at all.'

He nodded and said, 'Your wish is always the same, right, Mother? That I be happy.'

'May you be happy,' she agreed. 'But be careful, Hyacinthus. He has many enemies, and believe me when I tell you that they will not hesitate to use you to harm him.' She warned, looking into his eyes.

In them, Hyacinthus saw immense yellow-clad concern.

It was a tide contaminated by the toxicity of those creatures that would not hesitate to harm it. And she didn't know if Apollo would suffer, but he certainly would.

She was so convinced that Hyacinthus understood that she knew more than she would say. Indeed, her eyes revealed every little detail that was in store for him.

'Do you know fate, Mother?'

'No, I do not, and even if I could, I couldn't tell you anything either. I just feel that same pressure as you in my chest. It numbs my lungs, causing oxygen to not be able to reach them. Since my farewell, I say that I have many hearts. I know when one starts to beat slower.'

'Is that mine?'

'I hope not, but on the one hand it would make sense. Look at me, Hyacinthus, please.' The young man did so. His mother's hands caressed his cheeks. It was the first time she had touched him since the moment of his birth. It felt real, but at the same time it didn't. And it was the fog that really made contact between the two. 'You are incredibly strong, very intelligent, but sometimes you should leave nobility aside, leave sympathy behind... They are qualities more than defects, but people take advantage of them, and gods, who take what they want no matter the cost, even more so.'

'Mother, are you talking to me about Apollo? Should I be careful with him? I thought we agreed that he was in love.'

'And he is. It's not Apollo I'm worried about, son. There are so many deities that he has as enemies... So, so many! There can be danger around every corner. You have to get around it. Some will be obvious, others not so much. So, Hyacinthus, be very careful. You will have time to get rid of them, if you understand them. If you fear, ask Apollo. He loves you, so he will respond to you. If something worries you, tell him. He will take care of you.'

'This sounds like goodbye, mother.'

'Why do you say that?'

'Because it seems like you're giving me away to Apollo, like you have to get even further away.'

'I'm not going away, Hyacinthus, but understand me, son! With each passing day, I find it more complex to hold these meetings. You are growing up, and you no longer need anyone to look after you.'

'If I don't need it, why do you talk about Apollo as if he were my protector? Is this the situation?'

'No, Hyacinthus, but you are my son, and I will always directly or indirectly seek protection for you. This is how motherhood works.'

'You never told me your name. If this is goodbye, I would like to know.'

'I don't think it's possible,' she said, moving slightly away from him.

She began to walk like that, slowly, getting a little further away from him with each step, and the prince couldn't do anything. He wanted to scream for her to stop… Oh, he wanted it so bad! But he couldn't. That fog was escaping. It was moving away, beginning to unravel. And when he thought it was his last chance, he managed to run after her.

'Mother, tell me at least one reason! Give me at least one reason! Why are you running away? Why do you always do it?'

Upon hearing that question she stopped. Because her son had managed to master the dream, master that illusion, taking the reins of a horse that, although invisible, was still there.

She turned around slowly. Her dark eyes now took on an almost silver tone.

'History always repeats itself, Hyacinthus, that's why I run away.'

'What do you mean?'

'The world always has the same rhythm. They say that futures exist, and they are true, but only the names and leaves of the trees change. Disputes are always the same in the human realm. So simple are they, Hyacinthus, that they continue to fight the same losing battles. They kill each other over the same disputes. Forbidden lovers, they love even knowing the end, believing they have found the solution, having found the door, but they only have the hope that that fate will not come. Can I tell you something? It always comes, my son, it always comes. As far as the gods are concerned, they sometimes believe that there is nothing stronger than them. They think that everything will change just by thinking about it. Although they have created everything, they do not realize that they themselves are controlled by the fate that the Moiras weave. They have more power over matter, but in the end, everything comes down to the primeval forces. Among them is the destiny that both animals of the earth and spiritual beings fear so much. It cannot be tamed, nor subdued. It can only be ignored, causing it to hit us with the cruellest truth. Although sometimes, there are spirits that dare to risk knowing the truth.'

'Should I ignore it, reject it?'

The woman's eyes shone sweetly because of the innocence she saw in the young man.

'No, Hyacinthus. You don't have to do anything for me, you have to choose.'

'Even so… Mother, I would like to know your name. I would like to really know you. It is the first time I see you after years of meetings with a voice that was familiar to me, but I always questioned whether I was falling into madness, and now that I finally see your face, you have to go. I don't understand. Why weren't you there? Why weren't you present in my childhood? On the nights when I was unable to sleep? Why are you not in my life, but in my dreams? Who took you away from me, Mother? Who was cruel enough to do it?'

'Hyacinthus…'

'Don't say you can't answer, you should... You should be able to do it.'

'The thing is that I was in those moments, by your side, holding your hand, even if you didn't see me. There are so many ways to be present, that if I explained them all the world would end.' She paused slightly, reading the last question in her son's silence. *Me, is the response. I was the one who took me away from you. That cruel being was me. I walked away physically, but I would never walk away mentally.*'

'Mother, that's...'

His words were interrupted by a flash immersed in bronze, which made the fog that recreated his mother disappear, leaving him alone in the growing darkness, which preyed on him with icy hands, waiting for the moment when he was not alert.

He felt a strong, cold wind surrounding him, freezing his skin. He trembled under that density which the air turned into slowly. He felt thin fingers tearing at his skin, breaking his bones, penetrating his organs and destroying them as one would destroy the petals of a delicate flower. Lying on the ground, filled with agony, he firmly believed he would die. Then, the sun made way, driving away the darkness, caressing his naked and battered body with its rays, healing his wounds, turning that agony into pure joy. The lyres were heard accompanying the god, and the song words, despite being incomprehensible to him, assured him that he was safe, that he should not fear.

With the strength of the protector at his side, of the lover in love, he was able to find peace in a void that was not entirely void, since it was composed of the Apéiron, the unlimited, the indefinite. Nothing there had written limits. Everything was immovable, perfect and harmonious. Apollo had made way for that, banishing Tartarus to the shadows that hovered around it, to his worst nightmares.

VII

Gentle breeze of the years, the air on the mountain sang, the small birds making its choruses, which between flights caught a grape from the high branches of the olive tree. The tree grew, burying its roots in the earth itself, reaching the heart of Gaia, who calmly breathed. He breathed the joy of the years where peace still existed, banished to the shadows, hidden from the eyes of the simple mortal of human sentiment.

Apollo, with golden hair, walked through the world, after feeding the horses that helped him guide the light of day. His walks announced their arrival, and the nymphs, fearful, looked out. The few satyrs who were there silenced their flutes. They watched him with fulminating crystals etched in their eyes. How much greed! How much misfortune that soul gave off! What he caressed, rotted; what he loved, was destroyed He was the author of a thousand acts that did not please them, scared them, but they pitied him. Why did they if many hid when they saw his shadow? Because there was no greater misfortune than that which lived in the light of days.

His clear eyes were now beginning to take on a golden hue. They knew they had to look away, because watching him transform into his true essence could be deadly to the eyes of anyone who was not a divinity.

The winds continued to blow without fear, strongly moving the branches of the fine olive tree on which the birds had perched. All of them looking away, hiding their faces between their wings, protecting themselves from the splendour that emanated from the god.

Phoebus, now with bow in hand, quiver on his back, walked confidently and with a determined air towards the gathering breezes. They blew harder and harder. They gave the impression that they were chatting. The earth trembled as a result of the ferocity of his strides.

Because Apollo, who hurts from afar, could be fair when he wanted it, just as he still is when this work is being written, but above all he was a god, and gods as powerful and archaic as him sometimes forgot that they were not the only ones of their kind.

His hair, formed by threads of gold, had become brown. A light brown, with blonde highlights that despite everything continued to give off his energy. There was determination in his gaze. A look bathed in the waters of the *Mare Nostrum,* when the sun rose in the early mornings. And it existed in it, that light and intense golden tone, characteristic of dawn. He was, thus, the whole beginning, the start... For many, he could be considered in those moments the *arché* that the pre-Socratics looked for with so much enthusiasm. In a way, it was his beginning, because that's how he was born. With that same expression, that same hair, although this time already grown.

He kept a foreign heart safe, which did not belong to him, not even by right. A heart that he had risked to protect, when he knew he wasn't the best at protecting such things. He gripped his bow with a strength never used before. Inside him, a swirl of worries invaded him. He did not allow it to be reflected on the outside.

When he reached the top where the winds danced, Gaia knew that the moment had arrived where the sun and the winds would fight over a boy. Over a young man who, oblivious to all that, was dreaming under the sheets. An eerie tension ran through the body of the entire earth, from north to south, from west to east, passing through every town and city present, over every mountain, also shaking the seas. Shaking everything that was part of its being.

And all because he, son of Leto and Zeus, had fallen in love once again. All because he, son of Zeus, Olympian god, had decided to speak:

'Boreas, Zephyrus, come down from the heavens!'

He asked, still holding the heart of the one he loved. His friend, his beloved, the love of the moment. The symphony that he couldn't stop repeating in his mind. The same one that he longed to compose. A thousand lires would not be enough. Maybe infinite. He would never know... But, as far as he was concerned, everything was much better having that heart between his fingers, that young soul next to his.

The winds above him roared, filled with a frenzy that no person was capable of having. They seemed to be celebrating up there, where Apollo couldn't reach them. He understood that they celebrated the disputes that would take place, even before they happened. 'This is what the minor deities are like,' Phoebus said to himself. 'They feel so powerful, even when they are not so, that they are capable of believing they are the Moiras themselves.'

His face was hard, his jaw clenched. He gathered a large crowd of creatures behind him who simply listened. His bare back, built with the undoubted perfection of the golden ratio, was tense. And he had his bow ready, so that at any moment, if necessary, he could pierce the winds with an arrow as a warning sign. However, fortunately for those involved, it was not necessary, since they came down with mischievous smiles on their faces.

'Who do we have here?'

'It's Phoebus, who hurts from afar!'

Apollo ignored the tone they had both used. He had dealt with these deities before and understood that they were jealous of the prestige enjoyed by the Olympians. He advanced with splendid harmony until he reached where they were. He looked at them coldly. A coldness that could be deciphered in his gaze, which was usually warm, even friendly, although it never lost that shine, that nuance that showed that he was very wise.

'Boreas, Zephyrus.' He said, as a vague greeting.

'Apollo, sir.' The west wind made a rather awkward bow, which the son of Zeus knew well had been planned that way.

He wore his light hair in the same way as the last time he had seen him. He had a well-groomed beard, and his stormy grey eyes examined him with distaste.

The young man next to him was Boreas, North Wind, who had acquired the appearance of a child who had just entered adolescence. His short hair was snowy, and his ice-coloured eyes penetrated Apollo's soul with such force that anyone could have sworn he was freezing him.

Seeing that he said absolutely nothing, Phoebus gave him a warning look. It didn't matter if they laughed at the greeting if they at least had the respect to do so, but Boreas didn't seem to want to.

'Boreas,' he said harshly.

His detonating tone of authority caused the earth to shake beneath his feet once again. His jaw was tighter than ever, and fierceness flared inside his being, without hesitating to move towards the outside. This fury was so great that the birds that had previously been listening decided to take flight, leaving the poor olive tree naked, desolate, a victim of the loneliness that only the years can grant.

'Lord Apollo, god of Olympus, son of Zeus.' He said hastily, bowing his head slightly.

'That is more correct, although it was not necessary for you to say such words, a greeting would have been enough.' He walked again, facing the west wind. 'Zephyrus, I don't understand what you're playing at, but it wouldn't do you any good to get in my way.'

He preferred not to beat around the bush. He had to finish this as soon as possible, after all, the well-being of his beloved Hyacinthus was at stake. He didn't want that ruthless being to come after him. The prince only deserved the best, and of course, that god was quite far from Apollo's definition.

'Honestly, I don't understand it either, Apollo. I was the first one to see him, remember? It was I who saw him, who first approached him. Later, you, always envious, wanted to take away from me what was and remains mine by right.'

'You're talking about Hyacinthus, not an object. So please avoid saying that he is the possession of another being.'

'He is a mortal, perfect gift. You don't care about mortals either. Well, not even the immortals... You've murdered, wounded, and made them flee from you countless times, who's to say it won't happen again? Perhaps one of those fortune tellers of yours has told you that? Is it the prophetic gift that everyone thinks you possess? Or is it simply your desire to obtain a new lover, a new tragedy for the world to moun your misfortune? Oh, poor Apollo! So handsome and so unhappy in love! '

Zephyrus was naked, and Apollo noticed that his body was terribly calm. On the other hand, he himself had problems controlling his own, why was this happening? Maybe he was getting too carried away with his feelings. Holding on to these, clinging to these. That was what his muses had warned him about: 'Be careful, Apollo.'

They told him 'When you love, you not only love, but you feel a thousand other things.'

Yet there on that summit, with the winds before him, and the breezes still blowing overhead as the moon illuminated them, he did not wish to hear words. Neither those, nor any others, because that was not what mattered. There was something beyond that. Something that did not abide by rules or restrictions. It was a love so powerful and strong that he feared it would rot at the expense of a pair of ruthless beings.

The frigid air filled his nostrils. It entered his being, calming the emotion that instinctively uncontrolled his temper. He smelled the aroma released from the olive tree, which was watching them nearby. He felt the rays of the moon, the one that mortals had begun to associate with his sister. Somehow, he sensed the beautiful and wild Artemis next to him, at his side, calming him.

He thought of Hyacinthus. Of his eyes, his laugh, his hair, his face, his complexion, his energy... He thought about the intense emotions that he awakened in him, and he knew that it was worth being there to save him, to help him. It was worth it even if he might have to shoot a couple of arrows to remind the winds not to play that game.

Thus, those words that had unnerved him were transformed into musical notes that soothed him. He turned the enemy's weapons into his own. It was the only way to defeat a pair of minor deities who believed themselves to be the kings of the cosmos.

'It's nothing you should worry about, Zephyrus. I just wonder... And I would like to know the reason for your actions, because I suppose that if Boreas accompanies you, it will be for a reason.' He began to say with care and elegance. Am I wrong?' The only response he received was a stronger breeze, and the cold eyes of the north wind on him. 'You say nothing. I guess I'm not that far from the truth.'

'Apollo.' Zephyrus began to walk around him. He didn't take his eyes off the god. 'You see, I don't know if you understand it, because you really don't seem to. I saw Hyacinthus first. I was the one who discovered him. Why are you interfering in our affair?'

'Is there a *you and him*? Does he conceive of a *we* as you do?' The son of Eos made a grimace, which only gave way to Apollo to continue with his talk. His eyes on his challenged him in a way he hadn't known for a long time. The last time had been with Python, and the horrendous snake had not had a beautiful fate. 'Hyacinthus barely knows of your existence. If he loved you, the story would

135

change, the verses would be rewritten, but in this poem, I am the one who carries the pen.'

'And we are the ones who have the ink.' He snapped.

'You.'

'Us.' Boreas supported this time, who had remained silent for too long.

'Yes, Phoebus, hostile and greedy Olympian, Boreas also feels devotion to Hyacinthus.' The son of Zeus laughed bitterly.

'Here is a solar god and two deities of the winds, fighting for the love of a mortal.'

'We are gods too, Apollo.' Zephyrus corrected him.

'I haven't said otherwise.' He paused slightly. 'Tell me, then, why do you think you are better for Hyacinthus than I or any other being could be?'

'Look at you, son of Leto,' the north responded coldly, addressing him directly to embarrass him. 'Look at the mirror. You radiate beauty, art, elegance, justice, light itself... However, that is the complete opposite of what you really are. You have your hands stained with innocent blood. In your splendid smiles lie the diamonds of your victims. For every beat of your immortal heart, a defenceless body falls to the ground. For every arrow you shoot, someone dies infected by the epidemic you launch. For every verse you delicately compose, a nymph flees in despair. For every note you play on that lyre of yours, a satyr is skinned to death... And being aware of these acts, do you still wonder why one of us would be a better suitor?' Apollo knew that when Boreas decided to speak, his voice carried pure ice, freezing the spirit of the one who received his words, but he never really knew it until the arrival of that embarrassing moment. 'Are you really wondering? You who, more than creating, destroy. You, the cruellest of the Olympians by far. You, who kill for pleasure, and punish for fun. You, Apollo who hurts from afar, so naive and susceptible to the clouds that you harass those you theoretically love... You who punish the innocent, you wonder why we don't want you to get close to the beautiful Hyacinthus, do you really ask? Are you really asking yourself the question? We are the ink, Apollo. To write those verses you are talking about you need ink, and you don't have it.'

'For you Hyacinthus is a poem, for us it is the love we need.' Zephyrus supported, joining his withering gaze to that of Boreas.

The winds could hurt seriously, that's how Apollo saw it now. No wonder some animals feared them. The winds could be cruel at times. They were being so with him and twice as much, because above his head, dishevelling his hair and threatening to uproot that old olive tree, the air roared, screamed. Messages of hate reached his ears; in front of him, the personifications of two of these repudiated him.

'Speechless, Phoebus, god of words?'

The nerves from before the battle were the same ones he felt now flowing through his entire being. They went through his interior and challenged him, cursing him with the same misfortunes in which he had been a participant. These moved in waves, immense waves that awakened every atom of his being, causing him to dig his nails even deeper into the golden arch.

That weapon was no longer light, for now it weighed as much as such a quantity of solid gold would weigh in the hands of mortals. However, he did not believe that he would be able to surrender to the challenge that was being proposed to him. And that had stopped being a meeting to become an act of disrespect. One so immense that it would not be accepted by any god of his lineage.

His eyes, two sea pearls on calm days, were now intense fire. A fire tinged with blue and gold whose colours fought to find out who would govern that gaze full of light. They did not realize that they already had a ruler, since determinism had given way, driving away the fury, the anger that boiled in their veins, screaming at them to attack. He was owed respect, if only being feared he achieved it, he would do it.

'We are talking about a human like someone talking about a piece of food. We only take into account our thoughts, our desires, but have we asked him?' He began to say knowing that this could cause big problems in the near future. 'Have we asked Hyacinthus who he prefers?'

'Are you proposing something?' Zephyrus asked.

'That's right.' He paused slightly. 'Let's do something. Let Hyacinthus choose.'

'Sounds good to me,' the god of the west commented. 'It's the first good idea you've had in your entire long, horrendous existence. If Hyacinthus is smart, which it seems he is, he will choose me.'

'I'm not participating,' Boreas snapped.

'Why not?' The other minor deity asked him, while Apollo watched them.

'He is not only the god of poetry, or music, or medicine. Among other qualities, he is also the god of prophecies. Maybe he knows

139

that Hyacinthus is going to choose him. And that seems unfair to me.'

'That's not how it works, Boreas, but if that is your decision I don't care.'

'You're sure?'

The gaze of the north wind shone for a few moments.

'Sure.'

Apollo nodded accepting it and stared at Zephyrus.

'Let the game begin, then,' the wind said.

And although Apollo did not say it out loud, his mind had a clear answer: *If the love of the beautiful Hyacinthus is a game for you, I hope you lose for his sake. If love were something other than a feeling, it would never be a game but rather an art, because it does not entertain, but creates, if done in the right way.*

VIII

Hyacinthus woke up that morning with his face illuminated by the eternal and infinite light of the sun. Its warmth brought out a thousand different sensations in his inner being, and this light was so welcoming that many times he would think that it had its own attitude, consciousness. One that encouraged him to abandon everything superficial, say goodbye to comfort and go out to find what he really loved. That which filled his soul with new songs. And it was what emanated from that clandestine light that would lead him to happiness.

He got up from his bed and walked around the room. He stopped observing the clear skies over the lands of his birth, the lands of his childhood, of the beginning of his youth. They were bathed in golden tones, and the moon was still in the sky, threatening to fade away when the world least expected it. The birds were singing. They all seemed to sing the same name. 'Apollo', 'Apollo' they said. 'Come Apollo, welcome to the world.' 'Apollo we were waiting for you!' 'Beautiful Selene who has left hand in hand with Artemis. Now the sister runs through the hills with a thousand smiles and Apollo draws the world.' They exclaimed this in the avian language, and Hyacinthus understood them, because he was finally waking up.

He heard a flute being played. Its sound, although distant and weak, reached his ears. It was the first time he heard it. He did not even doubt for a second its origin. It was Pan bringing music to the world, the life that caused beings to flourish and awaken. The young prince felt cajoled with this playing, with this expectation, this reality that he was cherishing at that moment. If he had been able to see into the distance, he would have seen him dancing through the unknown, unexplored, wild lands. However, he was a human being, not an eagle.

Suddenly, a creature descended from a nearby tree. It perched on the window ledge, when Hyacinthus opened it. The coal-black animal looked at him with intelligent eyes. Eyes he had never seen in any living being. The crow watched him, and he knew it meant something. He tried to caress its plumage, but it did not allow it, as it moved away and immediately took flight. The prince followed him with his gaze, a smile on his face.

It was true, it had rejected him, but the world was immense, endowed with infinite beauties that he could never understand. However, he was still in that world. A place whose mysteries escaped his understanding, but at least they embraced him and accepted him as another inhabitant. It was said that nature should be protected, not allowing the sound of Pan's flutes to fade away at some point, even if it would benefit humanity. Because if

142

something was important it was that, Gaia, the entire world. And now Hyacinthus was sure that the Earth was alive.

With these thoughts stuck in his mind, refusing to leave, he dressed and left his room. He picked a peach from the lower branches of a tree, and without saying anything, he equipped his horse to get away from there.

As he entered the paths, he stopped and saw how his sister looked out the window welcoming the day. He couldn't help but smile. If she knew that he had seen his mother in his dreams that night, she would be terribly happy for him. He was surprised by the beautiful soul she possessed. He couldn't understand how in some places in Greece women could be looked down upon when they were pure strength, pure courage. It was said that they could be equal to, or be better than, any man. He soon turned his gaze towards the vast horizon and trotted towards it.

Everything felt in the most authentic way imaginable. The horse he was riding on was nature, the ground it walked on was also nature, the landscapes he saw... The sun illuminating him, being his light, that eternal light that would always return, reminding him that there were escapes even for the darkest moments. He wished for a moment that he could merge with that harmony that human beings were already beginning to spoil, and he well knew that later that would get worse.

He would look for Phoebus in the nearby areas, trying to go unnoticed and at the same time confirm his suspicions. If he was the god he thought he was, there would be no trace of him. His past told him to stop this nonsense, because it was clear that it was a simple coincidence. Instead, his soul, his heart, had seen him and they understood that he was the great Apollo, the one who owned sacred temples, the same one who was praised on countless occasions, who brought arts, healing, prophecies and epidemics, among other things, to the world. That was the being he had met. It was the only answer that made sense to him.

As he passed, Hyacinthus entered a nearby city, where he used to go regularly to think and go unnoticed, since very few there knew his true identity. Upon crossing the walls of that place, he became invisible, one more, another free young man. He liked to listen to the gossip about himself and the rest of his family that spread from mouth to mouth. Sometimes, it was thought that he was the son of a random local couple. It was something so different from his reality that it calmed him in a way.

He dismounted from the animal, and he felt various gazes on him. Murmurs came from their lips, and they gossiped among themselves without taking their eyes off the prince. Out of the corner of his eye, he could see that it was a small group of five girls, who were smiling at him enthralled. So, taking advantage of this attention, Hyacinthus approached them with the reins of his horse in his hands.

'Young people, do you know if a foreigner named Phoebus is staying near here?'

The girls looked at each other, completely bewildered.

'Honestly, I think none of us know anything about any foreigner,' answered the woman who seemed the most athletic, even though all of them were. 'If there were any around, we'd know.'

'Why are you so sure?' He had been struck by the determination in her gaze.

'It's easy to find out. Other human beings are not as strong as those we raised, not even a quarter. So, I'm sorry to give you this answer, but we haven't seen anyone. However, we will be alert.'

Hyacinthus smiled at her. She did the same.

'Thank you.'

'It's the least I can do.'

Without realizing it, someone had identified him in the crowd, and when he began to walk around observing the people, looking for some place where Phoebus could have stayed, this being followed him. He did not give importance to the constant feeling that someone was chasing him since at that time there was quite a lot of movement in the streets.

He saw an elderly man selling weapons and approached him in hopes of gathering information.

'Hello,' he greeted him. 'Do you know...?'

'What do you want, young man?' He interrupted. 'Look, we have a javelin that would look great on you! It would enhance your slender silhouette!' He exclaimed while showing him the weapon.

'Thank you, but I would like...'

'Oh no! How could that have crossed my mind! A bow would look good on you!'

'You don't understand how funny that is right now.'

'What?' he asked.

'Nothing, sir,' he responded politely. 'I wanted to know if you have seen a foreigner lately or if you know where one of them might stay.'

'So you don't want any weapons? I still think this arc would be good for you. What's more, we have the arrows at a very good price. You would look like Apollo himself.'

'No, thanks. I just want you to answer that question.'

'What question? Oh yeah! About the foreigner... Well, look, kid, I honestly don't know if I've seen any of them lately. I don't pay much attention unless they want to buy one of my products that I so carefully make. You know, about forty years ago, I had a good position in the army until I fell in love with a foreigner... Alas! The women of this land are so rough that I found her so sweet and manageable!'

'Very good. Thanks, sir.'

'But, boy, aren't you going to buy the bow?'

Hyacinthus rolled his eyes, and for a moment, he thought about leaving without saying anything, but that would be in very bad taste, so he was ready to respond when a familiar voice did for him.

'Don't you see, Anker? He has already answered you. He doesn't want anything.'

The old man stared at him, trying very hard to remember him, but by the time he had done so, Hyacinthus had already left, accompanied by the man who had spoken.

'So, are you looking for someone, your majesty?'

'Oh, Tamyris! I've told you a thousand times not to call me that!' The man laughed amused.

'I never imagined finding you in this poor area. You, who are used to great pleasures.'

'Tamyris, please don't distract me. I'm looking for someone.'

Hyacinthus continued walking, ignoring the man, but suddenly he snatched the reins of the horse from him and stopped him. He stood extremely close to the prince, fixing his gaze on him. The young man could feel his breath perfectly, as if they were waves caressing the shore... the shore that was his complexion.

Hyacinthus just smiled, amused.

'Who are you looking for so carefully, Hyacinthus, prince of these lands?'

'For a foreigner,' he replied bluntly. 'A foreigner who appeared at my house claiming to be able to teach me a thousand things.'

'Do you think that foreigner lives around here?' He asked with a very soft and harmonious tone as he noticed that Hyacinthus calmed down, freeing himself from the burden of the search.

'I think so, but it doesn't look good.'

'How long have you been searching, prince?'

'Not much.'

'But you haven't found him. Everything indicates that there are no foreigners, right?'

'That's how it is.'

'Perhaps your new master was afraid of falling in love with you and ran away. '

'Why do you say that? '

'Hyacinthus, dear, you are silly sometimes. Any living being with a soul would fall in love with you if you stopped to look at them. '

'I don't believe it.'

'Forget about your teacher. If you have to find him, you will find him without even going out to look for him. Instead, the Moiras wanted us to meet.'

'Did they want us to meet when really what you did was chase me?'

'I couldn't have chased you if I hadn't found you first, right?'

'Why do you turn things around?'

'Because that's what we musicians do, Hyacinthus. We turn everything around to make it even more beautiful. However, that matters little, prince, listen to me: the point is that we have met, and we are here talking. Come with me. Spend this morning with me. I know you want to, I can see it in your body. If you rejected me as much as you try to make it seem, you would have separated as I took the first step to shorten the distance between us. However, you have not done so.' He waited a few long seconds. 'And now that I've told you, I've reminded you, you haven't done it either. You want this as much as I do. Don't stay silent, what do you say to me?'

'Tamyris.'

'That's me.' He then switched to more colloquial language, as he always did after having exchanged several sentences full of formality. 'I could be yours for one morning at least if you gave me the chance.'

'What do I gain?'

'Not returning home as soon, and forgetting about your worries. Don't tell me you have to study. You deserve a day of rest, and you don't have to exercise either... What I see is already quite exercised.'

The man took another step, getting completely closer to Hyacinthus.

'Come on, give me an answer.'

Their faces were almost touching in those moments. Hyacinthus had to be honest, in some ways he was attracted to Tamyris, apart from finding him a rather pleasant person to deal with.

He was a man who was not very tall but had a very muscular and strong build. He wore his dark hair quite short. His skin, like that of the vast majority, was tanned, and he had light eyes. Despite all this, he was not handsome, although he was extremely attractive. He was in his early thirties, and many young women would have wanted to marry him, but he only had eyes for a person who, of course, was not looking to get married, much less was a woman. It seemed that for him, the only human being on the face of the Earth was Hyacinthus.

The prince smiled sideways at his in response, and victory dawned on Tamyris's face.

'Yes?' He insisted, wanting to hear it from his lips.

'Yeah. I'll stay with you,' he responded.

'That is the answer I was longing to hear, dear Hyacinthus.' He said very happily, separating himself slightly from him.

'I was planning to go play at the *agora*. You could join me.' He began to tell him.

'I don't know how to sing, Tamyris.'

'By the muses, Hyacinthus! We all know how to sing!'

'You say that so I sing with you, right?' He told him as he took the reins of his horse again and began to walk.

'Where are you going?'

'To the *Agora*,' he answered without looking at him. 'Wasn't that where we were going to go?'

'Indeed,' he commented, approaching him and gently taking his arm, 'but you won't reach any square that way.'

The prince looked him in the eyes. Tamyris smiled with immense tenderness without removing the physical contact that united him to the young man.

'I'm sorry. I was sure it was that way.'

'No worries.' He observed him carefully. He examined every feature, every particle of his complexion. He couldn't find words to define it other than perfection. Who would want a wife having that prince who was worthy of gods!

'What are you looking at, Tamyris?' he asked with winged softness.

'I looked at your beautiful face, Hyacinthus.'

'Not only you do, you're also thinking, right?'

'I think about why I can't caress it, kiss it, love it.'

'No one stops you from doing that.'

153

'No one except you.'

'I am pleased that you respect my decisions, Tamyris. This is one of the reasons why I have agreed to accompany you to the *agora*.'

'I'm glad to hear that.'

It didn't take long for them to return to their adventures. Hyacinthus let himself be guided by the musician, who soon began babbling about the thousands of new songs he had composed, and how wonderful they were. So wonderful that they would beat all the mortal musicians the world had seen and would see.

The young man had learned over time not to hurt his pride. He simply listened to him while observing the buildings and the people. He said to himself that, although the cities did not have half the beauty of the fields, they were also beautiful. If he felt overwhelmed, he could always look up at the clear sky and imagine that there were no buildings around him. Nothing that would destroy the perfect harmony of nature.

His thoughts soon diverted from the topic on which the proud Tamyris was conversing, moving away from there and returning to the god who had come to visit him. And it was clear to him that if he wasn't there, he would be on Olympus, or perhaps at his side, invisible, so that he couldn't see him. He was so surprised that Apollo had come down from his home with the sole objective of meeting him, that he had been unable to concentrate since the day before.

Spring had already made its way into the world, and it was felt with every second spent outdoors, but this time it was different. Its characteristic avian songs were still present, as was its soft aroma of familiar flower petals, but there was something changing that had never been there before, and if it had, he had never realized it. This difference was a sensation, an emotion that transported him to places he would never have imagined stepping on. He saw the world differently and felt it the same way. It seemed that an archaic force was watching his back, protecting him from all existing evil. He had no doubt that it was so, because he had the impression that Apollo loved him. He didn't know how, but he knew well that he felt devotion, or perhaps admiration, towards him, for whatever reasons. He wouldn't be surprised to know that the god was nearby, watching over him, keeping him safe. He must have thought that mortals were weak, and in a way they were.

Tamyris walked beside him. He kept talking about something Hyacinthus didn't understand. It didn't matter what his lips said, the only thing that mattered was the feeling that overcame him.

Despite this, it didn't take them long to reach the agora, where the aoidos began to play his instrument and sing ballads that reached the prince's ears, but he did not understand their meaning. He was isolated in his thoughts and, immersed in them, he felt fine.

As Tamyris was surrounded by many villagers who sang and danced with him, Hyacinthus knew that he would not notice his absence. When he did, he wouldn't be mad at him. He was too attracted to him to be angry. He smiled at him when he felt his gaze on him and immediately left that square followed by his horse.

He closed his eyes for five seconds as he kept on walking, because he needed to feel nature fully. And that was the best way to do it when you were in the middle of a place full of pedestrians who did not want to stop. Thus, with his eyes closed, Hyacinthus was able to appreciate the beauty that hid in earth's vibrations. It seemed to move under his feet, and he told himself that possibly that was the case. Who knew what mysteries she might hold! If, after all, it was the most primordial thing that existed in his world. The most beautiful, also the most powerful. He thought Gaia deserved more prominence. Everyone looked at the sky and imagined reaching for the stars. On the other hand, few realized how much beauty could be found in the earth that lies beneath the feet of the living being.

The sky was for the birds, because they had wings for a reason. However, the human being had to learn to find that same harmony in Gaia. Hyacinthus believed he was finding it after a lifetime of searching without result. The answer had always been in front of his eyes.

However, as he took a deep breath, he couldn't go any further. Not due to the crowds walking through those streets, nor because his horse had stopped, but rather because something or someone was getting in his way and seemed to refuse to move away.

'You're going to force me to open my eyes, right? Don't you think it's unfair? I'm feeling nature, Gaia herself! At least do me the favour of not interrupting me and moving away.'

The prince crossed his fingers that he was not talking to some object. It didn't take long for a voice to answer him, making him see that wasn't the case.

'You always have your eyes closed. At least you're dressed now,' he snapped.

Those volatile words were enough to make him open his eyes, meeting the person he thought he was.

'You're the one from the forest, right?'

157

'Yes, the one from the forest, although I prefer other nicknames.'

'Ha! We all want better nicknames! Look, I've been with a friend, his name is Tamyris... he wants to be known as the best aoidos, but he's just an aoidos, not the best. By this I mean that we all want nicknames that we will never have.'

He walked again this time with his eyes open, trying to find the way out of the walled city in order to return home. With any luck, Phoebus would be waiting for him.

'Hey, boy! We just found each other!'

'Yes, and we also just said goodbye, Mr. Unknown!'

Zephyrus ran to his side.

'I'm not your friend, you won't get rid of me so quickly. We just met, let me get to know you a little more.'

'Isn't it enough for you to have seen me naked?'

'It was not something unpleasant; however, I am talking seriously, Hyacinthus.'

'How do you know my name? I don't remember saying it.'

'You didn't say it, but I know that you are the prince.'

'How come?'

'Your features tell me so.'

'Sure.' He stopped then. 'Look, I don't know what you want, but please leave me alone.'

'Where are you going in such a hurry, if I may ask?'

'To my first lessons with my new teacher.' As he said those words, Hyacinthus noticed how a flaming fury grew in his counterpart's gaze. A fury that would burn the entire world if it sets its mind to it. 'Why do your eyes shine like that?'

'Like that? Like that how?'

'With fury, fierceness, as if you didn't like what I said. Do you know my new teacher?'

'Too well.' He answered.

'Too well? Tell me something about him.'

'He's evil. Don't trust him. He only wishes to use you, Hyacinthus. That's all he does: use people, but I won't use you. I only take part in this to save you.'

159

'To save me?'

'Save you from your crazy new teacher. Don't listen to him, he has bad intentions. Don't trust him.'

The young man was not pleased with the way the wind had begun to blow, icily. The way in which, suddenly, he felt tension in each of the particles of his body, much less the way that man's eyes popped out of their sockets, giving him a tinge of madness, doom.

'You tell me not to trust him... But to trust you instead, why should I trust you?' He asked while jumping on the horse.

The stranger grabbed the reins of the animal, preventing Hyacinthus from galloping away. Something he knew he wouldn't hesitate to do.

'Because he damages more than he heals, he destroys more than he creates. I, on the other hand, could offer you anything you wanted without even putting you in danger.'

'I'm not interested in what you propose. And besides, if those things are so horrible, why don't you tell me about them?'

'Because he sees everything under the sun.' he answered mysteriously. 'If you want to know the answers, meet me in the same forest as the day we first met when the sun is already hidden.' He only nodded in response.

'Now I have to go. Farewell.'

Seeing that the young man tightened his legs, asking his horse to gallop, the god of the west wind released the reins.

'I know you will come. I have seen it in your eyes, young Hyacinthus,' Zephyrus whispered. 'Boreas,' he said to the wind, 'please keep an eye on him, and make Apollo separate from him. If he is attached to the mortal all the time, even invisibly, we will have no chance of defeating that daring Olympian.'

IX

Apollo had been watching silently. Walking next to his beloved, without him being able to see him, while they searched for that Phoebus who was nothing more than his human form.

He had heard his voice. He had seen how not only the gods were devoted to his greatness, but also mortals. Mortals who knew art well and knew how to identify it when it took shape. He was not envious of Tamyris. Nor was his presence threatening, since it was clear that Hyacinthus was not interested or, at least, not fully. However, he had noticed the concern when finding Zephyrus. He also thought that his prince was a genius, rejecting that scoundrel who believed that one day Hyacinthus would be his.

He would have liked to continue being with Hyacinthus while he rode, but he decided to give the young man what he wanted: an encounter. So, he showed up at the house before he arrived. The slaves did not hesitate to open the door to him, and they took him to the *patio* where Polyboea was, with her eclipsing beauty and her long brown hair flying in the wind. She was wearing a long white dress, which seemed to be made of silk. She was bent over petting a cat, when Apollo stood next to her.

'In the most common creatures, one can find harmony, right?'

The princess looked up. It didn't take long for her to blush while straightening up and putting a wide smile on her face.

'Phoebus, isn't it?'

'That's my name,' he answered. 'Yours is Polyboea, correct?'

'It is.' She paused slightly. 'I am sorry to inform you that my brother is not at home.'

'I already know.' The god's eyes shone with immense intelligence.

'And then...? Let me ask you, what are you doing here?'

'Well, I had been told that you, Princess Polyboea, show many incredible aptitudes for dance, music and poetry.' The young woman lowered her eyes somewhat, shily. That gesture seemed terribly familiar to Phoebus. He soon learned that it was an attitude her brother also possessed. 'I know that I am here to teach your brother, but I am interested in restless, artistic minds, and from what I have been told, you have one.'

'I don't think it's that big of a deal. I only know how to do what they ask of me. I help Hyacinthus and my other brothers. I have free time, since I have finished my education and I do not wish to get married even if it is time, because I think that there are other

163

important things in this place... I could join the training of ordinary people, but my father fears for my safety, so I train with my brothers.'

Apollo smiled sweetly at her.

'It's a way of life, Polyboea.'

'What do you mean?' She asked interested, gradually breaking with the present shyness. The god looked at her sweetly.

'Art, Polyboea! Art! There are many paths we can choose to live our lives. Some are marked by humans as correct, and others are discarded, but they often bring happiness. Sometimes, more than those supposedly correct paths.'

'Do you believe so? Do you really think there is a path to art?'

'There is a dark path that leads to the most infinite happiness, and for you it is the path of art. Let yourself be guided by the muses! Feel them, they talk to you, they whisper to you.'

'But in some places in Greece they would think I couldn't do it.'

'Then, make them see that they are wrong. No one can tell you what or what you can't do except yourself. You must understand that.'

Suddenly, and after hearing those words, Polyboea remained silent, looking into nothingness, very thoughtful.

'How did we manage to have this conversation?' She asked, looking at his eyes. 'How did we start?'

'From what is said, and what I certainly know.'

'How do you know?'

The god realized that the young woman was soaked in, astonished, because after all, the world did not talk much about her, even less so far from her lands. He did little more than smile at her again, at the cost of the purity that she conveyed and even, he risked saying, represented. Apollo bent down, picked up the cat in his arms, and it immediately purred, resting its face on his chest. Those creatures were terribly sensitive, like the vast majority of animals that inhabited Gaia. It knew perfectly well his true identity.

'We are more than four walls. We are more than a body, Polyboea.' He told her without looking at her. 'Sometimes our eyes say what our lips don't. Sometimes, they shout what our hands omit. However, whether we try to repress it or not, our gaze is never silenced. Always speaks to those who know how to listen.' The sun surrounded his body. Maybe he did it on purpose, maybe not, but the sun's rays caressing his skin made him look like a god, and that was exactly what the young woman saw. 'What I mean,' he said, this time, looking into her eyes, 'is that you have tried to silence those qualities so as not to attract attention. However, I see the souls of mortals, and yours sings that song to me: A tragedy, which sometimes becomes a comedy, about the misfortunes of your life. About the way you try to follow the path of the muses without anyone noticing. I understand, Polyboea, the reasons that move you to act this way. There are a thousand men out there that you could choose yourself; despite this, you don't do it because you come before anything else, and that is not a bad thing. Ordinary people tend to put other humans, other beings before themselves, and it is one of the biggest mistakes they could make. One cannot be happy without loving oneself, much less can one participate in the love or joy of a group of creatures if one does not feel all these emotions about oneself. When human beings can spend, I'm not saying a year or a decade, but a measly day alone without getting bored or going crazy, they will have progressed more than ever. And you, Polyboea, are capable of doing it, which tells me a lot more about you than you might think.'

'You have immense knowledge... I would never have imagined it.'

'Sometimes, people surprise you. Do what your heart tells you, and you will find elaborate and complex happiness.'

166

'Do you know anything about art?'

. . .

Hyacinthus dismounted from his horse, helped the slaves remove the animal's equipment, and headed to the garden, where they had told him that they had seen Phoebus.

He was with his sister. Both submerged in an interesting conversation. Her eyes on his. The two of them with a brilliant smile on their faces. They seemed to understand each other. However, Hyacinthus did not feel jealousy, simply eternal joy and a certain degree of satisfaction. Polyboea was the sister he dealt with the most, the one he loved the most. Her advice was very important to him and seeing that the two of them got along well made his day.

Telling himself that they had made the best choice by accepting Phoebus, the young man walked towards them. However, he did not have to take many steps, since the man, whom Hyacinthus thought of as a god, saw him first. Saying goodbye to the princess, he walked to meet him.

'I had gone for a morning walk.' The prince excused himself when they were side by side.

'Good morning,' he greeted him with a tone full of harmony. 'Don't worry, Hyacinthus. Besides, we weren't going to do much today other than walk. Would you accompany me?' The boy nodded.

Over the god's shoulder, Hyacinthus saw a smiling Polyboea giving him her approval to go for a walk with him.

They remained silent until they reached the esplanade where the slender ephebe usually trained. He saw fit to tell him, so he did just that.

'Someday we will come.'

Hyacinthus was struck by the way he had said it as if they were never going to go.

'Your father has chosen to keep your former master, Hyacinthus. Polyboea told me that you left early this morning, so I suppose the king had not announced it to you yet.'

'What? So you won't stay here?'

'I'll stay, but we'll do different things. Your father, after meeting me, has decreed that I might prove to be a positive influence on you, although not in an educational way. Not at least in the subjects, but in life and in the soul.'

'What do you mean?'

'To the simplest things. Those that the vast majority of the population is not able to control.'

'Perhaps they are things that do not want to be controlled.'

'Maybe. But it is one thing not to control them, and quite another to fear them. I want to teach you that there are things that one cannot control, but that is not synonymous with fear in the least. Those little uncontrollable things can be the key to finding the Elysian fields in life.'

'What is it synonymous with, then?'

'With the Elysian Fields.' He responded with a half-smile on his face. He liked the interest the mortal showed.

Hyacinthus laughed lightly.

'You don't know me yet, and you already want to kill me?'

'Why do you say that?'

'Elysian Fields, you know, death.'

'You would have to be splendid to reach them.'

'What? Do you doubt me? I have a spirit worthy of that place.' He replied, amused.

'I do not doubt it, I just remind you.'

The prince said nothing, but stopped walking, and examined him in careful detail. The sun's rays seemed to dance on his complexion, and art itself was reflected in his eyes. Hyacinthus didn't know how no one had yet realized who Apollo really was, or who he had suspicions he was. Despite everything, he felt curious, was he so strange that he even attracted the attention of the gods?

'What's going through your mind, prince?'

Apollo's voice came so soft from his throat, with a tone so gentle, immersed in a love so deep as that which he professed for himself, that Hyacinthus could do nothing but answer.

But not before looking at his incredibly sky-blue windows. So beautiful that they transmitted to him the need to jump into them, to fall into that water and bathe his entire body in it.

'I think of a thousand things, Phoebus.' Phoebus, the brilliant one, as some called him. There was no doubt in his mortal creature that it was the perfect name.

'A thousand things can be dangerous, sometimes safe, sometimes complex and sometimes simple...'

'A thousand things can change depending on the mind. A thousand things can be one, and one can be a thousand.'

'That's how it is. What are your thousand things?'

'It's a concern, Phoebus. Something that eats me inside. Maybe it's simple nervousness, or maybe it's an unknown future. An uncertain fate that hovers over my being. I swear to you, Phoebus, that I feel that hands are crushing my heart, which is so fragile trying to win the battle. I fear that one day I will lose. I fear that it will end up falling apart, abandoning my soul in a limbo from which I will not be able to escape. I am not afraid of death. However, I do fear getting lost.'

It is knowing your true identity he wanted to say, although again his words silenced what his heart was screaming. *Knowing the misfortunes for which you are known. Knowing that all true loves end in tragedy. I don't want this to be true love. If anything, that's what consumes me inside, causing me to not want to separate from you, even though I don't even know you. If this is love, I don't want it to be true love. Not for fear of dying. To die for you, but for the fear that invades me when I think of you suffering my departure. You, who have so many enemies, Apollo. You, who have suffered so much... You, who have fought so much, Apollo, listen to me, I do not wish you to suffer for me. If what I feel is that cliché, I hope to keep it a secret under the guise of taboo until I am at least prepared to face it. I curse Eros and his damned little arrows!*

Apollo watched him, immersing himself in his gaze in the same way that the other had done. He listened to his cries. Those same ones that he tried to hide from him, but he did not rebuke him. He understood his motives. He would have done the same if he had been in his place.

But why wonder about the future when you could live in the present? When he could spend time with him? With these questions in mind, he set out to answer:

'Hyacinthus,' he said softly, 'they are the emotions of the moment, and even if they are not entirely pleasant, enjoy them, delve into them.' The formality had already been eliminated from his winged words, because he did not feel them as such. His lips formulated what his soul did not want to silence. 'Let them take you to the place where they want you to be. Feel them. Those sensations you

172

describe always hide what our mind is afraid to think. Find that worry and unearth it. Close your eyes, Hyacinthus.'

'Is it really necessary?'

He hadn't even realized that the god had opted for more colloquial language. He was too focused on him to make out exactly what he was saying.

'You feel nervous about something that has not yet arrived and that may never arrive. Allow your mind to really tell you what you fear. Allow me to tell you if there has been anything in the current present or in the near past that has caused your consciousness to stir. Do you trust me?' Hyacinthus nodded.

'Fully.'

'Good. Close your eyes, Hyacinthus. Close your eyes and look beyond your eyelids. Observe what surrounds us. Feel the earth, the breezes and the sun. Feel my energies, also yours.'

The prince did so.

He closed his eyes and suddenly, he could see.

He saw what lay in front of him. Those leafy trees that began the nearby forest. The short grass he walked on. To his right was

Apollo, although this time his mortal form was not so passable. A smile appeared on his face. The most perfect smile you would ever see. His golden hair had darkened slightly, and his lips formulated words that reached his bold ears. He felt the strength that his silhouette transmitted. A powerful and archaic force that pulled on his body or, at least, that's how it felt. However, it was not unpleasant, quite the opposite.

'Now travel, Hyacinthus. Let your mind tell you your fear. Let them appear here. Nothing bad will happen to you. I'm with you, remember that.'

His words gave life to his thoughts. They had cut the rope that bound them, and in those moments, unleashed and indomitable, they were fighting to make way for their vision. It didn't take long until he was able to visualize them.

They were two beings without bodies, not even eyes, they argued and went after Apollo. Apollo, who was now more god than human, seemed like an impenetrable wall. A bubble surrounded him. A yellow bubble that burned those figures. If he had stopped for a second longer to observe the panorama, he would have seen a flower with purple petals sprout between the feet of the god of arts, but he did not wait; instead, invaded by a terrible anguish, he opened his eyes.

For a moment, he believed that he would find those beings, but fortunately, that was not the case. Apollo looked at him, and his lips asked something that he did not hear. In his head, those unknown creatures continued to battle, and they did not disappear until the sun's rays surrounded him, embracing him.

Because he had never received a hug from the sun, but that was it, without a doubt. He felt all the rays of it on him. Although Apollo had not made any kind of physical contact with the prince, he felt his energies surrounding him. Those same energies full of power, but this time his eyes were open.

'Are you OK?'

'Yeah. Just a little self-conscious.'

'Lie down if you need to. Feel Gaia, she will help you.'

'I don't know if she will, but the sun...'

'The sun is the best healer,' he murmured. 'Are you sure you're okay?'

'I've been better. I thought it would be nice,' he replied, as he sat on the floor, following his advice.

'I knew it wouldn't be, but it was necessary for you to know the reason, the motive. Now even if you are not in your best condition, you will be calmer, am I wrong?'

'No, you are not. It is true that I feel more liberated, but at the same time, exhausted.'

'Then, recover your energy and feel everything that human beings miss out on by thinking about the past or the future, forgetting about the life that is only found in the present.' He made a slight pause during which he lay down next to him. 'This time, I'll do it too.'

'Do you think I've lost my trust in you because I had a bad time for a few seconds?' He asked, leaning on the floor with his hand, still half sitting.

His eyes were fixed on Apollo, although the latter's had already closed. The god only smiled widely, and Hyacinthus noticed the same smile as before. He also noticed how dark his hair now seemed. It was as if he had lost the gold that bathed him. However, the prince cared little. He was at his side, and his energies, in those moments, were much more noticeable.

'No, I don't think you have, but it's good for me to remember some things too.'

'Why? Weren't you an incredibly positive influence?'

'Even the most immense of forces becomes weak if it forgets to live. I don't want to forget to live, Hyacinthus, do you?'

'Honestly, I don't think I have lived yet. My heart may beat, I may breathe, but I don't know how to live. I don't know what life feels like... would you show it to me?'

'Of course I will,' he replied, 'but first, tell me, why do you think you haven't lived?'

'Well, human beings, although you may not believe it, tend to be very busy. Meetings, studies, jobs... Run looking at the position of the sun every second. Run and go to this or that. Do that thing you forgot about yesterday, but be careful not to forget this other thing. Think about the war that is supposedly approaching, but do not forget about the war that has already passed. Think about the future, but don't make the mistakes of the past. Live in the past, you will live in the future. Don't clear your mind, keep it focused and full of a thousand things that will only bring misfortune and make your existence bitter. If you do it well in the future you could be happy... In the future you could be happy. A future that may

177

never come. You see it? We humans only think about what happened and what will happen, we never stop in the here, in the now. We don't stop because we fear that, if we do, we won't be able to handle it, handle ourselves. We don't want to be alone for fear of loneliness, although being alone doesn't have to mean feeling lonely; likewise, we fear the crowd, because there is something inside us that assures us that we will not be ready until we first know ourselves, but we are still afraid of being alone because only the strongest souls could be with themselves for a whole day without fall into misery, thus finding in themselves the relationships they require.'

'Why do you think no one stops even for a second?'

'We are not brave, Phoebus. To stop, you have to be a person endowed with courage and wisdom. These are, unfortunately, qualities that are not usually common.'

'Congratulations, because you are going to be one of them.'

'Do you seriously believe it?'

'You are stronger than you think, prince.'

Apollo felt the young man lie down completely next to him.

'Will you talk while I keep my eyes closed?'

'Would that help you?'

'Yes, it would.'

'I will do it, then.'

'Thank you.' He murmured as he closed his eyes.

At that moment Apollo opened his, and gently rose to examine the noble face of Hyacinthus. He was very relaxed. All the tension had vanished from his body. The god felt terribly grateful to the Moiras for having put that mortal on his path. Because everything he was, everything he was made of, wrapped him in the most beautiful emotion.'

'Phoebus?'

'Tell me.'

'Will you speak in the end?'

Without saying anything, Apollo lay down again and closed his eyes.

'Breathe deeply. This will make your body calm down even more, reaching the vibrations of the animals. They see and hear before anyone else.'

'Okay,' the young man murmured.

'Don't talk, Hyacinthus, just feel. Trust in the knowledge that you will feel it. The Earth moves, and you will be able to see it, Hyacinthus, but first you have to wait. You have to relax completely. It's the only way to do it.

'Take a deep breath. Notice how it enters your nostrils, passing through the walls of your body. Notice how it goes down through it, caressing the interior and filling it with life. It keeps it alive like wood in a fire, but it has little to do with your true being. Release this same air and imagine how the negative, the toxic, the vile escape from you being expelled by that same air that escapes from your lips. Get that negativity away from you. That negativity should not surround you, nor any other self-respecting human being. That negativity is nothing more than all the worries that people usually have. Each of those questions about a future that has not yet arrived. Each of those regrets from a past that no longer exists. Let all that go. Let it escape. Let it get away from you... Now you only need the purity of this air, the blank mind attentive to the words I speak. Listen carefully, Hyacinthus, for what you will feel now you have never felt before, and when you open your eyes, everything will have changed forever. Your life will cease to be your life, starting again, rising from your ashes. Well, you know something, Hyacinthus? Humans are always so worried that they completely forget to spend time with themselves, to get to know themselves... Very few know how to answer the simplest question, who are you? Who am I? They don't know what to say, and it should be the first thing they know. However, I don't blame any of them. You have to be brave to risk knowing yourself. Most would not like to know how obscene they are, but you, Hyacinthus, possess beauty in every tiny part of the soul that peeks through those eyes of yours. You possess so much harmony that you manage to turn your body, which although perfect would never be worthy of your being, into a golden vessel where your soul rests. Now you vibrate trapped in your body. Get rid of the body. Let your soul be. Let it go if it wants. Let it see mine. Let it feel me. Let it feel the roots of those trees that reach us. Let it feel the earth, its movement. Feel the pressure of the sky. Allow yourself to feel the present, Hyacinthus. Allow yourself to live. Allow yourself to see. Allow yourself to realize everything you have missed. Allow yourself to wake up, Hyacinthus. Allow yourself to forget everything you have been taught and learn what you really know to be the truth. Reach that state, Hyacinthus. Feel. You breathe, so live. Don't tie yourself to the superficial, live truly. Live...'

Hyacinthus felt in an extraordinarily strange way. His body was no longer heavy. It was as if he had never been there. It no longer hurt at all, and he had the immense feeling that he could fly if he put his mind to it. The thing is that he noticed how something inside him, something much lighter, vibrated, threatening to rise to finally free itself from the burden of those four walls from which it usually could not escape. He also noticed an archaic strength beneath his being.

This force stirred, moved. It seemed to move forward and forward without stopping, turning around as if it were performing some unknown dance. For a few moments, he knew he was breathing. The Earth breathed beneath him. He quickly realized that he would never doubt again that the ground he stood on was truly alive.

The trees that had always caught his attention whispered lessons in his ears. It was true that they were far away, but their voices reached him because of the soft wind. Such a beautiful breeze... So beautiful that he scolded himself, wondering how he had never noticed that. The grass that grew under it danced to the rhythm of the songs that the birds spread through the skies. And the sky, desperate, tensed up trying to reach the Earth, but in a certain way it remained calm, giving the impression that it was relaxed, tranquil, as if nothing disturbed it, even though Hyacinthus knew well that was not the case.

And his hands... Now they were stiff, cold, dead, like the rest of his body, but that fact pleased him. He could be himself authentically. Himself in all his essence. He could escape and flee with Apollo. He could stay with him for all eternity, lose himself in his energies just as in those moments he lost himself in the vibrations of the entire world.

He had begun to understand, but only the tip of the iceberg... Now he was beginning to know everything that really mattered. Absolute truth, goodness, justice were before him... All of them before him on a somewhat distant mountain, but he was sure that he would reach them if he wanted to. He would achieve them if he began to reflect, to do ethics with respect to every small detail that surrounded him. But now he knew what the path was, where his soul should go. He also lived in the knowledge that he would never be alone down that path if he decided to walk it, because there would be someone by his side to help and support him. He was not talking about his father, or his mother, or even his sister, but about that equally powerful presence that was at his side, adorning his emotions with thousands of lyres that would never die out. He'd be surprised if he stopped listening to them. He understood that even after he died, they would still be there, filling him with life like nothing had before. However, he also understood now that his true being was enough for him. The one who had much more knowledge than he could have imagined.

He could answer that damned question and a million more about his being, even about life itself... Because, by the gods! Hyacinthus realized how beautiful life was! The mission of life! The mission of life, which was none other than to acquire knowledge, learn, and live! Live and live every minute! Every moment, without forgetting that time never existed in a definable way, much less controllable!

'Hyacinthus, listen, feel, smell life. Be alive, Hyacinthus! Don't even think about dying without having lived! Don't even think about being able to grasp all this and refuse to do so... Break with what you've been taught. Break with what you have learned and look, see, observe the reality, the truth. It lies here, next to us. It's a shame not to feel it. Listen, Hyacinthus. Pay attention... This is the real life, the one that your kind misses out on because of the worries that should never have replaced emotion, the celebration of life, the harmony of each leaf, each branch, each piece of tree bark, the notes that the birds sing, the beauty of the creatures you live with, the movements of the Earth, and the majestic clouds. Forget about worries, Hyacinthus... forgetting about them does not mean that they cease to exist, but rather that you will not let them take away your existence.'

The prince could not hold back his tears. These did not arise from Apollo's words, but from their meaning, accompanied by the sensations that surrounded him. He realized that he had always unconsciously believed himself to be the owner of the cosmos, the king of the entire world, as all other human beings used to do, but now he realized how small he was. So unimportant compared to what life really was. In those moments, even the way the tears fell down his face was different. It was beautiful. Everything seemed beautiful to him, but the point was that it had always been that way. However, he had never stopped to see it, to feel it, to listen to it. He had never realized the passion, the love he could feel towards life when he discovered it. Because before that it was a complete stranger. A stranger, who surrounded his places, who pursued him, filled him inside and never stopped in those twisted adventures.

Instead, life in those moments turned out to be the most beautiful thing he would ever experience. That paradise was within everyone's reach. It was before everyone's eyes, but few were able to feel it. Able to find the door to the hidden. That was the world. That was Gaia in her full essence. Such were the seeds that had sprouted thanks to Demeter. Such were the protégés of Artemis, the legacy of Pan. Such was the life that surrounded him. A life full of harmony that he had never understood.

And Apollo, lying next to him, represented an inexhaustible source of purity, of radiance, of power. It was not as much as what the

Earth, Gaia, transmitted to him, but it was so much and so gentle, that it still healed his broken soul. It healed his mind, and opened his eyes, removing the blindfold that had not allowed him to truly live for so many years. It was those energies that surrounded him and protected him. He didn't want them to get away from him.

'Neither darkness nor toxicity can touch you, Hyacinthus. There is no mortal, nor immortal, neither living nor dead, that can harm you. If darkness falls upon you, I will personally see to it that it fades away. If fear takes its place in your slender soul, I will make it flee away from your being. If evil stalks you in any form, if it manages to penetrate your interior, I will heal your wounds until they stop bleeding and heal completely. When you feel dead, lost, lie on the ground and feel us. Feel that life is much more than what humans define as such. Feel that there is beauty in every place, in every creature... Feel the energies and you will understand what the world is like. You will understand its harmony.' The young prince noticed how Apollo's fingers gently caressed his face. He didn't flinch. He liked the touch. It was so warm... 'Do not cry, Hyacinthus, for not having realized it sooner. Cry because you are realizing now. Shed tears at the shock, but never blame yourself.'

Those soft caresses continued over his face, through his hair. They were not the fingers of the god, but the eternal rays. These surrounded him, taking over him. They were not wrapping his body, but rather that lighter matter that still vibrated inside him, threatening to escape from its cage. The sun was undressing him without the need to remove his clothes. The sun was examining him as he was. He didn't see a face, not even a body, but rather a soul that was beginning to awaken in those moments. The sun embraced him. It merged with him, driving away all the darkness that threatened to attack him, protecting him just as Apollo's words had promised. They protected him and also loved him. Hyacinthus didn't need to ask to know.

'Open your eyes when you feel ready. You'll be fine.' His voice promised again. That voice that was not ordinary. That voice that was none other than the speech of the arts.

Hyacinthus was pleased because of the welcome of the rays that would never go out. He appreciated the way he heard the lyres being played in the background, and the grace in Apollo's words. Even so, he understood that sooner or later he would have to return, but never like before that experience. He now possessed knowledge that he would never have imagined attaining. At that moment, he was awake. However, he knew well that he had a long road ahead full of unknown learning. Life was nothing more than an enormous lesson given in the form of verse accompanied by clandestine symphonies.

As he began to move his fingers gently as the god recommended, his soul stopped vibrating, understanding that that would not be the day he would leave the prison that subjected him. Despite everything, the young man continued to feel the sun surrounding him, although now it seemed to be personified. Well, something that Hyacinthus did not know was that the energies of this star were immersed in the human body of Phoebus.

When the prince opened his eyes, he found Apollo surrounding him with his arms and looking into his eyes like one who observes the most precious thing one has, like one who observes the person he loves the most.

X

When the sun began to set, and after saying goodbye to Phoebus, Hyacinthus remembered the stranger's words from the morning. The same one who had examined him while he lay naked on the forest grass. The same one who seemed to be scandalized by even thinking about Apollo for a second. He remembered, thus, what he had said to him, the invitation he had made to him. Despite having initially refused to attend, in those moments, he felt an immense need to do so.

His suspicions were stronger than ever. Furthermore, he well knew that Apollo understood what he thought about him... He was a god, yes, but he would never look at him with different eyes because that afternoon he had really seen him, he had felt him. He had lived his soul, and it was full of goodness, of immense majesty. There were no words perfect enough to define him, to even be at his level.

He had an unsuspecting beauty, not only on the outside, but also on the inside. His essence was beautiful, although Hyacinthus had to admit that in those moments, he saw more harmony in the beings that inhabited the world than ever before. He couldn't have done anything horrible without justification. He was not like the others, Apollo was perfection, goodness, justice, the light that was so complex to reach for simple mortals. But he had had all those attributes at his side, narrating to him, even surrounding him with his arms... Apollo was nothing other than the most perfect thing he had found on earth, although of course Apollo was a greater force, whose origin many attributed to the cosmos. Hyacinthus firmly believed that no one and nothing would make him take a different look at him. Because the god could have murdered, tortured and condemned for no reason millions of times, but he was blinded and would not see it... He would try to justify him no matter what because the prince was in love, knowing it, but at the same time, hiding it.

Despite all this, despite his conviction, he found himself leaving his home after saying goodbye to Apollo. He found his feet guiding him towards the forest where he had encountered the stranger the first time. His limbs seemed to know very well where to go. In contrast, his mind was unable to get away from the emotions that enveloped him so powerfully. They welcomed him into an abyss full of security and fantasies. His mind dissipated along with his thoughts, and these were guided by his heart, which beat strongly as he thought of the man, the man who was above all a deity with whom he had spent the day.

Because his being reigned in his head and in the rest of his body. It was also the protagonist of his thoughts... However, he feared somewhat. Hiding that feeling that enveloped him, he tried to isolate himself from the words, from the emotions that a simple name could provoke in him. Likewise, he tried to consider the possibility that they would destroy everything that the god meant. He had to listen to the stranger without being blinded by an intense light coming from the eternal rays of the sun.

When he arrived at the place, he was not surprised to see the man already there.

He had sat on the low branch of a tree and was observing him from that height.

His gaze impregnated with blackness shone for a few moments, absorbed in the happiness that invaded him. Zephyrus did not think that Hyacinthus would show up, since from what he understood he had enjoyed Apollo's company that same afternoon. Apparently and according to Boreas, Phoebus had shown him the beauty of the world as his first lesson; the light of life. Something that was not at all surprising coming from a god like that.

However, despite the enjoyment with the Olympian god, the young prince was there. He was in front of him. He was somewhat dazed and even lost. The west wind realized that his gaze was alien, as if he were in a distant place, very far from there. It didn't take long to decipher his thoughts, thus finding out that what was happening to the mortal was that little by little he was falling in love with Apollo. He felt an immense admiration emanating from his being, a platonic one, which would soon become erotic, before turning into a forbidden and impossible love that he would try to hide until the moment when he could no longer do so.

That meant that Phoebus was winning the bet, and that if Hyacinthus was in his right mind, he would leave him forever as soon as he told him all the misfortunes and mishaps that Apollo had caused in millions of hearts and spirits.

He wanted to make him see that with the god of the sun one did not go far. The sun went out at night, leaving mortals alone, unprotected against the growing darkness. The one who guided him through the heavens did the same. He would hug him and kiss him. He would love him for a few hours, but suddenly he would abandon him to his fate. By then, Hyacinthus would be so dependent on him that he would not be able to bear having him and would die.

To Zephyrus' surprise, the prince did not get closer to him, he simply fixed his gaze on the other's and the tired words began to escape from his lips:

'You are a stranger to me, not gifted with any kind of education. An unknown being who forced me to listen to him this morning. The same one who found me naked in the forest and stared at me for gods knows how long. That stranger who claims to know the deepest and darkest secrets of the new teacher my father has hired, yet he remains silent even when I have been waiting for him to open his mouth for several minutes. You know me. I have the feeling that you do perfectly, but do I know you? Have you even told me a name or a nickname? Do I know where you come from or simply what you want from me? Because I don't think all this has to do with Phoebus.'

'You're wrong, Prince Hyacinthus. There is nothing else I want other than to warn you and beg you to be careful with that criminal who you think is a good person.'

'Criminal! Are you listening to yourself? Tell me who you are and maybe I'll pay some attention to you.'

'I can't tell you that yet, but, Hyacinthus, heed me. Phoebus will lead you to ruin.'

'Phoebus will lead me to ruin? All Phoebus does is take me to the Elysian fields. Are you aware of how much harmony that being possesses? How much justice and intelligence? Do you know? Are you aware of who you are talking about? Phoebus, a criminal! Phoebus is the rays of the sun, the songs being played by the lyres, the words that accompany them. Phoebus is the healing of body, soul, spirit and heart. Phoebus is the arrow from the bow that the poor shoot in the winters when the crops have died, and their relatives are at risk. Phoebus is the absolute and eternal truth that philosophers seek. He is everything and nothing at the same time. He is infinite beauty that can never be adequately described! Oh, if Phoebus were the criminal you say! I wish we were all criminals, then! It is the dream of the lost human. It is he, then, the light that dresses my agonies in crows with yellow beaks and intelligent eyes! It is he who will transform my melancholy into divine inspiration! If you didn't simply hate him... if only you felt him like I felt him today... you would discover that even the most important gods envy him. And if one day our gods are marginalized, Phoebus will be the envy of the god who rules in those days. Phoebus will be what hurts him the most, what will make him tear his head off... Because Phoebus is infinite things, and all of them beautiful.' Zephyrus jumped down from the branch on which he had been sitting. He listened to Hyacinthus, and did not want to believe his words. He walked towards him without stopping until they were side by side.

'Oh, you're so young! Don't you realize, Hyacinthus? The love that you think you don't feel yet, shines in you, wells up inside you... Why do you let a being like that blind you?'

'Why do you think that being affects my sight, Mr. Unknown?' He asked in a soft whisper, knowing that he would hear him, since Zephyrus was a short distance away from him.

'Because you hide the love that is beginning to emanate within you. And this is like a seed that grows and grows the more it is watered.'

'Why do you think it's love?' He asked again, taking a step back, because Zephyrus had advanced and they had found themselves a few centimetres from each other. He had felt his breath, and he had not liked the sensation, because it had reminded him of a soft breeze that would end up getting angry, becoming an uncontrollable wind.

'Because you defend it, saying that it is the best thing you have found even before hearing the misfortunes this god has generated. You defend him, because deep down you know he is evil. Do you want to hear the truth, Hyacinthus?' He said, approaching him again. 'Or are you afraid, young prince?'

'Do I have any other option? After all, I agreed to come, knowing that you would not let me leave until you had told me about all those horrifying actions that my new master has supposedly carried out.'

'You have no other option. Telling you that you do would be lying to you and I don't want to start our relationship that way.' Despite knowing that Hyacinthus was uncomfortable, he approached him again.

'Our relationship?' He asked strangely. 'I'm sorry to tell you that we don't have any relationship. I have not agreed to any of that. I just want you to tell me. Tell me the truth. That truth that you claim to know. If you know, why do you stop? Why do you approach me with your fingers crossed behind your back? I don't want anything other than to hear your words so I can return to the tranquillity of the four walls of my house, do you understand what I'm saying?'

'I understand it perfectly.'

'Then, don't delay in starting.' When he said that, he used a tone of voice full of authority that, coming from the lips of a prince like him, could not be disobeyed.

Hyacinthus clenched his jaw. He watched him with an icy face, crossing his arms. It made him look older, and much more experienced in those kinds of events. The truth was that, in a certain way, he had already matured more in that afternoon with Phoebus than most people would ever achieve in a lifetime. Now he waited for the stranger to decide to speak.

'If you don't want to talk, if you have changed your mind, let me tell you that you can turn around and disappear from my sight. I will pretend this meeting never happened.'

'You still insist, eh, Hyacinthus? You still insist, because you still fear. I go round in circles many times, and I take such a long time to start, just to be able to appreciate how the features of your face gradually tense.'

'Do you know that telling me those things won't earn my trust?'

'I will gain your trust based on the incredible truths that your beloved master...'

'That my beloved master hides,' the prince finished, rolling his eyes. 'I've heard about it, would you care to get started?'

'Of course,' he replied as he closely observed Hyacinthus's noble body. 'Phoebus comes from a somewhat distant place.'

'That's what he said.'

'A faraway place that really isn't that far away, either.'

'Remoteness is subjective depending on the creature that looks at it. Lesbos is close for a bird, far for a human, and an ant would never be able to get there.'

'Totally agree.' Zephyrus moved gracefully around the young man. As he did so, a soft breeze enveloped him, caressing both bodies.

Hyacinthus, for his part, felt it, but said nothing. He didn't want to let the stranger see that he was paying attention, although he was certain that he would already know that.

The breeze caressed him sweetly, this air was nothing more than the extension of Zephyrus' thoughts. Where his hands could not reach in human form, his wind would reach; where his words could not reach, his soul would reach. Apollo had reached the spirit of Hyacinthus, but he would take over his body.

'You completely agree, I see, but you still don't tell me anything.' He whispered, looking dangerously into his eyes with a hint of rebellion imprinted in her gaze.

'Wait, Hyacinthus,' the wind commented in his ear. 'You are little more than a child, and you want to go very fast, but enjoyment is achieved by going slowly.'

The prince clenched his jaw even more without taking his eyes off the opponent's.

'I don't know if you haven't heard, Mr. Nameless, but I'm not here for anything erotic, the erotic thing you're proposing by approaching me in such an inappropriate way.'

'Erotic things? Just because there are several adults who want that from you, doesn't mean that we all do.'

'Then why are you doing this?'

'What?' He asked, amused, pretending to be innocent.

'By the gods, sir! You know very well what I mean.'

Zephyrus brought his hand closer to the boy's face, but their skin did not touch. However, Hyacinthus felt an icy wind caressing him again. It was like an invisible hand that had first caressed his cheek and was now on his lips.

Zephyrus' gaze was placed completely on the young man's expressions. The west wind knew that Hyacinthus was feeling that tickling. That fact alerted the ephebe in a certain way.

'Tell me once and for all what you wanted to tell me, sir.' He insisted.

'I didn't hear you well, what were you saying?' The mischief in his pearls made Hyacinthus see that he had heard him perfectly. It only generated some kind of excitement in him to hear him say it again.

'Tell me, please.'

'About what?'

'Please tell me about the horrible things my teacher Phoebus has done. Tell me and go away.'

'Such manners for a member of royalty! You don't have to admit it, you don't even have to think about it, but I know perfectly well that this situation at the very least catches your attention. You are drawn to it like the sky to the earth and the sea to the coast.'

A kind of chill ran down his spine as he felt the breeze on his bare neck, and he couldn't do anything other than deny the continuous unknown sensation that was gradually invading his being.

However, he knew that the joy was reflected in his face, if not in his eyes, which, as was the case with all living creatures, were the mirror of the soul. They were incapable of lying or hiding anything. Humans were open books for those who knew how to read, and Zephyrus was a reader. A pretty good and experienced one. Hyacinthus did not represent any mystery to him, nor did his thoughts or the sensations that ran through his body at that moment.

The god of the west wind repeated the same thing to himself. It had been true that Apollo had reached his spirit first, possibly also his heart, but mortals had a very vulnerable body and were sensitive to stimuli. Fortunately, the pleasure they gave them was so great that they would sell everything they cared about to enjoy a measly second of bodily joy. The young prince before his eyes was no different. Humans, without realizing it, were slaves to their own cages, to their own bodies, and he would use that fact to his advantage if it meant he could have Hyacinthus to himself.

'Mister...'

'Hyacinthus.'

'Are you going to tell me?'

Zephyrus did not respond immediately, but waited for long minutes, without taking his eyes off the young man, and then spoke:

'Phoebus comes from a distant land. He has a sister, who he is quite close to, although she is quite unpleasant in my opinion. He was the second to be born, on the seventh day of any month. Both siblings are very close to their mother. One day, let's just say another woman messed with her. Phoebus and his sister annihilated her family, the daughters and sons of that woman who had little to do with the dispute.' Hyacinthus looked at him, trying to ignore the breeze that surrounded him. 'Aren't you going to say anything?'

'It's not something I would have done, but they messed with his mother, right?'

'That's right, but do you think it's fair?'

'I'm not saying I think it's fair,' he answered quietly.

Zephyrus approached him even more, their faces being extremely close. The young prince looked down.

'A little louder, please.'

'What?'

'Repeat.' Hyacinthus bit his lower lip slightly.

'I don't justify his exploits, but at least he had a reason.'

The boy did not know how he had managed to give such a long answer, without losing the firmness of his words. Because now that growing sensation was much more powerful. It didn't help to feel the stranger's breathing so close to his body either. Not even his voice whispering in his ear. And he understood that the wind came from nowhere else but the god.

He tried to keep his thoughts focused on something completely different: on the warmth of the sun that had already left him, on the beauty of the crescent moon that peeked through the clouds in the sky, or simply, on the beauty of the trees that surrounded him. Great and immense beings full of wisdom that would not stop observing him even when his heart stopped beating.

They were thoughts that calmed him, removing the feeling that did not allow him to be free, to behave as he should... It was true that it was not something vile, but that was not the time, and even less so when it was provoked by a person whose name he did not know. Although, to tell the truth, Hyacinthus already had an idea of the man's true nature.

'Continue, please, I'm sure you have more stories.' He stated.

At least as long as he continued talking, the prince would have the opportunity to place those stories he told him inside his head, try to find a similar myth whose protagonist was the god Apollo.

'He also cut the throat of a flute player who was a better musician than him.' He paused ever so slightly. 'The musician and your beloved teacher were competing against each other. The beings that made up the jury claimed that it was very close, so you master proposed making it more complicated. The winner would be the one who sang and played the best, but the poor flute player... He played a flute, and with his lips occupied with the instrument, he couldn't sing. However, your teacher, who owned a lyre for an instrument, didn't care. So Phoebus, being the only one who could sing while playing, won the competition. Although of course, so obscene is that teacher of yours, that victory through cheating was not enough. When they finished, he somehow got to where the supposed loser was and skinned him alive for challenging him. Does that sound familiar? Does it seem fair to you?'

'Yeah.'

'You think it is fair?'

'No, sir,a I say that it does sound familiar to me. It is similar to the myth of Athena and Arachne, am I right? Arachne is also punished for challenging Athena. Is the goddess Athena unfair to you, sir? Or do you simply think that Phoebus is unfair because he is Phoebus? Maybe you're just envious of him.'

'The difference...' His eyes burned with rage, although he remained calm. They burned like the flames of the braziers, not because of Hyacinthus's words but because of how Apollo's thoughts and presence had penetrated the young man. '...Is that Athena did not kill Arachne, and in a certain way, she made her do for eternity what she loved most: weaving. In contrast, Phoebus murdered for no reason... Apart from the obvious difference.'

'What is that obvious difference, sir? Because I am incapable of appreciating any.' Hyacinthus whispered.

Hyacinthus's dark eyes had taken on a very slight purple hue due to the moonbeams caressing his marine gaze. His noble features were even more marked, and his lips moved slowly as he spoke.

He felt floating, with no disturbances surrounding him other than that firm tingling, and those chills that continued to run through his body the more the breeze touched him. For this, he was in a certain way naked, since there was no rag or sufficient clothing capable of preventing the wind from moving over his skin if it required it.

There was nothing more than the body that Zephyrus himself had before his eyes, and it was even difficult for him to continue talking about the mistakes of the disrespectful Apollo, when he had him. Hyacinthus' soul already had an owner. He had found that out from the first moment of that night, when Hyacinthus's eyes resembled diamonds, reminiscent of the god of medicine. However, his body... was still mortal. He would surrender to its pleasures.

What Zephyrus did not understand was that Hyacinthus did not want followers who would try to conquer him, but lovers... Although of course, Hyacinthus did not know that.

'He also killed a creature that lived in a place that would later become something that represented him.' He did not answer the young man's question, but instead stuck to trying to tell the story of Python without being too cautious; Zephyrus knew that he could even say the true name of the boy's teacher, since he had seen it in in Hyacinthus's eyes that he knew hist true identity. 'And these are not the only things your master has done, because, believe me, there are more and they are all equally horrible or even worse.'

The prince walked a couple of steps backwards until he could not do so anymore, since the trunk of a tree prevented him from continuing. Zephyrus, however, despite realizing, walked right up to the young man.

Hyacinthus felt his breath on his face. The breeze that hovered over him was now much more invasive, and the hands of the god of the west wind began to gently caress his face. The boy didn't know how to act or what to do at that moment, so he just looked him in the eyes.

'What do you really want, Mr. Unknown? I know well that you have not brought me here solely to tell me about the evil deeds carried out by Phoebus.'

'What do you think?'

'I sincerely suspect that it wasn't enough for you to see me naked that first time.'

Zephyrus did not say a word, he simply looked at him with mischief reflected in both his smile and his gaze. Without warning, he joined his lips with the young man's.

The Spartan continued the kiss that, without realizing it, gradually turned into an action full of lust. Suddenly, the mortal heard a strange sound.

A sweet voice called to Hyacinthus. A voice called him by name that sounded distant but felt close. He listened to its harmony, and his eyes opened, finding Zephyrus on his face, thus understanding that he had been unwary. He had to leave right away. It didn't take him long to separate his lips from the other's and, without even saying a word, he left.

He felt overwhelmed by the event that had occurred. It wasn't wrong, of course, but he noticed something... Like a lump in his throat. Fingers squeezing his heart, also his soul. While he kissed those lips, while he felt the breezes and his hands running over his face, his neck, his body, he had not thought about Zephyrus for a single moment. There was only one being capable of blinding his thoughts, of causing such a feeling of elevation. And that being, so lucky or perhaps unfortunate, was called Phoebus.

XI

The Earth spun while Gaia breathed. The notes passed through the walls, the glass and even the rocks. The world was small, but humans were even smaller. They were these simple grains of sand lost on the beaches of the world.

The sounds of their voices could be heard. They sang in praise of those who had given them life. They didn't realize they could see them. They were lost in the irrational world, in the ordinary world, when they had before them the door to the gods and the Cosmos. They only needed to possess the key, which was none other than their own souls.

They would achieve absolute well-being if they focused on the present that is always unfolding. The gods live like this, feeling the world, being part of nature, protecting themselves from misfortune, without escaping their fears. Without escaping from themselves. They take refuge in themselves, and it usually works for them.

The world was so small at that time, the same size as it is now, but human beings had other objectives, other goals. And even in misunderstood Sparta, people still had a different vision of the world, although it was usually not the right one. Despite this, it was better than the current one.

Humans were simply a grain in the middle of a desert, the largest and most extensive desert that could exist. And a tiny part of that grain represented the love that Apollo, immense in comparison, craved. A love that he had to fight for. Even when he understood that he had already won, because he had seen the meeting of Hyacinthus and Zephyrus.

He had remained next to the young man, in complete silence, like an observer. He simply wanted to understand what the prince felt. He knew that morning as he crossed the sky, guiding the sunlight, that Hyacinthus was looking at him with peculiar eyes. His gaze shone at the thought of him, and he had rejected strong bodily pleasure for him. Without realizing it, he had conquered his soul or at least had it between his fingers. Now Phoebus would have to try to keep it. Make the boy realize his true intentions and the desires that were gradually beginning to invade his internal fire.

Humans were delicate, Apollo knew it well. They were so delicate that in a second they could die, even from the silliest thing. So, he would just dance. He would dance under the harmony of his lyres, under the songs of the nymphs. He would dance, and with the softness of the dance he would approach the handsome young man, Hyacinthus. The Olympian god did not desire his body, he did not crave his lips, nor his prayers, he simply wanted his soul to see and feel his own, to understand that the world was wonderful, and life was an eternal adventure that would never come to an end. Phoebus wanted to teach him that there is something that goes beyond the physical, that souls truly existed, and that bodies should not be important.

Apollo loved Hyacinthus. He loved him with all his being. He truly loved him. So much so that if his choice were any other way, he would let him go. He had to smile and laugh. That was what that prince who had dared, without even being aware, to steal the heart of the sun god had to do.

The path to the abode of love he sought was comforting. He had decided to walk, even though he could have appeared at the very door, but he wanted to feel the emotion of the moment. Live it like a mortal would live it. Live it as if it were his last. Apollo felt filled with a sensation. An emotion that blinded him, distancing him from the fears, from the misfortunes he had caused. Taking him away from the curse that Eros seemed to laugh at so much. He moved away from the nickname of being unhappy in love, and approached being Apollo, Phoebus, son of Zeus and Leto, brother of Artemis whose arrow never misses. Apollo, lover of Hyacinthus, prince of Sparta.

Trails wound their way through the rural landscape. The countryside shined, the men he met greeted him, without any of them even suspecting who he was. His steps carried him, almost in time with Pan's flute, whose sound reached his ears thanks to the wind from the distant mountains, lands that no human had yet set foot on.

He had to allow him to dream it, believe it, think that he could do it, change the course of the fate that was already sewn. He had to walk through his love until he had it in his hands, until he observed it and the other observed it. That was what he had to do and what he would do.

He hung his lyre from his body, and its notes could already be heard even if he did not pluck its strings. His life was magic, and his love was even more so. He had to fight for it as if it were a war he had to win. In fact, that was a war; a combat between him and Zephyr whose only prize would be the heart of a mortal whose life would be taken in a breath... But that mattered little! Oh, if love was felt the way Apollo felt it, the world would change!

The melody surrounded him, immersing him in the rising morning. In that complex dawn in which they would not see him in full for the sky, but only part of his being. His music grabbed his clothes, propelling him forward, while the whispers of his muses sang in his ear:

'Apollo, don't do it.'

'Apollo, it will go wrong.'

The voices warned. He, however, didn't care. He was the god of prophecies. If something bad was going to happen, he would know it, why should he fear if the only thing in his future with Hyacinthus was prosperity? Why should he fear? The fate could be unpredictable, and perhaps no one saw that he was capable of achieving a love that would not be lost, that would not rot, but he did see it and observed it in the boy. The world was small, he was a god. He would make it. That was what calmed him along with the desire to continue his journey.

His eyes lay immersed in the magic of the most complete of emotions. The thing is that love for a god is much more than what humans can feel. Love for a god is all the feelings that these creatures can achieve united, intertwined and multiplied infinitely. Thus, what emanated from Apollo is impossible to explain with the right words, since these do not exist. One could venture to say that they will never be created.

He felt free. He was flying in a world where that was not possible. He danced to the sound of his own music, whose lyre emitted a sound without even being pressed. He didn't understand what he was doing, but he let himself go. He could do it, would that lead to tragedy? It was impossible for his world, the one he was gradually building, to collapse at some point. He knew that, together with Hyacinthus, the two of them would be strong enough to overcome anything, and that, certainly, also included the threads that the Moiras had already woven.

The air caressed his face, and the rising sun followed him. His eyes shone with joy, and his feet seemed not to touch the ground. It was the force of love that motivated him. He had the impression that he would faint. That was what he wanted to do every day: relax, forget about his work and just be himself. Be himself so that, in the near future, he would be with Hyacinthus.

He could have stayed in his abode, following the advice of his muses, but then there he would risk losing the life that he could not get rid of. Hyacinthus was the reason the sun rose every day... If mortals had known, they would have crowned Hyacinthus! Not as the king of Sparta, but as king of the world, of everything that the light of Phoebus touched, and that was quite a few things. It was the fire of the braziers that he felt inside him. Not that destructive fire, but that light, that warmth that emanated from the bonfires on the icy winter nights. A restorative light, which healed each wound and eliminated memories that did not have to be remembered in order to be replaced by others starring Hyacinthus.

Between the push of the sun and the songs of the birds that accompanied his lyre, it didn't take long for the god of the arts to reach the home of his love. So, knowing that it was still early, he sat under the shade of a nearby tree, and simply began to play. This time, for real, making his fingers pluck the strings in a soft way endowed with a thousand elegances.

In his dreams, Hyacinthus could be free and equal to any other creature. In his dreams, Hyacinthus took refuge in the depths of his being. In his dreams, he listened to those who had disappeared. In them, too, he got what he craved in real life. And that dream had not been different:

At first it had turned out to be very dark. So much so that he could barely see the fingers of his own hands. However, soon all that darkness vanished as if something had chased it away, as if someone had sucked it in. In the middle of the esplanade that lay before his eyes, a human silhouette seemed to be waiting for him. Then, Hyacinthus approached him.

He didn't remember feeling his feet touching the ground. It seemed like he was flying, trying to get closer to that person with the indefinable face. This being was surrounded by an intense light. A blinding light that did not allow him to observe who the being was, and the notes of his lyre emerged from the particles of his

215

complexion. A melody that soon reached the boy's ears. Without even asking permission they entered and he, who had been deaf all the time, finally heard again. The sound returned like oxygen which turns out to be pleasant to one who has kept his head under the tide for a long time. It was an essential warmth; he could not believe he had survived for so long without having heard it.

It was a music that little by little made him open his eyes, revealing himself, forgetting the human figure that was so familiar and strange to him at once. At first, they did not focus in the right way. He saw everything blurry, but despite this, he continued to hear the lyre being played and its sound that seemed to come from outside. He felt the need to follow it. He didn't hesitate even for a moment, and so he did.

Without wasting time in dressing up in any way, Hyacinthus ran out of his bedroom. He did not stop at any time, not even when the slaves begged him not to go at such speed through the freshly washed corridors, but the young prince was not listening. The king's youngest son only followed what his heart asked of him. He would pursue that voice of shining steel, even unimaginable gold, until he found it. And if he did not find it, he would not stop until he found the origin of those lyres that, full of harmony, had managed to transcend the veil of dream to touch reality.

He knew well that when a dream managed to achieve that, it meant that the gods were present. Whether with him or against him. But the trust that he was beginning to acquire in Phoebus assured him that the sun was at his side, protecting his back from any enemy who dared to harm him. Therefore, he was not afraid that the supposedly invented melody had mixed with reality, because it surely gave a very good omen. One that spoke to him about the love he unknowingly craved.

When he went outside, he found a frog, which stopped in the middle of the road, looking at him with those enormous eyes that seemed to have been bathed in gold thanks to the first rays of dawn. Hyacinthus was surprised and stopped to listen to the little frog, and this beautiful frog was singing to him.

Singing a thousand notes in unison, the animal sang him a serenade, an ode, an epic set in an event that had not yet happened, which for that very reason was incomprehensible to him. But despite this, he knew that he would have to return the favour one day, singing to the little frog that sang to him, smiling at the sun that smiled at him, and dancing to the sound of that lyre that was so close. Because in those precious moments, so serene, but so full of nervousness on the part of the young man, he could see in the distance a figure sitting on a rock with the brightest instrument he had ever seen in his hands.

As he approached, he realized that it had undoubtedly been his imagination, but for a moment, he thought he saw the strings made of gold, the wood, of silver, and on top of it a golden insignia with a name written on it that he would force himself not to forget. He confirmed that it would not be easy, since he immediately realized that that silhouette was that of Phoebus, and that Phoebus was that same unknown being that had appeared in his dreams.

Apparently, not only the lyres had managed to pierce the veil between dreams and reality, but also the man before his eyes. That man who had stopped playing so he could fully concentrate on his being. He smiled widely, sweetly at him. So sweetly that Hyacinthus thought no one had ever smiled at him like that. He looked at him with tenderness in his eyes, with a kindness and even a love that the prince would have considered inconceivable if he had not seen it.

But he saw it, he was seeing it and he was beginning to feel the silence. The notes had gone quiet, and everything seemed to have vanished except for that look that loved him so softly, and that mystical smile that seemed taken from all the beauty in the world.

There was no difference between his dreams and the world. There was no difference between keeping your eyes closed or opening them completely. The difference was when one thought he was awake, but in reality, he had a blindfold that prevented him from seeing. However, now that he had truly woken up, he could appreciate in Phoebus all the strength of the previous days, of the night. All his skill, his bravery. He told himself that he could cause a thousand horrors, but that would only make him love him a thousand times more. Every action had consequences. He was aware of this, just as he knew that Apollo, who he never doubted for a moment the man was, was not perfect according to humans. And everyone who has known even just one god will know that not even the most archaic and powerful divinities are perfect before mortal eyes. Although this does not mean that they are not truly so. If there is any that comes close to the meaning that that word has, it is, without a doubt, Gaia. Despite this, not even Gaia, being so beautiful, being the home of many living beings, could be considered perfect in the eyes of many.

For that same reason, Apollo, despite representing perfection, was not perfect according to what society dictated. Hyacinthus was beginning to understand it. It should be added that he did not know to what extent those stories in which he starred were true, ergo he could not give an opinion, since he did not know the truth.

Even so, for the prince, Apollo was the most perfect thing he had ever found, because all his energy made him the most harmonious creature he had ever met. Likewise, he usually found peace and calm with him. In that era, as in all times, finding tranquillity as a human was finding the greatest of treasures.

'Were you the one who played?' Hyacinthus dared to ask.

'I'm afraid that's how it was, and since you're here it means that my lyre has kept you awake.'

'It has, but it was one of the most beautiful awakenings I've ever had. It's just that I feel everything differently since yesterday afternoon, Phoebus, birdsong has more life... My dreams are not dreams but realities, because what I find in them, I also find awake.'

'That's because you've woken up, Hyacinthus. When you get rid of the blindfold that prevents you from seeing, you finally see the most beautiful place before your eyes.'

The prince nodded, sitting next to him.

'I wish the others felt it too,' he whispered. Apollo looked at him sweetly, that same feeling that invaded him and which he could not get rid of every time the mortal was by his side.

'Someday they will and then they will understand what they don't understand now.'

'Do you think so?'

'No, Hyacinthus, thinking is not the solution, knowing is. I know they will.' The boy smiled softly.

'Are you always so confident? Don't you ever doubt for a second?' He asked interested, looking into his eyes. The god held his gaze.

'When you see it all, there is little time left for doubt.'

'I would also like to see everything.'

'Are you sure? Seeing everything also means seeing the horrors. Maybe your good heart couldn't handle so much injustice.'

Hyacinthus clenched his jaw in thought.

'But what is justice, Phoebus? I don't think it's something absolute. What may be fair for you may not be fair for me.'

'Are you asking me or are you wondering?'

'I ask you because I don't think I can get the answer.'

'Again, you speak of thinking. The word think, Hyacinthus, leaves up in the air what could be. It leaves it up in the air because it is the step between knowing and not knowing. People who fear use that word because they don't fully trust their own instincts or even because they aren't sure.'

'Can you be sure of everything?'

'Mortals don't find it easy. But do you, Hyacinthus, trust your instinct and yourself? It is normal that one, if one lacks evidence, is not sure about the existence of the gods, the origin of life, or even why in the warm months the sun shines brighter than in the cold ones... What is not normal is that someone is not sure of themselves.'

'Why do you think that, Phoebus?'

'Look at the world. The man who is lost, the man who suffers, is the one who is not sure of everything he can achieve; the man who laughs is the one who trusted in himself from the first second. This second man has not gone further because he is better than the first, but because he allowed himself to trust in his being. When the human being stops being sure of his own individual, everything else is corrupted, turning into a hurricane of misfortune that will never cease. When the human being is sure of himself, that hurricane fades away. It is true that many times it continues, but in the eye of that immense force of nature, humans can be happy.'

'That is very nice,' said the young prince, immersing himself in the opponent's gaze. 'Also, I risk saying that it is true.'

'Even in the clumsiest examples, beauty can be found. It can be found in everything. You just have to know how to search.'

Hyacinthus lowered his gaze slightly, and later fixed it on the horizon, where the sun was increasingly higher.

'Do you know if gods exist, Phoebus?' He asked, knowing that it was very risky because of the suspicions he had.

The young man felt observed by the man next to him.

'I know that most of the things that are talked about without evidence are usually real.'

'What do you mean?' He asked again, taking his eyes off the sun and looking at the god.

Apollo locked his eyes on his.

'What do you think, Hyacinthus? Your heart knows the answer to all the doubts you harbour. My answer doesn't matter if you already know the truth.'

Phoebus's starry eyes, more than stars, turned out to be two balls of blue fire. Blue fire similar to the sun. Hyacinthus told himself that he should not doubt it anymore. Although it was impossible, he had known it from the first moment he felt it for the first time. Now he had also heard him play, he didn't have to think about it anymore, the information was already in his knowledge.

The only thing the prince wanted was to travel even further through that archaic gaze. He also wondered what the other very ancient divinities that Phoebus possibly knew must be like. He couldn't imagine it.

'What do you think, Hyacinthus?' He asked him again in a very calm manner.

The prince turned his gaze toward the sun before returning to the god's face. When he did, he responded as he tried to dig deeper into his being.

'All gods are real. I know. There is not the slightest doubt in my being. They all exist.'

'You see it? Sometimes, you have to take a risk and go to one of the two extremes of knowing and not knowing. If we don't take risks, we will never achieve half of what we could.'

'Yes, but sometimes it's scary to risk choosing one of those extremes, even when you're completely sure of the answer. Possibly, this is because of the fear of being wrong.'

'The fear of erring is the most common fear that can be found in any creature that decides for itself.'

'How do you overcome that fear, Phoebus?'

'It can't be done. You just have to live with it. We can try to face it, put up resistance so that it does not sink us and prevents us from being or doing what we want, but it is a fear that will always live with us. The trick is not to let it overcome us. And if we make a mistake, nothing bad happens either. We have to learn from that mistake we have made, but that's all. It is also part of life.'

The Lacedaemonian decided to remain silent for a few seconds. He looked down from Apollo's gaze, beginning to reflect. He wondered if he could say it, if he should. There was no room for doubt in any type of relationship he had with him. There was no room for doubt, because the god saw everything, and his thoughts were possibly no exception.

'Phoebus,' he said out loud in a voice that seemed completely broken. He didn't want to use the name, his full name, even though something inside told him to do so. Apollo, meanwhile, did not say a word, he just looked at him. 'Phoebus, the other day I went to look for you in the nearest city. I thought you lived there, but no one had seen you.'

'Why were you looking for me?'

'I was simply curious. I wanted to know where you lived, but it was impossible for me to find your home. People I asked, people who told me that they were unaware of your stay or even your existence.'

Apollo was about to say something to him, but then some footsteps distracted his attention. These were followed by a cry calling for Hyacinthus. So the prince got up to see better, and Phoebus was not surprised to discover that it was Tamyris, the musician.

He remembered him from the previous morning, when Hyacinthus had encountered him in the city. Apparently, Tamyris had been dissatisfied when he realized, after playing the lyre a little, that Hyacinthus had left.

'Hyacinthus, are you okay?' He asked when he got close to him, without even noticing Phoebus' presence.

'Yes, perfectly, Tamyris,' he said, looking into his eyes. The young man felt the presence of the god and agreed to introduce them. 'By the way, this is Phoebus, my new master.'

'The one you were looking for?'

'Exactly.'

Tamyris nodded to the blonde, wary of making any approach.

'Pleased to meet you.' Phoebus murmured, getting up from his seat, in order to make a greater impression.

The musician took a few steps back, because he felt something strong splinter in his heart, like a shadow of grace and perfection that he lacked. He was condemned under metals that tied him to that force. He felt overwhelmed without knowing very well what to do in the face of such emotion that was beginning to invade him, gradually, dragging all his fears from that river into which he had thrown them, returning to him.

These fears moved like snakes that incessantly crawl across the floors with a single objective: To put an end to him.

Tamyris realized that he had not tried hard enough. That young man had been the one who had played the lyre in such a beautiful way. Those notes that he had heard along the path came from the golden instrument that was at the feet of the blonde, the stranger. He feared that he had not only taken the title of greatest musician from him, but also, much more likely, Hyacinthus's heart. He, who had been the first mortal man to love another man of the same condition, was being pushed to the other shore where his misfortunes rested because of the grace of a creature whose nature did not come from the earth, but from something higher, something similar to the Cosmos.

He understood without realizing that Apollo, who hurts from afar, was in front of him, looking coldly into his eyes, transmitting the same mental message that had plagued him in his darkest nights: 'Hyacinthus does not love you the way you love him.'

Could the clear message he received in his mind be true or was it, perhaps, an illusion from the young stranger? Tamyris knew well that there were many people, both women and men, behind the prince, but this was too much. The being before his eyes... Was not a human. He himself knew it, even though the renowned Tamyris was not one of the wisest creatures in this world. But you didn't have to be smart to figure it out. The only thing one had to be was completely sensitive. A soul dedicated to the arts would understand it, would see it as he was seeing it because what he had before him was none other than art itself in its materialized state.

His eyes sang it, his hands wrote it, his lips narrated it, his unprecedented presence, to which no one's could compare, composed it. His being expressed it. That perfection that only the arts can contain. That magnitude of expression embroidered on his face. This was such that all the arts in the world fell short of describing it. That was not a human being, he knew then. He was a god, Apollo himself. There was the ruthless one, looking into his eyes and reading his soul as only the deities know. However, he was petrified.

Was he falling into lust? How could that be Phoebus Apollo, who hurts from afar? That same Phoebus whom the poets praised? That Phoebus, son of Leto and Zeus, brother of Artemis? Was that even possible? He said to himself that it could be. He had more need, then, to strut before Hyacinthus and his singular guest about his way of living life.

'Hyacinthus, I wanted you to come with me for a walk.'

'Sorry Tamyris, but today I was planning to spend the day with Phoebus.'

'But, prince, you will have a great time. Come with me.' Hyacinthus looked at the god out of the corner of his eye, and he simply anticipated his words.

'It's okay, Tamyris. It is a good idea. Hyacinthus,' he told the boy, 'we should go.'

'"We"?' Tamyris asked. 'You mean Hyacinthus and me, right?'

'I mean Hyacinthus, you and me. I promised his father that I would not be separated from him today. As I am a being of my word, I won't.'

The musician did not like that at all, especially because he had planned an entire morning of solitude with the son of the king of that region. On the other hand, the voice of his intuition telling him that this was Phoebus, Phoebus, not the human, but the god who guided the sun at every dawn, encouraged him a little more. If he could convince Apollo how good he was, he might turn him into some minor deity. If that wasn't the case, he would settle for surprising Hyacinthus.

'Okay,' he finally said. 'You've been playing before, right?' He asked, looking at the lyre resting at the god's feet, in an attempt to get closer to that god who turned out to be warm, but at the same time cold.

'That's right,' he replied. 'I would ask you, but I already know the answer. You are Aedo Tamyris, the musician who is talked about so much in this neck of the woods.' He said as he picked up the instrument and began to walk alongside him.

'Phoebus, should I take a horse from the stables for the return trip?' Hyacinthus asked, surprised by the tense atmosphere that had been generated between them.

'It won't be necessary,' he replied. 'But if you're going to feel safer, go ahead.'

The prince nodded but preferred not to separate from both of them just in case.

Phoebus and Tamyris were talking or, at least, they seemed to be talking. The boy they were both in love with just walked in the rear, trying to understand the reason for their behaviour. They were treating each other in a polite manner, but at the same time, they gave the impression of being hostile. Well, there was something, a challenge painted in their looks. In the case of Tamyris, admiration and respect could also be seen. Phoebus's eyes turned out to be deeper than they had ever been before. Hyacinthus told himself that he was reading Tamyris perfectly and had found out so many things that he didn't know what to think of him.

The prince was immersed in a very strange sphere whose nature he did not understand. Nor did he have enough knowledge to change that tense environment that invaded even his body, passing through his skin and reaching his bones. It burned him inside, also freezing him in a certain way. At the same time, it turned out to be a destructive fire. Hyacinthus was not able to describe it. A pressure in the chest, a pain in the temples, and an immense emotion capable of destroying gigantic empires. All of this intermingling, becoming the same essence that was something unpleasant for him. He felt dizzy because of this.

It was like smoke that enveloped him. A smoke that would not allow him to escape. The voices of both began to dissipate in this environment. It seemed like a bubble was surrounding him and their words couldn't penetrate it. On the one hand, he appreciated it; on the other, he cursed it.

Hyacinthus knew well that Tamyris could become too vain and build himself up greatly with respect to the art he created. It was something that should not be allowed, because Apollo could see it as a threat or even a challenge. He was aware that his god was not evil, but it was an archaic force that could be quite changeable, in the same way that all those of his nature tend to be.

However, Tamyris was often so blinded by his own narcissism that Hyacinthus was sure that he had not grasped the powerful aura that enveloped his opponent's body. And if he had, he was too busy trying to surprise him. That would lead him to the path to perdition. The same one that, without being aware, he was about to take at the crossroads at which he found himself.

However, Apollo seemed to be in a good mood that day, as well as calm and gifted with immense patience. Possibly, this was not the only attribute that inhabited his being. With some luck, he also possessed some perseverance, prudence. The prince did not know it, but he suspected it because of the relaxed gaze of the divinity. He seemed calm, as if nothing could disturb him. Hyacinthus knew well that that sensation could fade in seconds. He hoped that wouldn't happen, for the musician's sake.

So, with that walking accompanied by a rather peculiar conversation, they arrived at the city, which they entered without hesitation.

It was here that Hyacinthus came back to reality. He was used to raising murmurs and sighs when arriving at such a place, and this time was no different: Whispers surrounded them. They followed him well into the heart of the place, and he also realized that this time, despite being the bearer of an almost unattainable beauty, he was not the one raising those gossips, but rather one of his companions.

Phoebus walked, and all the citizens fell lost in his being. The force that emanated was so great that more than one knelt thinking that he was some king. In a way, they were right, for he was one of the sons of the king of the gods.

His beauty overshadowed everything, and the harmony that accompanied it, caused Tamyris to become somewhat more jealous. So much so that he dared to say something that in a moment of sanity he would never have said.

'I am such a good musician, Phoebus,' he began to say, capturing the god's attention, 'that even the very muses are simple novices compared to me'.

Hyacinthus then saw a slight tinge of anger in the gaze of the god Apollo. He knew, then, that Tamyris had made a huge mistake. He also realized it judging by his countenance, which surely changed to an expression of pure fear in a matter of seconds.

Apollo clenched his jaw and didn't take long to speak.

'Even when nervousness invades us, Mr. Tamyris, we must remain calm, because jealousy only brings misfortune. Consider your words before you say them. You will remember the mistake you have made.'

This is how his winged words sounded.

Passersby had stopped to listen to the conversation. No one doubted Apollo's words. Not because they were superstitious, that too, but because of the confidence with which he had pronounced them.

'Forgive me, please, I beg you.' He pleaded kneeling in front of him.

'It is late, Aedo Tamyris, the muses are everywhere. They come when they are named. They have heard your words, and will act accordingly. If I were you, I would enjoy the time I have left doing what you love most, in case you can't do it again.'

Without further ado, Tamyris began to play the lyre. That day he composed the saddest melody that had been heard to date. A melody full of pain and regret. A melody that screamed suffering, also begging for hope that his beloved's teacher would err, but he well knew the rudeness of his words, the mistake he had made. He didn't need to look into Apollo's eyes to know what would happen. Voices came to his mind as he played: *Enjoy the time Apollo has forced us to give you. Enjoy it... because there is something much worse than death: being dead while alive. Living without being able to do what you love. That will be your punishment: a long life without art, Aedo Tamyris.*

XII

'Have you heard about Tamyris, Hyacinthus?' A girl's voice stopped him as he walked through the hallways of his home.

The prince turned around and managed to see a young woman with dark hair and brown eyes who immediately seemed extremely familiar to him. When she approached, he realized that it was one of the girls who had trained with his older brother on many occasions years ago.

'What exactly happened?' he asked, expecting the worst.

'He dared to defy the muses, prince. Apparently, gossip says that he had boasted about his skill and his singing, saying that they were better than those of the muses themselves. So, they did not take long to punish him. Now Tamyris lies blinded, and all musical ability with which he was once endowed has been deprived of him.'

'How did they blind him?'

'I don't know, but many claim that the muses tore out his eyes; others say that they burned them... I don't know what the true version is, but discussing it with your brother, he told me that you were a friend of Tamyris, and he believed that it was necessary for you to know. Since I suppose you won't be interested in a cripple continuing to court you, assuming that man dares to do it in his current condition…' Hyacinthus gave her a rather harsh look and continued walking. The girl followed him. 'Sorry if my words have offended you. What I meant was that you could take this opportunity to take on the role of courtship, and start approaching other people, especially women.'

'I'm not interested,' he told her without stopping. He wanted to get outside in order to find Phoebus. He wanted to know how he would act when he told him. Hyacinthus knew well that Apollo had no say in something his companions had decreed, and at least he had managed to give him some time to say a proper goodbye to what he loved most in the world. Despite this, the prince found it very cruel. It was said that, possibly, the muses were not vile, but rather that they were very little valued. Therefore, when a mortal challenged them in such a way, they had to act in the cruellest way they could devise. Hyacinthus realized that art was like them, like the muses, its bearers. Art could save, but it was also cruel if the author intended it, if inspiration required it in such a way. Weren't the muses, indeed, inspiration itself?

'Excuse me?' The girl was unable to accept what she heard. 'You are not interested in me or the topic in general?'

'I'm not interested in you or the topic. I have many things to dedicate myself to. Many things to think about before courtship,' he responded very coldly.

At this singular response, the woman whose name Hyacinthus did not know stopped, somewhat in a bad mood. The young man heard her snort and complain behind his back. Then, he realized the intentions that the girl had had from the beginning.

He didn't like the feeling that came over him. Something told him that he was attracting attention for a physique that would someday die. A physique that would soon rot. A physique that was nothing compared to what he was. He told himself that no one would understand that feeling. No one mortal, at least.

With his mind working, he arrived at the garden, where he closed his eyes and wished with all his being that Phoebus was there. So, when he opened his windows, he found a very slender human figure, full of harmony in front of him. His hair was dark. It had stopped being golden and had become such a light brown that, looked at by many, it would have been considered dark blonde. The moon illuminated him, and the plants that swirled at his feet. It seemed as if they were singing to him. His gaze, blue like the sky on sunny mornings, rested on Hyacinthus. He could do little except

239

walk towards that man, who managed to consume the negativity that, from time to time, crept into his being.

It was true. He attracted glances because of his slender body, but he understood that the being he was now looking at, gazing straight into the soul, loved him. Not because of his beautiful frame, but because he had been able to feel, see and understand his spirit. He repeated himself for the eleventh time, that Phoebus was none other than Apollo who strikes from afar. After all, there was no human on the face of Gaia who was capable of matching him. He also suspected that there was not even another divinity endowed with the same beauty, harmony and perfection that Apollo possessed.

When Hyacinthus reached him, he felt the cold moon. It was similar to the embrace of the sun, yet at the same time, completely different. It was a cold breeze that was beginning to gather around them. It was not invasive, rather healing, although it did not last long. He understood in those moments why the sun and the moon had been associated with a brother and a sister, because these two spheres seemed like twins. One full of invasive joy; another, happy, but always in the shadow. For the sun, happiness was found in brightening other lives; for the moon, it was found within itself.

Apollo's fingers gently caressed Hyacinthus's face. He looked into his eyes, seeing the truth in them. He saw sadness in them. An immense melancholy. At the same time, joy lived in them. He didn't know how to interpret it. He felt sorry for the prince, just as the prince felt sorry for him. Hyacinthus had always quite easily known how to interpret expressions on human faces, but he had to remember that what he had before him was anything but a man.

'Gossip has reached me,' he told him. That was what Apollo feared. If only Hyacinthus had known the reason for the misery in his eyes! He didn't feel sadness for the musician, that was what the prince felt deep down. He had simply transmitted this feeling in the form of energy to Apollo, and he had accepted it. He shared his pain. He knew that it was the only way to understand human hearts, which, in a certain way, were similar to his own, but at the same time, they were completely different things. The melancholy, however, had a remotely different origin. 'I have been told that the muses have blinded Tamyris, and who knows what else! Do you know the truth, Phoebus?'

'I haven't seen the musician, if that's what you want to ask. Hyacinthus, however, I cannot deny the possibility that these rumours are completely true. Not even other deities should challenge forces as powerful as the muses. Much less if one is human.'

'Tell me, Phoebus, is it bad that it seems unfair to me?'

'No, it's not,' he whispered in a very soft voice, a tone that Hyacinthus found angelic. This caused his fears to dissipate. 'It's normal that it doesn't seem like a good thing to you. You don't understand what moved the muses to act that way.'

'Could I ever understand it?'

Apollo smiled softly, looking into his eyes.

'Can the bird fully understand what it feels like to dive? Can the horse fully understand what it feels like to fly? Can the human being fully understand what it feels like to be free?' Hyacinthus clenched his jaw gently upon hearing these words and later shook his head. 'Hyacinthus, we can try to put ourselves in the other's place, but we will never fully understand what that other being feels. We can get an idea, but many times, it will be very far from what it really is.'

'So, what can we do?'

'Live,' he answered sweetly. 'Live, my prince. Living is the only thing we can do. Live trying to achieve what we believe is good.'

'If good is an absolute value, why does it seem good to the muses to punish Tamyris like this, but not to me?'

'You see, Hyacinthus, we can compare good to a puzzle divided into millions of small pieces or, perhaps, to a board where the absolute value is in the centre. We have to advance squares to reach it. Each square gives you a piece that is equivalent to knowledge, a situation that will tell you what is good and what is evil. The more squares you advance, the more pieces you will have and the closer you will be. The more squares you go back, the further away you will be. Both the muses, you and I have gone through boxes, picking up the pieces that tell us what is right, but this does not have to be maintained. It varies depending on whether we move forward or backward. Has it ever happened to you that you thought something was right, and then later, you realized that it wasn't?'

'Yes, on numerous occasions.'

'Many times it was something that others followed and still think is good, right?'

'Yeah. In most cases, I'm the only one who thinks that way.'

'That's because you were in a square, and you have moved in some direction. Maybe you have gone backwards or maybe you

243

have moved forward, you don't know that. The muses are in a different square, one that they have reached by accumulating many other goods, passing by other squares that have allowed them to gain more pieces. They took another path to goodness, which is why you differ. None of you have achieved absolute goodness yet. If, say, they had, you wouldn't understand it until you got to the centre.'

'It would be a horse trying to understand the eagle that has wings and can fly. It could try to find out what it's like to fly, but it would never know one hundred percent. In the event that they have achieved absolute goodness, I would still think that they are doing it wrong because I have not got there yet. They are the eagles, and I would be a horse that does not yet have wings, ergo, cannot fly. Flying would be that absolute value. However, if one day I got wings, I would fly and then I would prove them right... If I achieved absolute goodness I would know the true meaning of it. I would know what is right and what is wrong. So, if their actions were carried out while they were aware of the one true goodness, they would be good and I would understand it, but I would not know until that day.' Apollo nodded gently along with a half-smile that appeared on his face, letting Hyacinthus know that he understood.

'Although I insist, there are few beings who have reached that value and have been strong enough not to retreat.'

'Do you know any?' Apollo looked at him playfully.

'If I told you all the beings I have known, the world would come to an end and I still would not have finished. However, yes, I have known beings who have managed to do it, although few have lasted for long.'

Hyacinthus smiled softly upon hearing his voice. He still remained quite close to the god. Even though Apollo had stopped making physical contact with him some time ago, he felt his strength surrounding him, healing his wounds, both psychic and physical. His soul found calm with him.

'Despite this, Tamyris worries me,' the prince confessed. 'He is not very cautious. He doesn't think when he speaks, but he is a good man. He is on top of me too much, but he has always treated me well. Me and everyone, and that should have been something that the muses took into account.' Realizing that the prince would begin to tremble with helplessness, Phoebus allowed his own emotions to drive his acts, and gently kissed the young man's forehead.

'Calm down, Hyacinthus. Believe me, they have taken it into account, and if they have not, in the future, others will.'

'How can you sound so confident?' he asked, resting his forehead on the other's chest, while he hugged him. He appreciated the warmth of his body, the relaxation it transmitted to him, the peace he found in his words. These were the only reasons why he did not curse the muses on the spot. It wasn't that he was a very good friend of Tamyris, but he was annoyed by the fact that the muses were so cruel on certain occasions. He said to himself that they were still divinities, and that if humans sometimes made horrible mistakes for believing themselves to be gods, the true forces of the world would do so too, even with more reason.

'Because I know, Hyacinthus,' he whispered softly. 'I know. Just as I know that the decision they have made corrodes you inside. I do not justify them, but I also assure you that they are not creatures who impart their punishments lightly. They always think deeply before selecting one. Furthermore, the punishments of the deities end up, on many occasions, being blessings. Theirs are not the exception. They are not vile either. However, they are immortal beings, and they tend to lose their patience quite quickly. Likewise, they are often very undervalued, and they must show that they are strong. Nevertheless, you don't have to worry about the rest of Tamyris's life. At first, he will fall into darkness, but he will find something, someone, to help him get out of there. Then he will be happy, much more than he had been before. It should be added that he will be happier than he would have been if this misfortune had not happened. And when that happens he will thank his mistake for everything it has brought him. Sometimes, to find true happiness we have to make mistakes infinite times. We must cross our own personal Tartarus, Hyacinthus.'

The prince completely believed his words. He had said it with implacable certainty, with an aura that confessed that he was not lying.

He blindly trusted the god. It was clear to him that no falsehood would be uttered by his lips. He was the son of Zeus, the light of day, also the brightness of the world. It was difficult for him to imagine a life in which Apollo had never crossed his path, and he had only known him for a short time, but he felt that he had loved him for an entire existence.

Phoebus was silent for long moments, letting Hyacinthus wander in his thoughts, reflecting. It was something he wished all humans were capable of doing. If so, the world would never be lost. However, Apollo knew well, even in those early days, that the time would come when the Earth would be lost due to the flaws of human beings. How could some be so horrible, and others so wonderful? He would ask himself this question throughout his entire existence, even when the human species came to an end. He would never find the answer.

'Hyacinthus, by the way,' he said, drawing the mortal's attention after some long minutes.

'Tell me, Phoebus.' His brown eyes locked onto the god's blue ones.

'I thought that tomorrow, with the first rays of the sun, we could go hunting, for example.' He remembered that it was something that humans liked to do. He, sometimes, did it with his sister, but they did not usually hunt animals, but rather other types of much more dangerous beings in whose existence humans had little belief. 'I would talk to your father personally so there would be no problem.'

'How long?'

'Hours, or maybe days. As you wish.'

'Sounds good to me,' he replied. 'Stay tonight, Phoebus,' he added after a slight pause. 'Stay. I don't know where you are staying, but it is the dead of night, and I wouldn't want you to walk along the roads in the darkness.'

Apollo, endowed with immense softness, brushed a lock of hair from Hyacinthus's face. And in this way, he told him that it was okay, that he would stay with him.

So, both of them stayed a few more moments in the garden, under the beauty of the moon, which was little more than the presence of Artemis, who was always observant, judiciously examining the mortal to whom her brother had felt attracted. She was surprised to realize that there was no lust in his being. What she found in his gaze, what she found in his energy, was the deepest love she had ever seen.

Then it happened; the moon smiled on the lovers. She didn't like romance, but he was happy for her brother. He had found what he had always looked for and, with any luck, it would never be taken away from him. But if the Moiras tend to be twisted, the threads they weave are even more so. They would manage to destroy this beautiful story.

. . .

He trembled slightly on his bed. The cold wind seemed to have blown in through the window. He didn't understand why this was happening to him. However, despite this, that sensation continued to surround him, and Hyacinthus feared that it would refuse to leave him. He had an idea in his head. An idea he did not want to accept, because doing so would mean being able to realize what he was really participating in, and that was something the prince did not want to do.

This icy breeze began to caress his back carefully. Hyacinthus felt it as thin, agile fingers that knew how to touch his body. They knew its secrets, thus understanding how to reveal them. His body was a lyre, and the wind, a musician gifted with the talent of Tamyris along with all the other musicians who had once existed.

Surrounded by this imminent sensation, it did not take him long to get rid of the lethargic dreams that came to his mind. So, he opened his eyes seeing the darkness that was gradually decreasing. Apollo, next to him, was still resting or, at least, that was what it seemed like. The sun's rays were still not visible. Hyacinthus guessed that there was still plenty of time left until dawn.

However, there was a word that filled him, a voice that called him. The prince knew well who it was, and to be honest, he did not like it at all, since that same creature he was thinking of possibly only brought misery to his soul. However, he knew that the fingers of the wind would not cease until he came to meet him. Without stopping to think too much about it, he got up and prepared to leave his home.

As he had suspected, there was the stranger who had seen him naked, on a rock, javelin in hand. The same one who harboured an eternal hatred towards Phoebus. His eyes lit up when he saw him, and Hyacinthus just looked down, recognizing that weapon as his own.

'I hope you had a pleasant awakening,' he said approaching him. The prince tried to grab the javelin, but Zephyrus pulled it away at the last moment. 'Not so fast, young man,' he said as he stopped him.

The teenager crossed his arms, looking at him in a very distant and cold manner. He didn't understand the reason for that behaviour.

'Do you not want to talk?' Zephyrus added.

'Not with you, so I ask you to please return my javelin.'

'The other day I remember you were more willing for me to keep it, what has changed since then?' His tone was polite, but at the same time tense. It gave the boy a very strange feeling.

'That day was another day, not today. So do as I ask,' he demanded. 'You are on my father's land, in front of our house. You could be damned if I raise my voice just a little bit more. So, if I were you, I would do exactly what I say. Give me the javelin.'

Zephyrus, who did not expect that reaction from Hyacinthus, gave him the weapon without hardly resisting. He said to himself that Hyacinthus had taken on very haughty airs since meeting Apollo, son of Zeus.

The boy grabbed it, squeezing it tightly. He continued to find a coldness in his gaze that would have even frozen Boreas, and that was saying a lot, since it was the north wind.

'What are you doing here?' he asked again.

'I thought you didn't want to talk,' he snapped.

'What are you doing here?' he repeated with a much harsher tone.

It had bothered him that he had spoken so badly about Apollo. He had been upset that he had kissed him. It had bothered him that he had appeared there before the sun woke up, probably trying to keep Phoebus from spotting him. Hyacinthus did not know who he was, but he understood that something was happening between him and the god. Something he, unknowingly, was involved in.

'I have come to bring you the javelin.'

'Now allow yourself to tell me the truth.'

'Do you forgive your master Phoebus for allowing Tamyris to be cruelly punished?' He asked bluntly.

Hyacinthus understood that the stranger had made an enormous effort to say Phoebus, instead of Apollo. Another test for the consistency of his theory.

'What are you talking about? Phoebus has little to do with the muses. He is like you or me. Saying that he could have prevented it is like saying that I can control the course of time,' he told him, acting surprised by such a strange question. Despite believing that he had acted correctly, he knew immediately that Zephyrus had not been deceived.

'You know exactly what I'm talking about.'

'Tamyris' punishment was doled out by the muses,' he said, challenging him with his eyes. 'It has little to do with Phoebus.'

'What is happening?' A voice spoke behind him.

Hyacinthus didn't need to turn around to discover who it was, because Zephyrus' eyes said so much.

Behind him was Apollo, who had looked out the window just when Eos, the one with rosy fingers, had appeared to the east of the horizon, bringing with her the first rays of the sun. The prince looked at Zephyrus to examine his reaction. He simply clenched his jaw, and fixing his gaze on Apollo, spoke:

'I was leaving,' he said with reluctance.

Zephyrus realized that he had not approached Hyacinthus in the best way. The west wind understood that Apollo had managed to dig a deep hole in the mortal's heart. A well so deep not even his erotic caresses had been able to overcome.

Hyacinthus had given his heart to Apollo, and he knew then that it would not take him long to give him his soul. Boreas whispered in his ear that he had already lost. Zephyrus feared that the north wind was right. Despite that great possibility, he could still try a little more. He did not want Phoebus to get his way as he always did.

However, without trusting his words, Hyacinthus followed him with his gaze until Zephyrus vanished into the distance. It was then that he had the luxury of turning around and looking up. Although he was unfortunate enough that Apollo was no longer in that place. Instead, the young man heard a voice asking him. A very soft and sweet voice that felt like it had been millennia since he had last heard it.

'Hyacinthus, Phoebus told me that he was going to prepare the horses that you will take. I was wondering if you would like to take a walk with me before you leave.'

The young prince nodded. His sister Polyboea deserved that and a thousand more walks.

'You surprised me by getting up so early,' he said when she got closer.

'That's how it is. Lately I do, because I am incapable of resting properly. There is so much running through my head!'

'Are they pleasant things or worries?' he asked, as they both began to walk.

'It's a very strange feeling. I had never felt it before. And on the one hand, I'm grateful I hadn't felt it. However, I didn't want to take this conversation in that direction, since it seems selfish of me to worry you before you go out with the splendid Phoebus.'

'Don't worry, Polyboea. You know you can count on me for this kind of thing.'

'I know, but I still don't want to worry you,' she paused slightly. 'Rather, I wanted to congratulate you.'

'What are you talking about?'

'You do not know?'

'No.'

'Haven't you noticed?'

'What are you taking about? Be clear!'

'I'm talking about your friend Phoebus. You have enchanted a heart, a spirit as archaic as his, even before you knew that he already knew you.'

'What do you mean?' Hyacinthus asked, trying to sound surprised. He knew well what the girl meant by such gossip. He remembered then the time when he had found Apollo and his sister chatting in the courtyard. He was sure that that day Polyboea, a very wise human, had been able to understand his true identity.

'You know perfectly well.' She paused and she looked him directly in the eyes. He smiled sideways, realizing that he had understood her words. 'You are the bearer of an essence that is too striking, and of course, that was what attracted him here. That other one who just left also seems to be like him, but at the same time, he seems completely different to me.'

256

'He was the one who saw me naked in the forest that morning before I met him.'

'The one you thought was Phoebus?' Hyacinthus nodded. 'I understand now your mistake. They are different, but both have that mystical energy that surrounds them.'

'I guess you're right.'

'Don't assume, you know I am. I know it by the way your eyes have sparkled. We are both fully aware of who this being who claims to just be called Phoebus is.'

'In a way his name is also Phoebus.'

'But it's not just Phoebus.'

'There I have to agree with you. There is something inside me that always knew, but every second I spend with him convinces me even more that my own suspicions are real.'

'There is no one in the mortal world like him. I risk saying that there will never be, due to the simple fact that he is not one of us. You have to look at the sun to see the proof. You have to listen to the music to understand it. You have to observe him and see in him all the spheres with which he is associated, because, honestly, he possesses all of these in his very essence.' Polyboea paused slightly. 'In dark times, when my soul was locked up, depressed, I used to believe that the gods were little more than gossip. I think that, deep down, the idea has always been on my mind, but now I know that I was truly wrong. They are real, but they choose us. We do not have enough power to subdue them. They decide who to talk to, when to appear, when to act... Now I feel very grateful. Not because Apollo who hurts from afar has chosen you, brother, but also because we shared beautiful thoughts the other day. It's not exactly how we imagine it but, at the same time, it's exactly the same. It's such a strange feeling that it causes a lump in my throat, making me unable to explain it.'

'I know what you think, Polyboea, what goes through your mind. It is impossible for any human to be able to imagine such grace and joy altogether because we do not believe it exist. However, there you have him, brushing the horses, who know very well what his true identity is. In his eyes are a thousand treasures that many would dream of. Treasures that can never be reached, not even by friendly hands, much less by enemies.'

'Do you love him?' the girl then asked, in a very low voice.

Her brother looked her in the eyes. For a few moments, the princess thought he would refuse her question. However, finally, he answered.

'How could I not love him if he represents everything I love? How could I not love him if he's everything I adore? How could I not love him? It would be impossible not to love him.'

'So it's true, you love him how much?'

'It is. I love him like no one has ever loved before. I love him with everything my little being possesses. However, I know well that he loves me much more.'

'Why do you think so?'

'Humans are corrupted creatures, Polyboea. Instead, he is a god. His way of loving will always be purer, more real than ours, ergo, he loves me better. He loves me more, because due to my human condition, I am incapable of reaching the level of emotions that he can have.'

The young woman remained silent, she was looking for something else to say, but she found nothing. The only thing that made its way through her thoughts was an immense joy coming directly from her heart. She would never understand how one could be so happy about someone else's life, but she was capable of being and, in those moments, she felt it. His brother deserved someone who understood him. At first, she had thought that this someone was the aedo Tamyris, but she quickly realized that he was too proud. However, Apollo had turned out to be the best option Polyboea had ever known. From the first moment, she knew that it was his soul that searched for her brother's, not his body wanting to possess him.

She heard horse hooves behind her and knew that the time had come. She hugged her brother tightly as a farewell. He would return, but it could take a little longer than anticipated. She said to herself that if it was like that, so be it. Hyacinthus deserved a break.

XIII

His body was completely pressed against his. His hands caressed his, which rested on the arch of his back. His voice asked him in a whisper to look up slightly, to relax his entire being, because he was too tense. He asked him to please put all his strength on the arm that was pulling the bowstring.

For Hyacinthus, having him so close simply made a great impression. It was true that it was not the first time, but despite this, it still seemed strange. Feeling his perfect skin on his, noticing his breath close to his body, listening to his voice, which gravely advised him in a whisper, unleashed a torrent of emotions, sensations that he had rarely experienced before.

When he finished correcting his posture, he separated from him. This made Hyacinthus wish to return to the previous moment.

He had within easy reach the trunk of the young tree with which they had decided to practice, so that later, if the prince achieved a good technique, he could go out and hunt creatures. As long as this was the boy's wish.

'Now remember everything we said and simply let go of the bowstring,' he told him softly.

His voice had come out very softly from his lips, but it mattered little, because in the middle of the field, they could find little noise.

Almost without being conscious, Hyacinthus moved the position of the bow a millimetre. Apollo noticed this but said nothing. So, without paying attention to that mistake, Hyacinthus fired. His arrow grazed the trunk and simply fell to the ground.

The boy grimaced, clenching his jaw.

'What have I done wrong this time?' he asked after a few long seconds.

'You stopped putting enough strength in the arm holding the wood, so the direction of the bow moved. You should have checked that you had everything right before you risked shooting.'

'What nonsense,' he muttered.

'The simplest things are the ones that end up having the most importance. Next time, don't skip points that you think are insignificant. Everything has value, even the simplest things.' His advice was full of wisdom.

They had just got off their horses, and Apollo had had the idea of seeing if Hyacinthus really knew how to be an archer. He discovered that this was certainly not one of his strong points.

When the young man failed, he said to himself that after all Hyacinthus, despite being wonderful, was still a mortal. He couldn't be perfect. He had already been good at reflection and exercise in general. Therefore, he didn't take his own ruling very seriously.

'Will I end up getting better?'

'If you practice, you will,' he paused slightly. 'When I spoke to your sister, she confessed her love for archery. I asked her how good you were at it and, I'm afraid, I should have trusted her words,' he responded with amusement.

'It could be much worse.'

'That's true.'

Minutes passed, hours passed, and the days seemed to fly by. Next to Apollo, Hyacinthus felt freedom. Together he admired the world, and learned what happiness was, because this was what he found when he was next to the god. If he ran along the roads and stumbled, he would get up with a smile on his lips. If he bled, he laughed and continued. Even the tears seemed to be different.

Apollo was nothing more than an archaic force that sheltered him from the depths of his being. His gaze shone all the time. It seemed like it would never go out. The prince hoped that would never happen. This unique look brought warmth to his life, positive energy that helped him calm down and bring out the best version of himself. He also loved his words, which never ceased to surprise him, because they were endowed with the greatest wisdom he knew. It was something he would cherish forever.

The mortal told himself on numerous occasions that he would not have minded if his life were limited to that. To be in the countryside in the mountains, with two horses to take care of, sleeping on the grass. The first thing he saw when he woke up was the clear morning sky, and the last thing was the mysterious beauty that only the night possessed. He would have been happy in a world absolved of worry, where he could stick to being with the love he would not have suspected he would find.

Apollo, for his part, had dedicated a large part of his entire being to Hyacinthus. He had been warned a thousand times, not just by his muses, but also by his sister under his father's orders. Since apparently and in the eyes of the other gods, he was neglecting his divine tasks; however, who could he not neglect them having Hyacinthus at his side? Who could refuse the prospect of spending long days with the prince of Sparta? He, of course, was not capable. He had tried, but it had not worked. He felt that with each passing day, he was eager and eager to spend more time with the young man. He was seeing in him everything he had dreamed of.

He remembered in those moments, during the night, his previous lovers, while he tenderly observed the body of Hyacinthus who was resting deeply asleep. None of these were even half of what the boy before his eyes meant. He thanked Eros silently for having finally allowed him to enjoy a love that both hearts desired.

He was not afraid. However, he suspected something would happen. There was a heaviness in the air, along with the overwhelming emotion that someone was present there. So Apollo stood up, with the bow in his hand, protecting the body of the sleeping one.

The wind began to blow stronger. It was colder and came from the north. Then Phoebus knew well who it was. Who knows how long he had been watching them, but he didn't care. If the god had appeared there, it was because he wanted to communicate something to him.

Thus, the icy breeze began to take human form. Before his gaze, a boy with platinum hair appeared.

'Boreas.' Apollo uttered the word with politeness and harmony.

'Apollo,' his opponent greeted. 'Don't worry, I'm not here to bother you. I simply wanted to tell you that despite not being an official player in this game, I am completely withdrawing. I do not intend to waste my time for the love of a young man, whose heart I well know has already chosen.'

'It's okay, Boreas. I allow you...'

'No,' he interrupted him, 'I did not come for your approval, son of Zeus. I simply came to inform you, but despite being an Olympian god, nothing grants you the privilege of allowing me or preventing me from playing this game.'

'Anything else?' the god of the sun asked him when he noticed that the god of the north wind had almost said something else.

'No.'

With that simple and cold word, the child's figure dissolved, turning into an invisible wind that soon moved away from there.

Apollo heard a very familiar voice. Then he looked up at the sky.

It wouldn't take long for the moon to reach the highest point of the celestial vault. He felt his sister's call. He felt warned, again and again. Artemis watched over them, protecting them from any enemies. He was aware that if there was any danger she would warn him, but that night Apollo was restless and not only because of Boreas' visit, but because of something else that he could not identify.

Hyacinthus, meanwhile, was in a state of shallow sleep from which it did not take him long to wake up, seeing the silhouette of the god against the sky. His voice called him softly and Apollo soon headed towards him. Phoebus's eyes were still blue suns. A color so intense that Hyacinthus didn't think he could have seen it anywhere else.

He observed the stars surrounding them, since he had gone to bed at sunset, since he was tired from such a long day. He had not been able to see the stars that at that moment illuminated the entire world. There were thousands and millions of them. He was very surprised, since there were not usually so many of them or, at least, not many could be seen from his home. However, he was in the countryside, in the mountains. He was closer to Uranus than he had ever been, and there, at that height, he was already able to appreciate the beauty that the sky possessed. He also admired the moon and his sisters, to whom he had always been accustomed to pray.

On numerous occasions he had said that the moon reflected so many things, that it had so many mysteries that no human being would be able to discover them. On the other hand, he no longer felt the need to unearth those secrets, since he already had everything he wanted. He was in nature, his true home, and next to him was a deity he had drawn the attention of without even being aware of it. A deity, to whom, without exaggeration, he felt more united than to his own body, than to Gaia herself who supported his being as he walked through her fields. However, Apollo was endowed with something that attracted the soul of Hyacinthus. Its strength was such that the prince had the feeling that he would never notice anyone else.

He wanted to know what Apollo that hurts him from afar felt towards him. He wanted to understand once and for all what it was that united them. It was not just friendship or the search for knowledge, justice or passion for the arts, but something deeper. Something like the romantic love that the prince was undoubtedly already beginning to feel inside. Although he was sure that this had emerged from the first second the god's gaze met his.

He also wanted to understand who the stranger who had seen him naked truly was, the one who seemed to hate Apollo with all his being.

And that night, when he woke up and heard two voices talking, Hyacinthus knew well that something was happening. Over time he would confirm that at least Boreas and Apollo were participating in the game, and only the gods knew who else was trying to conquer him, but despite his little fortune, there was already a clear winner:

The one who brought enlightenment to the world. The one with the golden lyres that he would never stop listening to even if he died. The one with the silver bow. The same one that had made entire cities sick. The same one who had also saved a lot. The divinity who had a fortune teller in distant Delphi, a woman whom all of Greece respected and would respect for centuries of existence.

If there was someone he should embrace, someone he should worship, someone he should pray to... If there was a god he would never renounce no matter what, it would be Apollo who hurts from afar. The same being that looked him in the eyes after having come to meet him.

Hyacinthus didn't have to say anything for Apollo to realize that he had woken up before the end of the conversation with the north wind. The son of Zeus did not say anything either. He waited in silence, while he observed him. It seemed like that was all he did: watch him, letting him make the decisions. He was the embodiment of justice. He would never risk putting him in a bind, making him believe that if he did not continue things, even against his will, he would be punished for having rejected a deity.

He wanted him to be the one to say it, for the prince to be the one to act, for his lips to be the ones to caress him first. He wanted him to be the one to call him to know that he was not forced, and that everything he did, he wanted. Those were Apollo's thoughts. Because, for the first time, he understood that that was love. All the positive emotions that he could perceive intermingled, forming a single feeling that, despite having believed he had experimented it in the past, he never had. Love was not about forcing, but about giving freedom, allowing the other's wings to open. And if he couldn't take flight, he simply had to be helped.

Hyacinthus showed signs of standing up. But Apollo, realizing this, crouched down next to him. The prince looked into the eyes of the god. He felt like he was lost in the sun's rays. He felt that before him was the sphere that no one would ever stop praising. He did not know how to proceed, since he did not want to offend the divinity either. He didn't want to be confused, but he had talked it over with him: making mistakes was nothing to be ashamed of.

But despite all this, when he finally dared, joining his lips with those of the other, thus feeling in his own skin the warmth that only sunny mornings transmitted, he was afraid. It didn't take long for the prince to gently separate himself from the god.

Apollo, hearing the young man's thoughts in his own mind, caressed his cheek gently. A cheek that gradually took on a reddish tone. That which was only revealed on the faces of mortals when they suffered terribly from shame.

'It's okay, Hyacinthus. You can do it,' he said with a voice full of sweetness. To which the young boy did not take long to respond.

'I already know who you are, Phoebus,' he confessed, looking into his eyes. The prince's gaze was full of a thousand emotions that even Apollo, being a god, had a hard time identifying. It was fear for what could happen, also, dare, joy, satisfaction, love and even a hint of sad melancholy. 'I know who you really are, and I just feel something so strange towards you, that I don't know what it means. I don't know if it's because of your glorious identity, or what my heart has been warning me about for a long time.'

'Who do you know I am?'

'I know you are Phoebus, Apollo; Apollo Phoebus who hurts from afar, who protects and attacks from the heavens.' When pronouncing his name, Hyacinthus's eyes turned a beautiful purple because of the light of the firmament bouncing off his gaze. 'Son of Zeus, born to Leto on an island called Delos, also brother of Artemis, the one with the arrow that never misses. You are that young man who once had cattle that Hermes stole. Thanks to a lyre, you forgave him and since then, you carry their music wherever you go. These notes have also reached my heart and not from the hand of an aedo, but from the god of music himself. You are the god of the sun, of the arts, of diseases, but also of healing, of beauty, of poetry, of oracles, of light... Also in you we mortals see protection against evil, harmony, balance, perfection, justice... You are the god who managed to kill the Python snake, turning its home into your own temple. The one we turn to for advice. I speak of all of them, but, especially, of Delphi. You are a god, one of the most influential I would venture to say, and you noticed me, a mere mortal, what am I to deserve your presence?'

'Hyacinthus,' he murmured. 'I might be a god. I might have millions of spheres, and might have had thousands of adventures, but you are no less for being mortal. What's more, you are luckier. You mortals are able to appreciate every second on Earth if you put your mind to it, because you know that there will be a day when your time is up. However, we will still be here, even when you mortals forget our names.'

'I don't think anyone will forget your name. What kind of society could forget you, Apollo?' Saying that last word was like medicine for Hyacinthus. Something he had wanted to do for so long that it was terribly relieving to dare to say it. At the same time, imagining a world in which no one would be able to remember the god he had before his eyes filled him with sadness. Since he had met him, he had been unable to imagine a life without him by his side. A life lacking the knowledge that he was real, like all the other gods. He didn't realize that he had doubted that not so long ago.

'A society that has been forced to forget because of submission. A society that wants to live without being persecuted. For this reason, one day my name will be forgotten, and I will be here seeing it every day. Instead, you, Hyacinthus, will live a life in which you will always be remembered. When you die, they will forget you, but at least you can say that you lived. However, whatever happens to you, I will always remember you at every dawn and every midnight like this. I will remember your eyes that seem bathed in purple waters as I watch the world change.'

'But you have avoided my question, Apollo, what am I to deserve such an honour? I have even doubted your existence. I have come to believe that you were a figment of someone's imagination.'

'We gods do not have to focus on those who are truly devoted to us, even if they believe blindly. We gods look at the mortals that fill our soul, at the beings that give us hope, at those that transmit to us something different from the ordinary.' Then Apollo, who had lowered his gaze slightly, raised it again. He looked into his eyes without any desire to move away from them. 'Hyacinthus, you transmitted something unique, authentic to me without even realizing it. I then began to observe you more closely, because some time before I was not aware of your existence. However, your soul managed to reach my gaze. It managed to penetrate my senses. You managed to make me feel emotions that I should not have noticed at any time, but I was unable to control them, so I let them flow. They ended up leading me to materialization, to acquire this human form so that I could be with you, so that you could see me and I could give you the opportunity to feel the same thing that invaded me. But your soul, Hyacinthus, is tremendously desired, and other humans like Tamyris, as well as other gods, like Boreas or Zephyrus, were attracted to you, drawn to you. I didn't know and I still don't know if I'm enough for you. They say that I am the most beautiful of the Olympians, but beauty does not conquer a heart, much less a soul.

274

'You raise admirers wherever you go, prince. It is not only because of your physical appearance, but also because of the heart that beats in that body of yours, because of the spirit that lies trapped there. You have so much light that you managed to overcome that of the sun. You managed to dazzle me, and I couldn't miss the opportunity to know who you were. A life to you, Hyacinthus, is a mere sigh to me. However, in no second of my existence have I found someone like you on Gaia. No one has made me feel as alive as your presence alone. There have been others, but I have never felt love as intensely as this. I have never felt something so big blooming inside me. Nothing as immense as what you manage to birth in my being. I could have a thousand things just by snapping my fingers. I could achieve infinite goals if I set my mind to it. I could subdue, I could force, I could run to capture as I did long ago, but I did not want a simple path. Nor do I want it in these moments in which I look into your eyes, confessing that you are and will always be, even when you no longer breathe, the art that inspires me, the reason why the sun rises every day, facing the clouds in order to illuminate the world... It is you, Hyacinthus, human mortal, a tiny being that has captivated me so much that I could not imagine even a second without being by your side. The stars shine tonight with a brilliance that I had never seen before meeting you. I know well that they will not shine like this again when you leave sentient life, when you return to Hades. Then the stars will matter little. The days will matter little, the land itself. Music will be insignificant and poetry useless. When your soul leaves me, the world will no longer be the world I knew. The lights will go out, I will sink into darkness, but then, when I am ready to abandon everything, your memory will plague my nights, your memory will sneak into my thoughts and I will finally be able to come out, because your presence will save me again. If I lost you, Hyacinthus, I would not stop until I found you. Since I am the god of art, and you are this personified. Since I am the god of light, and only you are the focus of it. If I could stop you for a second, singing to you everything that sneaks into my mind; If I could even tell you exactly what no one has ever thought, I would do it without hesitation, but I can't find a way to make a being like you understand what I'm talking about just like the way I feel it. I can't find a way to tell you how much I love you without falling into verses, but I doubt that they have enough power to sing to you what you have caused inside an immortal creature that I had thought would never love again. I cannot sing to you what my lyre would sing. I cannot love you as I would like to, because a thousand tragedies follow me wherever I go, and I have a thousand more misfortunes in mind in a future that is gradually becoming closer. If I could perhaps...! If I could, I would do it!'

'Then do it,' Hyacinthus murmured. 'Sing to me what your lips are unable to pronounce. The same thing that I am incapable of

276

feeling. Sing it to me, play it to me. Play the lyre and I will try to understand what I have created inside you. If only you tried! There will never be another love like this. I know that, but not even I am aware of the breadth of my emotions. Apollo, my heart is yours. It moves away from my possessions and becomes yours... And now I am aware that it was never mine, it was always yours. Always! Even when I just heard your name without completely believing! Even when doubts came to my mind! Even in those moments, my heart was already yours, but I was unconscious. I was a child who didn't understand. I can't explain how grateful I am that you chose me, that you came, that you came down, that you appeared to me... I don't think I deserve this. I don't think I deserve your presence, so divine, so archaic... Oh, if only I understood it! I have thorns as a head. They dig into my skin, and I don't know what to do. Then, you arrive with your morning lights and remove that crown from me that hurts me as much as the human knife does to the earth itself. I had a blindfold as eyes. You ripped it off helping me see. If I should remember anything in my life, it is that mere moment in which I entered the room and there I found you. For the first time knowing that you were not who you said you were, that you were much more than a human could be. I want to know, to feel at least what I am unable to understand through words, but perhaps through notes I will understand something. So please play the lyre,

Apollo. God of the sun, play the lyre and make me understand what is in your heart.'

Apollo didn't need Hyacinthus to insist much more. Thus, the lyre appeared in one of his hands, and without further thinking, the god began to play. The prince lay down again, closing his eyes, as he thought this would help him.

The son of Zeus, before starting to play, looked at him with a sweetness never felt before. There was so much that neither words nor music could encompass. It was a sweetness that screamed his entire being, if indeed a human could feel with the grace that the gods did. If only a human could feel with the same purity and intensity that not only the gods did, but also other creatures. All of them, when they loved, truly loved. When they wanted, they really wanted. When they were sad, they were really sad. The human was a liar even for the most beautiful feelings.

Apollo's long fingers began to caress the strings with immense softness, because he did not pluck, he touched with the elegance that swans had when taking flight, with the majesty that wolves possessed when singing. As his fingers moved, his curly hair darkened until it reached that black colour with bluish reflections of the *kouros*, the petals of thought.

And as the *kouros*, the petals of thought, he silently prayed that his emotions would be conveyed by the lyre. He wanted, despite knowing that he didn't need it, that Hyacinthus would understand that he was not somebody else, but him, who had really marked him. The one he would not forget even when long centuries passed. His legacy, his dynasty would be forgotten, but he would never forget the humans, thanks to that young man with the dreamy look. He would not do it.

When the snakes stopped crawling on the ground, when the dolphins stopped playing, when the sunset of the swans arrived, when an eternal morning awaited the wolves, when the crow stopped observing, when the roe deer disappeared from the forests, when the kite and the vulture vanished, and along with them also their fallen feathers... When the human era erased the name of Phoebus-Apollo from his history, he would continue remembering, dead in life, that time in which everything still shone.

Apollo would listen to the calming sounds of the sea from his island of birth, Delos, the one that would never forget him, remembering the clandestine tonality of those beings who had once worshiped them, and the only voice that would come clearly to him would be that of the prince of Sparta. The prince of his life, art in person, art in soul. A creature carrying so much beauty that not even he was a match. When darkness enveloped him, a laugh would be heard. That would be that of Hyacinthus, the boy of his eyes, the young man he loved with all his life. If he noticed nostalgia growing in his soul, there would be someone who would push it away. If, at any time, he thought about throwing himself into Tartarus, it would be the face of Hyacinthus who would come announcing to him that a new day would soon dawn, that he should not give up even when nothing seemed to matter, because life continued even though his heart no longer beat.

That melody had infinite meanings, an ode to nostalgia and the love of a long life! And Hyacinthus felt it.

These notes filtered through his ears, reverberating throughout his body, creating echoes in his being. He didn't understand it. A thousand emotions seemed to be found in them; another thousand appeared when he least realized it. All of them intertwined and transmitted a message that he described as the true love that humans were not able to access. But Apollo, oh Apollo! He wasn't human, even in that form he wasn't even close to the word! Oh, Apollo! He wasn't trapped in a body, much less tied to a society that made him forget what really mattered. Apollo was a free being. A wiser, more developed, more powerful being... So much so that he had managed to achieve an authentic love, free of impurities; a love that no one could be able to achieve. Nobody who wasn't like him.

It was normal for mortals to praise the gods, since they were the closest thing to perfection that humans had known. Hyacinthus knew well that this was the case; however, he also understood that the feeling that Apollo found when thinking about him was much deeper than his own and that he loved him, he loved him with all his little soul! With all his fragile human body! There was no one he loved as much as he loved Apollo. However, his excitement was very small compared to that of the god. But this did not cause him any trauma, since the only thing he found in his being was eternal gratitude.

A gratitude that Hyacinthus felt throughout his being. He knew Apollo understood. The song he played calmed him. He also felt completely understood, loved and cherished as he had never been before. The lyre told him what no letter, no word would have been able to pronounce. *How beautiful the music was!* Those were the ephebe's thoughts in those moments. Thanks to the music, he understood what Phoebus was trying to say. He knew he wouldn't want to be separated even for a second.

When Apollo stopped playing, Hyacinthus opened his eyes. The god's hair returned to its natural shade. There were tears in his eyes, he was not surprised that they could also be found in his lover's eyes. However, both seemed to refuse to let them fall. What's more, they couldn't let them go, because those tears didn't want to leave them. The prince sat up, unable to take his eyes off the god's face. He simply approached him, caressing his cheek with those same fingers with which he had played the lyre so harmoniously. The voices were unnecessary, the silence was their words. The gaps in their gaze were their music. The energies were the meanings. Matters foreign to both of them mattered little.

And during that night they risked loving each other, but not in the way that anyone would do, but in a way so spiritual that many would envy it. It was the feeling that grew in both of them that was incredible, because it was not ordinary at all.

Apollo could have been with Hyacinthus in that way until infinity. However, the last one was still mortal and sleep soon came to him. So, Phoebus simply let the young man sleep with his body pressed against his, while the god gently caressed his curls, letting him know at all times that he would not leave his side.

However, Apollo was not free from dreams, because being the god of oracles, visions used to attack him when his subconscious realized that he had not accepted something that would happen. Without realizing it, that's what happened. So it was that in this state he heard what he feared most. He had been fearing it for a long time.

In a way, he still saw the plain before his eyes, just as he felt the soft breeze, the grass on which he was lying. He also noticed the prince leaning on his body, but his mind was much further away. And he knew it.

He felt overwhelmed by the burning feeling filled with darkness that had been following him for a long time. This energy spoke to him. Possibly, it was his own future self. He warned him carefully: what he loved most would be taken from his hands, because misfortunes surrounded him, and he would never be able to get away from them. What he loved most would be lost to him.

Then, Apollo truly feared as he had never done before, and he soon told himself that at dawn they would abandon that excursion, thus taking Hyacinthus safely to his true home, the one from which he should never have left. He also set to distance himself from the prince, at least romantically. He knew well that if he maintained a relationship with him full of admiration or cordiality, nothing bad would happen to him. However, Apollo already loved Hyacinthus, and that fate had already been sewn.

XIV

After a few hours riding, they arrived at their home. They had been in complete silence the entire way. Hyacinthus kept asking himself if it was wise to bring up the topic of conversation that he so wanted to address. On the other hand, Apollo was immersed in a darkness that the boy was not able to perceive. A gloom that kept his mind distant, questioning himself if the omen was true or just an expression of his greatest fear.

From time to time, Phoebus looked at Hyacinthus, making sure he was okay. There was something so dark following them, he feared it was actually true. And in a certain way he knew well that there was no room for falsehood within him; however, there were circumstances that not even he was able to accept.

As they got off the horses, Apollo gave him the reins of his mount. Hyacinthus took them, looking into his eyes. He was questioning him about whether he would come back. Apollo, the young man with golden hair and sweet eyes, looked at him, surrounded by a mysterious aura that the prince could not decipher. Ergo, he risked asking:

'Will you come back?' Phoebus, who was very close to him, brushed his hair away from his face.

Apollo answered him like this:

'I will, Hyacinthus. Don't doubt that I will. However, I have to do things that I have completely forgotten about. And unfortunately, this kind of work requires my full presence.'

The boy nodded his head.

'Alright.'

Apollo, with a broken heart inside, smiled sweetly at him, and started walking away slowly until there was a moment when he vanished from the young man's sight.

Hyacinthus stayed there for long minutes with a bitter desire to see his return, even though he knew he would not come back. At least, not during that day. The prince did not know that Apollo would be there next to him anyway. Watching him with immense sweetness, accompanied by each and every one of his muses, who had advised him to do so for his own good. It was better that he separated from him for a while, but they all knew, just as Apollo himself was aware of it, that it would not take long for him to return to his beloved. However, he had to find out what it was that bothered him so much.

Hyacinthus stood staring at the distant horizon for hours. The slaves had already spotted him, and they had taken charge of the horses without even asking their young master. He had an indecipherable look. On one occasion he felt a hand gently rest on his shoulder. Despite this, he did not take his gaze away from the distance. He had his heart in his hands. He knew Apollo did, too. He felt that he was still at his side invisibly, and he was not wrong.

Mere hours had passed, but not finding him physically at his side devastated him. He didn't know why, but he was losing the magic that the moments with him gave him. He wasn't dissatisfied either, quite the opposite. He was baffled by how strange everything seemed to him. Because it was strange not to find that strength next to him in a completely palpable and visible way. The young prince still felt it, but far away. At the same time, it seemed to be close. What was felt in those moments was so complex that not even by asking the petals of the Hyacinth one could find out.

He was calm, yet completely excited. He felt the adrenaline boiling through his blood, but his body would not run. It would remain idle, standing at that same point, while his mind tried to accept everything that had happened. His sister, at his side, remained silent, accepting his decision.

The memories of those days illuminated him, surrounding him, overwhelmed him and he could see them: Apollo with his bow. Apollo and his smile. Apollo and the birds that seemed to observe him from the heavens. Apollo with his clandestine voice. The kindness that was in his eyes. The beauty of which it was composed. The harmony that he transmitted even through his own arrows. The elegance of his adventures. His impeccable way of doing everything, even riding. His lips next to his reliving memories that he would cling to tightly. His strong arms guiding his body trying not to make mistakes... His voice speaking, bringing out great truths that if he, Apollo, had not come across his life, he would never have known. And that last night under the stars where his lyre had sung the love he professed for him.

Hyacinthus knew then that if at any time Apollo left, he would give his life for him, joining a group of priests who would pray to him, since Phoebus had saved him. He had made him bring out his best version, tear off the blindfold. Apollo had taught him to see, and very few were capable of doing so. The god had given him the greatest gift anyone could give: knowledge of the world, the feeling of the universe. He felt grateful, thanks to him he would abandon the customs of men in order to return to nature, to the wisdom of the gods.

He had helped him become what he had always dreamed of, something that he had never before believed possible, but that could nevertheless be achieved, because at that moment, he had it in his hands. He knew he was with him. He would not leave his side, because he understood that Apollo also reached some peculiar state with him. Life had never been so clandestine, so mysterious, so full of riches as it was in those moments, allowing his gaze to get lost in the twilight, in the farewell of the sun. If anything, he was barely aware of everything that had happened, because he lived it like a dream. It had been so surreal! However, he understood that dreams would not come disguised in that way; knowing, possessing the knowledge that Phoebus was Apollo, that his beloved companion in adventures, his teacher in life was, in reality, Apollo, son of Zeus, that being of ill-fated lovers, stirred something inside him, an effort to distance himself from the god that had unwittingly returned him to true life. Because that was what Apollo had done. And Hyacinthus told himself that without his help none of this would have been even half as possible. He had always considered himself a great expert on the world, above all, because of what he learned in the scrolls and his level of culture. However, in those moments he also reminded himself that the music of the earth could not be learned. It had to be heard.

Humans were commonly too busy with their own business, so closed in on themselves that they couldn't even manage to listen for even a measly second. Nor could they say that they felt Gaia's movement, because if they did, the vast majority of them would lie; nevertheless, people did not usually boast about their feelings on the places they frequented. Something Hyacinthus believed was indispensable for a creature that lived in Gaia. After all, she was his home more than anything else. Gaia was a goddess, but she was the only one that everyone saw, that everyone could feel. Still, no one dedicated the required time to it. Apollo had shown him that he could appreciate her beauty, even when he doubted it, since everything horrendous, everything horrible was a product of human greed, but everything beautiful that could be thought of came from nature. Because even the arts, which seemed to be a grace only managed by humans, were also managed by Gaia herself and her other inhabitants, the birds, the animals, the gods who collaborated with her. Also, in her fields, which were no other than her body, one could hear a silence that possessed art, and that without even understanding it could be classified as music, since it was the grace of the sounds of the forest.

On the other hand, everything horrible, what made many humans hate their lives, hate the Earth, was, redundantly, what those same humans did, what they caused with their vile acts: the blood spilling on the floors, the screams of a woman who had lost a child to the edge of a knife, the pleas of the slave who was beaten in a corner of the home. The suffering that caressed the souls... In the vast majority, so as not to disagree and generalize, they were caused by humans. Suffering was a human art. Many times, it was unnecessary suffering. Hyacinthus knew it. There was light in the world, that same light that Apollo represented. There was light, an immense and brilliant one to which Phoebus-Apollo could be compared, for he himself was it.

There was light, it existed and it was worth fighting for it, trying to see it. He was understanding it. He already did, dared he say, but it would never have been in such a way if the Olympian had not appeared before his eyes, if his voice had never spoken to him. However, it had done so, and thanks to him, in those moments, Hyacinthus was completely awake, feeling fully alive and grateful for being there, even if this time it was without him at his side.

Polyboea looked at him in a tender way. Her eyes were two moonstones that asked him to tell her what had happened, since in his eyes one could easily find the curiosity that long ago had led the talented Pandora to make a huge mistake.

'What are you thinking, Hyacinthus?' she dared to ask. 'What's inside that elaborate head of yours?'

'I simply tell myself that the world has never been as beautiful as it is now. The world has never been as gorgeous as it is right now, the breeze has never blown this way before. Not even the clouds above us have long had those shapes. Birds have never sung this way. Never before had Apollo hidden the sun in the way it is being hidden today. I have never been as aware as I am now.'

'What are you trying to say?'

'That I have never been so awake, nor as alive as I am now. Because today, Polyboea, I am able to see the light of the Earth; because today Polyboea, I not only feel and listen, but I also understand, and understanding is the best gift that someone could have given me. And all thanks to him, Polyboea, the son of the king of gods, the one with golden hair and clear eyes, the one with the golden cows, the one with the lyres with extraordinary notes, the guide of the sun, the voice that advises my soul, the healer, the poet, the musician, the artist, the most powerful and beautiful creature I have ever had the luxury of knowing before. Today, dear sister, I am realizing that the only dangerous thing in this world is to love. Love is confused with wanting, and wanting generates chaos.' He paused slightly. 'The most beautiful and dangerous thing there is is to love. The most horrible thing that exists is wanting. They seem to go hand in hand, but I hear the voices of the gods, and I know it is not true, it is not true! They are different... Love builds, wanting destroys. Love frees, wanting enslaves. Do you hear me, Polyboea?'

'I hear you, Hyacinthus, but it is difficult for me to follow your train of thought.'

The young man then looked into the girl's eyes.

'It's like the day I told you that the sky was endowed with beauty. You were unable to see it, but now between you and I, I repeat it to you: someday you will see it and when you do, you will not believe that it was there all the time without you being aware of it.'

Polyboea smiled softly.

'Do you understand?' Hyacinthus asked, carried by hope when he saw the soft smile that was drawn on his sister's face.

'No, Hyacinthus, I do not understand it, but I am sure of your words: today I do not understand it, but someday I will, and then, I will know what you are talking about.'

'When you understand it, you will hear their flutes playing in the early mornings. You will hear the lyres, the war songs, you will understand the meaning of life, of nature, of our own soul. On that day, you will open your eyes and see.'

As he finished his words, the sun finally set. And without saying more, he turned on his heel, heading inside the home. His sister followed him.

'And what have you done?'

'We've talked. I have heard him play the lyre. We have also gone hunting, since I insisted on doing so, because we had not brought much food, and I had been very hungry in the few days before.'

'Did you manage to hunt?'

'Indeed. A spectacular piece, I must say.'

'I thought you would come sooner, did something unexpected happen?' Hyacinthus stopped at that moment in front of his room and shook his head.

'Simply that at his side, minutes do not exist, nor fears. Just this internal fire that burns me every time I see him, feel him or listen to him. We could have been out there for years, and I wouldn't have realized it, because at its side I find a world unaware of time and limitations, where the only guidelines are set by us.'

. . .

The god searched and searched, trying to find an answer to the weight he felt on his shoulders.

There was something that damaged his soul, like a storm that suddenly makes its way through the calmest and most beautiful mornings. He didn't really understand why this situation was delaying him. The agony was devouring him. That same bad air he felt in his chest consumed him at levels he wouldn't believe possible. It destroyed him, turning him into such a tiny figure... In a being so tiny, that Apollo could not be able to understand how this could happen to him, him that would forever inhabit the history of humans, the history of the world and of the cosmos itself. And still, it did. Apollo understood that when one approached the little clay creatures, it was very likely that one would make the same mistake as Prometheus: loving them without even being aware of it. Loving them, even more than one's own being. However, Apollo did not love the entire species as the aforementioned Titan had done, but only one individual. An individual he couldn't imagine not having by his side for all eternity. And his plan seemed to work. He wouldn't force him, of course he wouldn't! However, he would suggest it. He would look him in the eyes, while his lyre was being played. He would look him in the eyes, piercing his sincere gaze into that of the young man, and then he would speak to him. He would tell him how much he loved him. He would confess to him the fear that surrounded him at not being able to continue by his side for thousands and millions of years, all of this to end up asking him if he wanted to join him.

He would make him a minor deity as he did with his son, Asclepius, and then they would be together. All his nightmares would fade, but in those moments, there was a new fear that was gaining ground. Perhaps he had long thought that the wind gods were his enemy, but maybe that was not the case. Maybe there was something else, someone else. For once he was afraid to know the truth. For once Apollo, who in the depths of his conscience knew what would happen, did not listen to himself and began to doubt the fate of the young boy whom he had grown so fond of.

His presence before his lovers was usually fleeting. At the same time, all of his lovers were, too. Both those who had accepted him and those who had fled. It was the only thing that united them all. That feeling of expiration. Someday, either he would have to leave, or they would. Apollo had counted on it throughout his entire existence, because he was a god, and they lived much more than the vast majority of the creatures that populated the Earth. They will still be alive even when humanity becomes extinct. They will always remain alive, because they do not know limited times. Nor is there any biological clock whose sand is destined to run out, since they are composed of other materials.

They are formed by the same matter that forms the spirit of creatures and the cosmos itself. However, they do not have to be reincarnated, much less do they have to learn the lessons of life. Death cannot touch them with its sweet caresses either.

So, being aware of all this, Apollo had never forgotten about it. He remembered it every time he found a being for whom he lost his soul, but he had never expected that the day would come when that want would not exist, and would forever become a love impossible to achieve for the creatures who do not possess his divine condition. He was not losing his mind, nor his thoughts, nor his wise spirit for Hyacinthus, but he was giving him every single thing he was.

The young man was endowed with a thousand gifts that he admired. He took his breath away, and even as he crossed the beautiful firmament, sometimes he had the desire to only illuminate him. It wouldn't have surprised him to do it. If he had, he would have made a fuss, but it didn't matter since the sun would be shining on him.

Illuminating the being he loved, the being he sang for, the one he played for, the one he lived for. Well, Apollo knew that death was a rest before the next game. However, the worst death was that which occurred while one was alive. A death from which he was not protected. The only truly true one, he said to himself. Hyacinthus was his shield against that death.

He lived in the knowledge that, for some time, many humans would forget him and his entire dynasty. An oblivion that would lead them to misfortune, to death in life, to death in the abyss of faded memories. An abyss it would take them a while to abandon, but Hyacinthus at his side would take him out of that dark place. And despite being able to immerse himself in that melancholy for a yesteryear that might not return, he would not do so because the prince would be next to him, filling him with life. He adored the young man. A thousand emotions could try to define what he really felt, but none would completely convey his feelings.

He loved him and wished no harm for him. What's more, he would protect him from any being that tried to harm him, since if there was someone who should not be harmed, it was his beloved Hyacinthus. However, despite swearing that he would protect him, there was something that escaped him. Deep down he knew it. He knew it, but he didn't want to know it and when you don't want to know something, even when you really know, you end up ignoring it.

He was looking for an answer to that darkness that surrounded him. While he was thinking about his being, about his energies, about how these had become so sweet. They had become a tender symphony as he felt an internal fire that was the driving force that led to their kiss. An internal fire that had led the boy to do something of which he himself was ashamed. Despite knowing well that Apollo understood the feeling that motivated him to do it. After all, it was not very different from the one who had made the god engage, without moving an inch away from the other's face.

Apollo recalled the tender way of looking he had. Also, his sweet, tanned face that turned reddish when something brought out a shyness that at first glance he did not seem to possess. He smiled, seeing in his mind Hyacinthus grimace as he failed to master his bow, and his joy when he hit the target. He got lost in the harmonious way he walked, because it gave the impression that he was dancing on invisible clouds. His slender form, and that tender smile endowed with a thousand colours, taking over his soft and delicate lips... Apollo had had many lovers, but none were like Hyacinthus. None was endowed with everything that made up the young prince. At times, he even wondered if he was truly completely mortal. He always told himself that he knew the answer perfectly.

His eyes, endowed with a light akin to two stars, when illuminated by the moon's rays resembled purple petals of a flower that did not yet exist, but which, without a doubt, would be created. When it was created, it would be in his honour. Those two stars were nothing more than an open door that led to a soul more beautiful, talented, and delicate than it had ever existed before. Apollo, at least, had never met one, and he saw everything. Ergo he supposed that thus far there were no others, except Hyacinthus, and his was unique.

His sweet features, his peculiar personality, gifted with that immense intelligence, that respect, that desire for knowledge. That archaic force that Apollo felt growing in him every time he opened his eyes a little more, thus realizing what the place he inhabited, the creatures he lived with, was truly like. He wouldn't change a thing about the young man. He couldn't imagine that anyone would want to harm him. How beautiful he was! He was the most beautiful piece of living art you would ever see!

Despite all this, he continued to notice that negativity that hung over him, around him. That dark cloud that alerted his being, and that asked him to please leave him. It yelled at him that they could not maintain a romantic relationship, as this would be the young man's downfall. He was very wrong. And if he had listened a little more to his instinct, he would have known the truth, but love makes a wise man an ignorant man, and an ignorant man a wise man. Not even the one who houses all the knowledge in the world is often capable of knowing all the meanings. Or maybe he did know, but he didn't want to.

It was a pulse, an emotion, a bond, a thread that tied him to the soul he would never stop loving. And Phoebus Apollo knew well that when that connection was formed it was impossible to break it. His insides would ask him to look for it even when he didn't realize it. They asked him to find him so that he would never leave him, because it was true that he could live without being dependent on him, but next to him, he found a world immersed in silence, a peace, a freedom that he had not experienced for a long time. Next to Hyacinthus, Apollo felt fully alive.

Phoebus, moved by the feeling, continued wandering for long periods of time. He asked the muses, while telling them what was happening. He also spoke with his sister, Artemis, who did not like romance very much, but he did not find any answer to his questions. He knew then that the only one who could advise him was himself. He said to himself that the darkness that fell upon him was simply caused by Zephyrus, who had not yet retired from a game that had already ended. Boreas had already abandoned, therefore, Apollo felt nothing on his part. On the other hand, he continued to feel a great weight when he stopped to think about Zephyrus, the west wind that should soon withdraw from this. When Zephyrus surrendered, everything dark would fade, because this deity was the one that caused that cruel internal emotion that did not allow him to return to the one he truly loved.

So, with this reflection in mind, Apollo went in search of him. Before long. he found him, and the answer he would give him would not be the one desired.

'Are you asking me if I'm going to abandon, son of Leto?' he said in response.

'That's right, will you?' His voice sounded very elegant, full of grace despite being quite tired of those talks.

'You will see that for yourself, Olympian god.'

XV

'Tamyris, I am Hyacinthus, am I allowed to enter?' asked the voice of the young prince at the door of the Aedo' dwelling.

He heard footsteps approaching, and in the blink of an eye, the door opened. Before him lay a man he barely recognized. He still had the same haircut, also the strong arms that characterized him. However, he had lost what Hyacinthus had always loved about him: the sparkle in his eyes every time he saw him. And since he couldn't see it, he had to remember. However, a soft smile appeared on his lips, possibly because he imagined the young prince before him. Well, Tamyris had always gone looking for him, and now, for once, it was the other way round.

His gaze was lifeless, and Hyacinthus clenched his jaw, trying to stop himself from cursing the muses right there.

'Do I look so horrible, Hyacinthus? So horrible that you stay silent for so long?'

'No, Tamyris. I was silently condemning the women for weaving your destiny in this vile way, is this true justice? A great wise man told me that it was so. At least, that's how it is in the eyes of ancient beings like the muses, but to me, what they've done to you doesn't seem fair.'

302

'Come in, then, my prince. I think we should talk.'

Without further ado, Hyacinthus entered the interior of the dwelling and closed the door behind him, but not before letting in a slave that he had brought with him.

'You're not alone?'

'No, Adelphos is with me. He has been serving us for a long time, but he is now an old man, and I do not think it is appropriate for him to continue in our home, doing a thousand jobs that are not good for his body. I convinced my father to offer him the long-awaited freedom, so that he could live his retirement as he wished. As a free man he could return home, but he himself rejected this.'

'Yes,' the old man confirmed. 'I cannot return to my homeland, since it is far away and I am very old, but I can continue living here as I have always lived, as I have always liked to live. I asked my masters to give me one last task to help with until I board the boat that takes to Hades.'

'But,' Hyacinthus began to speak, 'our household jobs tend to be hard; perhaps not hard, but rather they require you to walk too much, because you know, Tamyris, that we have a big house. However, this place is ideal for Adelphos and I think you also need some help.'

Tamyris smiled widely again. The sweetness and kindness of Hyacinthus could not be described. He was not at all surprised that a god had noticed him. Yes, that human being was one of those graceful beings that were scarce in the world.

'I couldn't refuse this gift, Hyacinthus, even if I wanted to,' he said gratefully. 'As long as it doesn't bother you, Adelphos.'

'No sir, it will be good for me to keep you company.'
The prince smiled widely. He was sure the two would get along well.

It didn't take long for him to feel an archaic force that began to surround him like the soft breeze that wakes up sleeping bodies after the long and cold night. It was a force that felt so beautiful; in the same way, it made him want to be touched, caressed, in order to understand that it was not his invention, but reality. The love he thought he might never see again was there. In the musician's house, at his side, smiling as he smiled, enjoying his joy, praising his beauty. He was protecting him even when he didn't see him. He loved him even from a distance. He did not know any being as splendid as Apollo was. He was surprised to hear his voice inside his head, that same voice that had appeared but this time it was endowed with a harmony that it had never possessed before.

Hyacinthus was told that this was due to, possibly, the voice coming from a higher plane.

'You see it? Even the simplest decisions can brighten lives.'

The smile that was already on the young man's face widened even more.

Apollo, I thought you wouldn't come back. He thought without even hesitation. It was something that came instantly. He had not considered for a second whether this was appropriate. He cared little, because he knew well that the god had seen it coming even before it appeared in his mind.

The only response was silence, accompanied by the distant conversation between his former slave and that musician, whom by now he considered a friend. However, Apollo was still present. He felt it. He knew it. He thanked him without saying a word. He thanked him for having crossed his life, for changing his way of thinking, the way of seeing the world, of contemplating every small circumstance of that long lesson that was life. Apollo had helped him be truer to himself, so he thanked him. He could not deny that he would have wished the deity had materialized at that moment next to him, but he understood that he had his reasons. He harboured in his little heart the hope that Phoebus would return in flesh and blood. He needed to love him, even when he knew it was dangerous. He needed to worship him, his entire being needed him in order to live.

What could he do other than worship the one who had saved his life? The one who had turned him into the best existing version of himself? And, in those moments, he looked at Adelphos, being able to see the joy in his eyes. That joy that his decision had caused. He said to himself that human beings could still help other creatures achieve happiness.

'Hyacinthus.' Tamyris pronounced his name; despite being blind, he knew that there, in that room, was the essence of Phoebus - Apollo. This essence did not live in the prince, but it was near him. The son of Leto, the music in creature, was visiting his abode. He didn't know how to express his gratitude.

Seeing that he received no response, he prepared to speak again, but then Hyacinthus answered:

'Yes, Tamyris?'
'Take a seat if you haven't done so yet, since what I have to tell you may be long.' Upon hearing this, the little prince, trusting his words, sat down next to the former aedo.

'You can start whenever you want, Tamyris, what do you want to tell me?'

'First, I want to thank you.'

'You should not thank me for anything at all, because I have not done anything that could save you from this cruel fate to which you have been subjected.'

'You can't save me, because this is the punishment I deserve for having crossed a line that I should never have crossed. However, I have nothing to offer you anymore, and you have shown up at my house with a man who will help me with whatever I need, do you know what I mean?'

'You appreciate me.'

'Apart from that. Hyacinthus, I thought I loved you, now I know that I love you and that I was afraid to do so, you know it well, even if you love another.' He told him without thinking about it. The slave looked at the young man out of the corner of his eye, pleasantly surprised by the spontaneity of the man he would soon live with. After all, Tamyris was being the first man to love another man. 'And I don't blame you for doing it. That other man... I shouldn't even call him that. That other creature, that other being, you know who I mean, is infinite times better than me. Since I am human, but he... he never was.'

'Tamyris, there is no need...' The son of the king of Sparta began. He was aware of how the former aeda felt towards him. No special qualities were needed to figure it out. He didn't want him to say it out loud, because in a way Hyacinthus was surprised by the number of souls he inadvertently eclipsed.

'Yes, it is necessary, Hyacinthus. We have to normalize it, we have to tell that person we love our feelings to their face, because sometimes this can mean too much to the other person. Listen to me when I tell you that I have wasted a thousand days wandering from land to land while playing the lyre, when I could have been by your side. And when I was next to you, I didn't realize anything. I do not regret it, not even that nonsense I said about the muses, because it all led me to you. All this made me close to you. Maybe I could never have you, but that doesn't mean I will stop loving you, because listen to me prince, I am happy when you are. I am blind, there is a growing darkness. That's the only thing I see with these eyes whose ability was taken from me. However, I continue to see, if differently. Sometimes, I see shadows within that blackness. Sometimes, I can appreciate the colours that the birds sing to me, the leaves of the trees, the rays of the sun, the moon, its sister, which hides in the early morning. Sometimes I would venture to say that now that I can't see is when I'm really seeing. I can't play the lyre, that gift was also taken from me, but I know that I will see again, and when I do it will be for real. I don't need to see with my soul, as one day I know I will be able to do to tell you that you are even more beautiful than before, and not because of your face, or the way you wear your hair today, but due to what I capture with my other senses. You are happy, Hyacinthus. You are immensely happy with him. Happier than you ever were with me; however, I repeat, I do not blame you, but rather, I am happy for you. I may be a somewhat self-centred human, but, nevertheless, I am able to appreciate the joy that your world houses during these days. I may be selfish, but at least I am still so human that I can thank that deity who is next to you right now, because you, Hyacinthus, are worth it. So much so that Uranus itself could fall on Gaia again if necessary, so that you can smile for eternity. You are so worth it, Hyacinthus, that for you I would lose not only my sight, but also my legs, my hands, my touch, my tongue... I would lose my entire life, my existence so that you could be happy, I would even lose my soul to make you laugh. A smile, a laugh from you, prince, is similar to a thousand new lives, a thousand perfect harvests. The strange thing would have been if no god had noticed you, that no one would have done so... That would be the strange thing, but once again, the cosmos tells me that I was not wrong. You are gorgeous, Hyacinthus. Much more beautiful than most mortals, and not only because of your splendid physique, but because of the soul that lives in your body. It is that spirit of yours that makes you unique. It can be seen with the naked eye through your eyes that, transparent, welcome the purest heart.'

'Tamyris.' He whispered the name.

'Hyacinthus, I haven't finished yet.'

'I don't deserve the words you're giving me.'

You deserve them, and even if you didn't deserve them, he loves you, Hyacinthus. Let him speak to you, allow him the pleasure, because, sometimes, although other people's emotions bother us, in them we can find great treasures, relics that rather than condemn, save. It was Apollo's voice again. He returned to fill that void that remained in his mind with his sweet prose dressed in beautiful colours.

'You deserve them,' he assured. 'Prince, my prince, if the gods invented a new word, I could write a sonata to the beauty you contain. If only the gods would give me back the gift of music... But you know what, Hyacinthus? I cannot be angry, because they allowed me to know true love. Maybe you don't love me, but I do love you, and it is better to love than to be loved. In the end, no one could be loved if no one took the risk to love. And I risk loving. I have taken the risk of loving you. I may not be worthy of your love, but that doesn't worry me. What, then, is love if it is not this? Love is desire and happiness; wishing the happiness of the individual you love, even when this means disappearing from their lives. Those who truly love understand that there is nothing more important than the happiness and well-being of the being they love. True love knows no jealousy, nor selfishness. Therefore, I thank the muses for having punished me without anything but this thing I feel. True love is seeing that other soul happy, and being infected by that same happiness. Love is the constant search for the happiness and well-being of the being you love. The muses took away my musical gift, but music is something that many mortals have access to. Yet few know true love, and I do, Hyacinthus, I do. I risk saying out loud that I enjoy happiness when I see you happy. May the muses punish me again if I lie: Hyacinthus, a thousand humans have related to me, thousands much more experienced than you, but none were endowed with half of what makes you unique. I have not loved any human yet as I have loved you.'

'Tamyris, I don't know what to say.' The prince whispered, somewhat self-conscious because of the aeda' words.

'Do not say anything. You don't have to say anything, you just have to listen. Don't worry about me, I'll be fine. I'll take some blows until I get used to not seeing, but I'll be fine. You are too and you will be, even when the one who cares most about you thinks you aren't.'

'How can you be so sure?'

'Sometimes they say that when you deprive yourself of sight, you learn to really see. I think that's what I'm dealing with now, the new skill I'm learning. My intuition tells me that I will be able to do what I set out to do. However, it also warns me, begging me not to waste my time listening to the rest; they will never understand when I truly wake up.'

'You don't know how much I identify with those words of yours.'

'I don't know, but I can imagine.'

'So, you don't have mixed hatred towards the muses for doing this to you? Don't you have, perhaps not hate, but disgust in your soul when you think about them?' The blind man shook his head.

'For a long time, prince, I prayed that they would visit me and prove to me that they were real; At last, I know. They have punished me for a good reason, although I must say that I do not consider it a punishment, but a gift. It may be a nuisance now, but I have heard and felt things, Hyacinthus, that I had never been able to experience before. I have felt and heard things that will be the basis for a future in which I will thank them for doing this to me.'

The prince was unable to fully understand his words. He somewhat understood what he was saying, but also, there was something that didn't add up. Tamyris was completely relaxed; however, the god's lover found in him a shade of madness that he could not fully discern. He told himself that maybe he wasn't crazy. Maybe he simply knew more than him, or maybe that was the feeling that was generated in the minds of others when they heard him talk about the beauty of the world that he had discovered thanks to Apollo. He told himself that Tamyris was waking up, in a different way to him. It didn't take him long to wonder if pain wasn't the key to life.

To which Apollo, around him, did not take long to respond:

Life is not only the good things, or what humans know as such. In life there is also suffering, and it must be accepted, because it builds and teaches us more than it damages us. There is no such thing as pain in earthly life, even when it is firmly believed that there is. It is simply a phase that is somewhat less pleasant, but nevertheless, it must be passed if we want to achieve an objective, a goal, if we want to be the strongest and fullest version of ourselves. If we want to learn, the best way is not to avoid pain or suffering, but to live it fully. Anyone who says otherwise wants slaves, and the world, believe me when I tell you, Hyacinthus, wants warriors. These need obstacles to appear along their paths, together with the possibility of giving up. If one does not give in to any, even the most bitter pain, one can say that one has truly lived. The subject who comes to life must take advantage of his opportunity and live the experience in the most complete way he can think of.

So, is pain the key to life? Is it pain that makes us live? The youngest thought, eager to know the answer.

If there were only one key to existence, to life, a key that everyone knew, there would be no grace or mystery in it.

Despite not having asked about this, Hyacinthus thanked him silently, understanding that perhaps not even a god's lover like him should know such things. It would be one of the thousands of secrets that the gods hid, that nature itself hid.

'Tamyris,' the boy murmured, taking the former musician's hands in his, 'if I could give you back your vision or perhaps your gift for melody, I would... You are aware of this, right?'

'I am, sweet Hyacinthus,' he replied softly. 'But I know well, even with a lot of imagination, that that will not be possible. Medicine is at your side, the future too, art too, but that does not mean that it can alter the fate which is already woven.... If he, being an elemental part of the future, is incapable of helping me, how could

I possibly think you could? How would I ask you to heal me if not even the healing released as energy can do it? I would never ask you for something impossible.'

'Why have you always been so good to me, even when I didn't pay half as much attention to you as I should have?'

'Because I loved you, Hyacinthus. Furthermore, even the god that is present with us, the same one who walks alongside you on numerous occasions, knows well that love makes us blind, drags us like the waves of storms.... Until we find ourselves in the middle of the immense ocean, without even understanding where we are... I was floating there since I began to feel this thing that was eating me up inside. From that very moment, I was a shipwrecked man who saw a boat every time I saw you. Maybe you didn't treat me in the best way, but I was on a cloud, wanting to show you my world, everything that I was, which, without realizing, was yours. I loved you, that's why I was always good to you. Maybe if I hadn't loved you, if I had wanted you like the vast majority of people who are attracted to you, I wouldn't have been so kind.'

When one loves, one desires freedom; when one wants, one longs to possess. Apollo whispered in agreement with the mortal's words, who was getting closer to the reality of that ambiguous feeling, which humans so rarely really felt.

Hyacinthus kissed Tamyris's hands gently and repeatedly, not knowing how to thank him.

'Hyacinthus, do not delay in leaving, for I feel that night is falling. However, please, young prince, no matter what happens, remember that there are people who love you, who would give their lives for you. Be happy with the love of your life, I will be happy too because you will be. When you smile, I will smile. This way, we will both be happy without even realizing it.'

'You have taken the words from me, Tamyris. I came here to encourage you, to tell you not to give up, because I had imagined you dejected by the misfortune that has befallen you. Yet here we are, and you seem to be the one cheering me up.'

'The thing is, Hyacinthus, this is not a misfortune. It is the greatest joy that has ever happened to me. Only you are not able to see it yet, but you will be able to. He will explain it to you, he will tell you, and you will know it. His prose has much higher quality than mine. That will help you.'

'Tamyris,' he whispered.

'Don't delay leaving, prince.'

'I will visit you again. If you need anything,' he continued as he sat up, 'don't hesitate to send Adelphos to my home. I will try to help you.'

'Believe me, it won't be necessary, young man with a good heart and beautiful soul.'

'Isn't that what one of the verses of that song of yours that became so famous was like?'

'Yes.'

'How do you remember it? Why do you dedicate it to me?'

'Because you were the protagonist of that song. They are the only words I can still sing, the only words the muses allowed me to keep. Possibly, because they were also surprised by my way of loving.'

. . .

Hyacinthus rode that day alone under the stellar mantle, which, little by little, took over the entire firmament. Under the light of the moon, he managed to decipher an immense beauty, so, carried away by the gorgeous nights, the prince took his time to reach his home.

His horse moved slowly beneath him. From time to time, the animal seemed to tremble on the verge of uncontrollability if it heard a distant sound whose origin it could not make out. However, Hyacinthus calmed it with soft words. These had an effect on the creature, causing it to relax and be able to move forward without any hesitation.

He breathed freedom, filling his being with a sensation that would take time to fade. He still felt Apollo at his side, and he knew that he only had to say his name or perhaps think about him, so that his presence would be stronger.

However, there was no need, nor did Hyacinthus want to bother him. He knew that he would have a thousand matters to deal with now that he had returned to his divine duties. However, he did not rush for a moment to reach his home at the earliest hour.

The path was very calming, even when he himself felt the caterpillar of anguish inside him, which was gradually making its cocoon and later turning into a butterfly. A tiny little butterfly, but one that would not hesitate to hurt its fragile being, the one endowed with weakness as its only weapon.

He felt a small sensation that grew as he went. A sensation that increased as Apollo moved away, dissipating his essence in an air that would not bring him back until the return of dawn. Although he didn't pay attention to it, so he didn't slow down. And Sparta was so beautiful, illuminated by the platinum of darkness, that it mattered little what could happen to him along the path as long as he enjoyed such a spectacle.

For the world immersed in night was endowed with such a different nuance that not even the same places seemed the same. There on that road, the trees on both sides resembled titans with blinded gazes whose eyes did not shine. To titans silenced by the passing of the years and the defeat of the Olympians who ruled then, the entire world known by the slender Hyacinthus. The moon illuminated them, giving them some life. Its stars, faithful warriors, shone, giving soul to the landscape that lay before him, to the landscape through which he rode, neither stopping nor rushing.

A thousand sounds could be heard in the night, before Pan's flute woke up the wildlife. A thousand incomprehensible sounds if taken as words, but understandable as emotions, because the prince received in silent messages those that the illiterate nocturnal voice wanted to transmit. He welcomed them with open arms, with an immense heart and a spirit eager for knowledge. He well knew that the world was the wisest thing existing on his plane. He knew well that if he wanted to grow, the best thing was to listen. Listen to the singing voices of the trees, in those moments, immobilized titans;

319

listen to the melody of the bow of Artemis, the sister of Apollo, who knew that she would be running next to the lunar moon that was in the sky. Stay silent to capture the notes of the dryads, the oceanic girls, the beautiful nymphs.

At night the world was silent and gave way to those creatures endowed with the most mysterious and beautiful femininity that anyone had ever known. If the world fell quiet, if everything stopped for a single day, Hyacinthus told himself, humans would understand. If humans were to keep their lips sealed for a single day, they would understand, when they could speak again, the remarkable and ardent beauty that the places they frequented possessed.

Because Hyacinthus shared a great number of things with each tree; the same with each rock... This is what happened with each small being, animated or non-animated that existed, because in the end and in a certain way, all of them were the same: dust from the lights that illuminated them. Stardust.

His horse probably understood him better than most people. However, it got very scared, since it was a fearful animal by nature, and even when Hyacinthus calmed it with his words, with which without even being aware he was already forming verses, it felt a horrifying sensation. Some melodious verses that perfectly accompanied the surrounding music. The creature, despite all this, always feared, so Hyacinthus, who had been attentive to it, was not taken by surprise by the way in which the entire body of the animal began to tremble until finally it could no longer stand, rushing forward.

The prince squeezed his legs, trying to get a firm grip, while his beautiful steed galloped completely out of control. The kicks he launched trying to get rid of an apparently invisible enemy did not cause him to lose his balance to the point of having a strange encounter with the ground, because from above the young man did not pull the reins to tighten the bit. He well knew that this would make the situation worse, since it might frighten that creature of Gaia even more. He focused on being calm. Despite the adrenaline coursing through his veins, he did not fret. Then, when he saw the landing in front of his home, he tried to make a wide circle as he continued to whisper to the animal. This circumference began to decrease in size, and thanks to this, the horse soon fell into a trot, then a walk. When he managed to completely stop the animal, he stroked its neck, thanking it for having stopped. Without thinking, he dismounted.

Perhaps he found walks under the light of the stars very pleasant, but it was clear that his four-legged friend strongly disagreed.

The animal shook itself, and Hyacinthus simply stroked its sweaty neck, took its reins, and prepared to lead it to the stables.

It was there that he came face to face with someone he had said he never wanted to see again. But, obviously, he simply ignored him. If Apollo was a god, that nameless stranger must be another.

He spoke to him, but the king's son had decided to ignore his words. He was focused on his task, not only removing the saddle or the bridle, but also examining its legs, its entire body more thoroughly than other times, since it had been such an uncontrolled race. As he dried the horse's hair with straw, he noticed that his back hurt. Minutes before, while he was leading the horse into a circle, he had noticed a kind of pull that had prevented him from moving one of his arms freely enough. However, it mattered little to him, since at that moment, he had to concentrate on his horse. Without it he couldn't go very far, so the mínimum was to take care of it… The máximum was to give it his heart.

When he was sure it was okay, he released it, allowing it to begin eating its much-deserved dinner. It was then, the moment when he turned to coldly examine the stranger, who was nothing more than Zephyrus, the West Wind.

'I don't like seeing you, so allow me the pleasure of leaving,' he snapped as he left the area dedicated to horses. 'Thank you,' he whispered beforehand.

'Listen to me, damned prince!'

'The only thing you do is bring me bad omens, but above all, bad words towards one of the sons of Zeus. And believe me when I tell you, I don't care what you bring me this time. I know how he is. I'm not going to care what the myths say about him. We well know that a large part of them have been modified by humans for their own benefit, even created by them. They are often stories that people develop, choosing them as protagonists, but they have little to do with reality.'

'I'm not here to talk about myths.'

'You never come to talk about myths, but you always return to them. It is not my fault that you have some kind of pessimistic feeling against an Olympian god.' The god remained silent, because he was aware that Hyacinthus would continue speaking. 'Besides, who are you? What is your name? You have been warning me, asking me to choose you, and not him, but I don't even know who you are, so how am I going to choose you?'

The wind then blew softly on that night lacking breezes. The prince knew then that he had something to do with that. He could feel the air behind him, coming from the west. A western air that the other soon called:

'Zephyrus.'

Zephyrus was the fruitful wind, messenger of the springs, son of Astraeus and Eos, brother of Boreas, north wind, if he remembered correctly. He looked down gently, suppressing the urge to kneel that suddenly came over him.

'You might be a god but, despite this, I do not desire your presence, even when I am aware that you can punish me. I'm tired of the game that has already ended. The same one in which I have participated in without being conscious of it. The first ray of sunlight illuminated me after the longest storm my soul had ever seen, and since then, I was blinded, sealed by the imprint of light. If you have to tell me something, tell me now or silence your voice forever. Tell me now or shut up.'

'Is that an order?'

'That's a request, Zephyrus.'

'It seems that you already know what I was going to tell you, and right now I see clearly that you have already chosen. You speak the truth when you claim that you were blinded by the majesty of the sun. Likewise, I risk saying that right now you are only listening to his lyres. Those whose notes are so beautiful that they bring you back to true life. You are not attentive to anything else because he has made you pay attention to everything. He has taught you and makes you see and understand... It is something that almost no one is capable of experiencing, so I think it is normal that you feel that immense devotion for him. He is the way that life has shown you, he is the key that has opened the door that separates humans from human life, from the rest of mortal life. You have found so much beauty in this new world —which, in fact, had always been there— that Apollo should invent a new word so you can thank him.'

'You are right; if Apollo invented a new word, I would be able to convey my most sincere gratitude, accompanied by a longing that I am still unable to explain. This is how I would explain to Apollo what I feel. This strange conjecture that devours me internally, causing me to suffer, because I am not able to classify this. Or perhaps, I am simply unable to accept it.' He paused slightly. 'I like how the wind blows during the days, but I am so tired of this game, Zephyrus, that I just want to retire.'

'That's because, now that you know the truth, reality falls on you, Uranus himself, because you understand in these moments that Apollo is a god. It will be temporary, much more than any human being, and he will disappear from your life. Maybe he has even already abandoned you.'

Hyacinthus clenched his jaw. He knew he was trying to provoke him, but he wouldn't succeed.

'You are also a god, ergo, you would vanish just like Apollo.'

'You are right, but at least I allow myself not to break your heart with false promises.'

'Don't you understand, Zephyrus?' The prince asked, approaching him. 'Don't you understand? I don't care if Apollo disappears from my life, I just want to remember this. And, if one day I return, not to forget it... If life came back, I wouldn't ask for anything apart from knowing for sure that he exists. I don't care if Phoebus forgets about me, what would bother me would be me forgetting him. Do you know who the real wise man is? Well, he is the one who knows the line between what is in his power and what is not, what can change and what cannot. I can't make Apollo not forget me, nor make him keep an eye on me all the time. However, I can make sure I don't forget him. And that's what I plan to do. I know I will always end up remembering him, I know I will always know

326

he exists. Maybe he is not by my side, not even in a spiritual way, but he is an entity of nature as you are too, and whether I like it or not you both are everywhere. Every time I feel the sun, every time I hear a measly musical note, every time I compose a clumsy poem, every time someone claims to be able to prophesy the future, he comes to me. Those two suns that he has for eyes return to my mind: His voice, his temperance, his energy, his *you can do it, don't give up yet,* all of this rises from the ashes, simply by seeing the sun every day. It is impossible for me to forget him, may the siren songs end me if I do, if I forget... He who is life, he who is art, should live in all of us, without leaving our minds, much less of our hearts. Anyone who has played the string of a lyre has known Apollo. Everyone who has created art has met Apollo at least once in their life. Everyone who has enjoyed the sun, or who has seen it, has known Apollo. His essence is found in all these things. However, many people don't realize it. Humans will one day forget him only to remembering him soon after, because he is beauty, harmony, and the world knows, even inadvertently. Apollo is someone so engraved in my soul that even if I don't know his name, I will know of his feats. I will recognize his presence in the beauty of writting, in the harmony of music, in the warmth of the sun, in light, and even in truth. Apollo… Apollo is and will be the reason to live for many. Apollo has kept at least a little piece of my soul. Part of my spirit belongs to him. It will always be like this.

As long as another little piece remains inside me, a fine thread will continue to connect me to him and it will guide me when I am ready to return to him, thanks to which he will find me when the time comes.'

Zephyrus remained silent, looking at him, full of admiration. His words revealed the love he was processing. A love so immense that it was not as selfish as that feeling usually was in humans, but instead so large that it resembled being in the middle of a desert, something so huge that the West Wind, despite being a god, was not able to describe or understand.

'Zephyrus, may I go to my room? I'm tired,' he asked.

The wind nodded gently. So the prince, seeing this, prepared to leave, but then Zephyrus's voice did not take long to stop him:

'Do you think people will also remember me?' He and so many other deities knew well that one day humans would forget the old gods. These would be lost not forever, but for a long period of time.

For a moment he thought that Hyacinthus would not stop, much less respond to him, but he was surprised to hear his voice:

'Of course, Zephyrus,' he replied. 'The wind will continue to blow even when the sun goes out. The wind will continue to blow even when the arts are lost. The wind will continue to blow until the end of life itself. And the west wind is also wind. Maybe my name will be lost, it will move away among the human waves. Perhaps I will not be remembered, but you, Zephyrus, you, the gods, will be, even when they try to extinguish you. Your voices will resonate throughout the Cosmos. Your names will be recorded in writing so that one day you will live with us mortals again.'

And with those words, Hyacinthus left there at a moderate pace, in a somewhat strange manner. After all, the boy's back hurt much more at that moment than before. He told himself that if he continued like this in the morning, he would ask his father to bring him a doctor.

As stealthy as he could, he entered his dark room without even using any type of lighting. He realized that someone had entered there before, since some things were not in the place where he had left them. However, that fact did not worry him. He closed his eyes and, being aware that the fire was burning in various parts of the house, he thanked Hestia for taking care of his home. It was a habit acquired recently, because if Apollo and Zephyrus existed, there was also Hestia. She deserved recognition too.

It didn't take long for him to lie down on the bed, with a small moan because of his annoying back. He calmed himself by thinking that soon the pain would subside, it would fade away and he would not notice anything.

Hyacinthus was about to enter the world of dreams when he felt a presence behind him, from whose body emanated the most beautiful source of heat he had ever felt. It was a presence that enveloped him. He felt like he was being healed. He knew without having to turn around that no one had materialized, but that Apollo, whom he was beginning to consider his beloved, was there. The young boy noticed how his skin began to burn because of the heat that Phoebus gave him. It was waves of fire that instead of burning him, healed him. A tide in a transparent dress that managed to penetrate his delicate skin and reach directly to that muscle, which, in an attempt to protect himself, had been damaged. Still, there it was. Being healed thanks to the medical arts of a being that, in theory, should not have existed, but did, and was there.

Hyacinthus asked himself again for the thousandth time why those deities, who would have a thousand more importantly and infinite tasks of more interesting beings within their reach, visited him; still, they chose him. He didn't understand why they did. So, it didn't take long for his mind to find itself full of unknowns with no apparent answers. And the feeling that invaded him was such that during those days in which he had not seen Apollo, he said to himself that perhaps he had invented him. Perhaps he had been a product of his imagination because, how come a god wanted to meet him? Although he was a prince, there was little else that stood out in his small and fragile creature. But, when he suddenly felt it, all the doubts vanished; was the human being prepared to imagine so much beauty together, so much light, so much justice? No, of course not. To think otherwise, to affirm that this was the case, was a complete aberration. An idea that comes from a radical and completely extremist anthropocentrism. So much so that its supporters were blinded to what the world truly was; not only what they could appreciate with their bodies, but the rest of the world. The same one whose end would never be discovered, possibly because it did not even exist, or was so far away that even the gods would have a complicated journey.

However, Hyacinthus cared little about the extension of the universe and its various planes. The only thing he needed to know was the answer to that question that, from time to time, wandered through his mind. He knew well, even when he was very young, that he would never have it responded, because the gods knew the answer to that and to all the questions that one could ask, but they were secrets so well kept that they even ended up forgetting their existence. Apart from not sharing them with mortals.

With the fears fading, the unknowns gradually receding from the flow of his thoughts, Hyacinthus closed his eyes, previously open to try to observe whoever was with him. An attempt that had been unsuccessful. However, and despite closing his eyes, his goals were not to fall asleep in those soft arms of Morpheus, but rather to fully feel the energy of Apollo trying to heal his delicate body.

Being stripped of all senses other than touch, the prince managed to glimpse, faintly, what, he risked saying, few mortals had ever felt. Because Apollo could be known in the music, in the clear mornings not foreseen by clouds that would take the view away from the golden sphere, in his fortune tellers through whose lips he pronounced his words, in the writings endowed with a certain harmony, in the light, in its sacred creatures... In a thousand things, without forgetting diseases and medicine. But not many people could say that they had been cared for by Apollo himself. Hyacinthus, however, could. In fact, he could say so many things about Phoebus that he was somehow scandalized by everything he had done, even by the thoughts he had had in which the god was the protagonist. Apollo, who saw everything, must also have seen what was so hidden in his being, in a certain way fearing to come out.

He did not understand how, even just the thought that Apollo could be treating another mortal the way he treated him, which was quite likely, caused a species of caterpillars that lived in his stomach to turn into unruly butterflies which caused waves of a sensation that was somewhat reminiscent of nervousness. He was thinking about it at that very moment, while the aforementioned continued providing his body with what he believed was necessary. Hyacinthus bit his lip slightly, realizing that he was letting his thoughts run wild, even though Apollo, or at least a part of him, was close to him. It would be much more complicated if he did not see what was going through the boy's mind, similar to a frightened horse that galloped and galloped without apparent direction, afraid of reaching its stables where it would be locked up. Or with the fear that only the anger of a human or the modesty of a hungry beast can generate.

Apollo, then, seeing this flood of thoughts within the mind of the one he loved, endeavoured to simply remind him that each being he dealt with was completely different from the previous one. Thus, his relationship with each of them was different. He loved Hyacinthus. Although he did not say it in an extremely explicit way because everything he wanted to say he had already done so before, and if he hadn't, his actions had said it to him. These said more than any words that could be uttered by his lips.

Hyacinthus was lost because of his unresolved unknowns, but at the same time, he was at home. At least, in a place where safety lived, and with Phoebus that was the case. When he heard his sweet voice inside his head, he simply smiled, realizing that it certainly wasn't in his mind, but that it was really happening. He was calmed when he heard his words, although they once again confirmed what he already knew: It was impossible to hide anything from Apollo, because Phoebus saw absolutely everything, even those things deeply buried in mortal minds. Phoebus saw what should never have been seen. In the same way, he managed to penetrate the minds of mortals without even wanting to. This was a being from whom no one could hide anything at all or lie to, and Apollo was partly grateful for that. However, he also found some drawbacks in this. A way to save himself from the sorrows that he would never be able to possess, but thanks to seeing everything he had become, possibly, the wisest and most conscious being and deity in the world or perhaps, one of them. He had built upon who he was and still is, even if humans have forgotten his harmony.

The prince felt that wave of heat, which in turn repaired everything that needed to be fixed, running through his back, his skin, destroying every inch of complexion, bone, and muscle. He felt how everything was beginning to heal. He was sure that the next morning it wouldn't hurt, or at least, not in the way it would have if Apollo hadn't been next to him. A part of his soul wished he could turn around and find him there. See his eyes, his face, his body. A part of his being so of this earth that it was soon silenced by the constant sensation that the presence, the essence of the beloved deity gave him.

Apollo was there, even without manifesting himself and that was all he should care about. However, that mortal, completely human part of his being prayed for him to be there physically, but unfortunately, or perhaps fortunately depending on how you saw it, that was not the case. His energy embraced him and healed him. He wouldn't exaggerate by saying that his energy loved him, and Hyacinthus still couldn't explain what he felt, because he did not know. He didn't know if that was love. That love that was talked about so much, or perhaps another emotion that could be confused with it, like desire or simple admiration.

He didn't know what he felt, but he was sure that if he could explain it, he would. Likewise, he understood that he did not have to look for the right words, because Apollo understood the nature of those butterflies that, from time to time, took flight inside his being. It was true that the son of Zeus was a superior being in some way. So archaic that few beings surpassed him. Likewise, he was endowed with great knowledge. He was sitting at the top of the absolute, a place very few achieved. This fact made him a creature endowed with very wise information, almost unattainable in his knowledge. Meanwhile, Hyacinthus was a simple mortal whose biological age was quite low, whose spiritual age was not even close to that of Apollo. Apollo was a venerable creature, from yesteryear, as was the golden sphere he led. Hyacinthus, however, was a small plant that was gradually beginning to grow. In some way they understood each other, no matter their origin, their nature, the fact that they had little to do with each other. They started from the basis that they both possessed a non-earthly part, their soul, that spirit that, in the case of the boy lay trapped in the prison that was the body. Apollo, however, was spirit at all times. He was essence, energy with the ability to materialize when he wanted and how he wanted. On the other hand, Hyacinthus did not have that option at hand.

A thousand things would not be important, if only his presence remained by his side for infinite time. If only he enjoyed the essence of the divinity that loved him like he had never been loved before. If Hyacinthus feared anything, it was forgetting about him. Forget about his always serene aura, his wise words and healing energies that, similar to the sun's rays, healed his body as if they were sunflowers, which even at freezing temperatures, seek the light as if nothing else mattered. And perhaps, only that was relevant: waking up in the morning and enjoying the gift that Apollo had given him. A gift that he could not have achieved in any other way.

The gods were not essential in the lives of mortals. That is, it was not necessary to know them to breathe, but in a certain way, it was necessary, at least, to feel them once to start living. For life and breathing seemed to go hand in hand, although in reality they did not: Hyacinthus, for example, had not lived until he had been reborn. That moment had been when Phoebus had appeared in his life bringing new lights, lyres accompanied by the singing voices that surrounded him.

He flew like this, without having wings, through places that he had always known, but now he saw them from another point of view, managing to capture the beauty in each tiny piece. Something that only the most ancient souls were capable of doing. Still, there he was, feeling it.

He then appreciated, while Apollo healed him, the dark figures that the furniture drew in the darkness of the night. He also felt the beauty that Phoebus possessed. Likewise, he was also able to notice Gaia's movement under his body, even when he was not in fully direct contact with her.

The sensations that lay in his being so calmed him that, without realizing it, he closed his eyes to unknowingly fall into sleep. With the soft voice of Apollo, as far away as the stars, singing soft notes of a song that was never to be sung again. The lyres transported him to a place where pain and suffering would never be known, where life was beautiful like Phoebus was. He understood that when he opened his eyes the next morning, he would continue living in that place endowed with such beauty, and therefore he slept peacefully.

XVI

That night was the last night he felt Phoebus, and even then, Hyacinthus wondered if he would ever see him again, or if, on the contrary, he was the only 'lover' of the deity who would not end in disgrace.

He didn't feel him, nor did he hear the god. He had not spoken to him at any time after that day. If he had done so, it mattered little because the young man had not heard him. He felt in a certain way that he would never leave him, because if he had given him anything it was a full life, a life that deserved to be lived in the best of ways.

At night, every time he went to bed, his name, Apollo, would sneak into his thoughts, keeping him awake for a few long minutes. Although he always ended up falling asleep at some point that he didn't remember later. When he woke up, his name also came to mind; even in his daily life, it was almost impossible not to remember the deity who had visited him.

Despite all this, he tried to live a normal, ordinary life, like the one he had led until the god had appeared in his world. He used to wake up at dawn, when the birds began to sing their songs. He woke up next to the rays of the sun, which again brought him those same words: Phoebus... Apollo....

Before having breakfast, he used to train in a thousand different games. Now he did it in the company of one of his brothers. This did not surprise his father, since he had already accepted that the man he had once invited, the same one who showed so much interest in his son from the first day, was none other than the god of medicine. If he wasn't there, the father thought, he must be taking care of more important matters. Or perhaps he had simply lost interest in Hyacinthus, which would not have surprised him, since after all, he was a god who was said to see everything. Possibly, there was another mortal dancing on Gaia who caught his attention.

Then, his daily routine guided him to take some fruit from the tree. After that, he used to lie under the sun in his beloved garden, while he dedicated himself to the study of theories, generally philosophical. He also used to read many scrolls filled with the history of his ancestors. He immersed himself in these and did not put the texts away until they had been engraved in his mind forever. Afterwards, he ate. Sometimes, with his father and brothers in the dining room only intended for men; many others, he would sneak away with the desire to have a picnic with her sister, Polyboea. It was to her that he expressed his longing, his nostalgia, and even his feelings every time he heard the name of the one for whom he felt more than admiration.

When the sun had only a few hours of daylight left, he would saddle up one of his family's horses and go for a ride. This was his favourite time of the day, as it was dedicated to full reflection. On his horse he could go wherever he wanted. Plus, his mind seemed to empty. On the back of his horse there was only one thing, and that was the freedom that only full concentration can harbour.

It should be added that there were many days when Hyacinthus, the one who looked purple under the moon, went to visit his old friend, Tamyris. He always welcomed him with a huge smile, repeating it a thousand times if he felt like doing so. The ancient aedo had developed a wisdom that few mortals would have been able to achieve, except for the great philosophers of those days. It had done him immense good to be punished. So much so that Hyacinthus was already beginning to think that perhaps Apollo was right when he said that despite sounding unfair, or appearing to be so, the acts of the deities went beyond that. On many occasions, even what had been horrible at first, benefited the victim in the long run. Of course, the prince thought, that was the case of the musician.

He had been a good person all his life, but he had always had huge problems regarding his own personal ego. Likewise, he was a very proud person who firmly believed that there were few people in the world who could be even half as talented as him. This same pride which he was endowed with was what had dragged him to the point of uttering the words that had condemned him.

Words that had condemned him at first, but which, as both the Aedo and the prince already appreciated, had ended up saving him. He supposed, then, that the muses had appreciated him for his mastery, so when giving him the punishment they had selected one which would thus teach him a lasting and good lesson. Or perhaps they had simply decided without thinking about it. If Apollo was difficult to understand on numerous occasions, Hyacinthus could not imagine how complex his friends, the muses, would be.

After his walks with the horses, which commonly led to a spontaneous and unannounced visit to Tamyris, who cared little if the prince told him beforehand or not as long as he came to see him, Hyacinthus returned to his home when the moon had already taken over from the sun. It was only then that he allowed himself to breathe easy. He took his time unequipping the animal, always staying with it for a while, caressing it, thanking it and giving it some fruit that he well knew these beings adored.

Then, when the moon shone with special beauty, he would lie down in front of his dwelling, close his eyes and force himself to remember Apollo's words, apart from his face, his archaic look. He forced himself to slowly relive each lesson, each moment spent with him. Sometimes, he just needed to remember his way of slowly pronouncing the words, giving them a musicality that no one had done before, that no one would do later.

If any servant saw him, they would approach him and ask him what he was doing. He always responded the same, always after a light sigh:

'I remember Phoebus.'

He said it, generally, in a heavy whisper, filled with immense melancholy. The servants did not take long to accept that behaviour. So, when the months passed, and they saw him lying outside late at night, they rarely stopped, and if they did, it was to let out a few words that usually escaped quite softly from his lips: 'Our poor master who lives in love with the sun! He prays to his sister, the moon, to talk to him. Our poor master! At least, it hasn't ended badly. Someday he will get over it.' They assured each night, trying to make the cosmos listen to them, and pay attention to their words.

One night, to the astonishment of the servants, his siblings, and everyone who lived in that place, I would even venture to say that the animals were also surprised, Hyacinthus, after giving an apple as a reward to his horse, stopped for a moment in that clearing where he used to lie down. He looked at the moon, almost begging it, but he knew well that it couldn't do anything.

Without even thinking about it, Hyacinthus finally got going and headed to his room. No one would see him that night lying outside, waiting for the arrival of dawn. Nobody, absolutely nobody, would see him. Such was the astonishment that many servants became worried and went to look if his favourite horse was in the stables. They smiled when they saw that it was.

The young prince then lay down on his bed. He bit his lip lightly before speaking.

'I want to see you, at least feel you, Apollo, just one more time. I'm selfish. You have every right to call me that, but I don't understand anything that happens to me. I implore you. You don't seem to hear me; at the same time, I feel like you do. And still, I seem to get lost in this place. If something happens, I know that you act in the way that is best for me. All your decisions seek my

wellbeing, but for now, I don't see why, I don't see the reason.'
Suddenly he fell silent. It had enlightened his mind somewhat. A
goal, a plan. Maybe she did listen to him.

He closed his eyes, concentrating in turn on the woman who used
to appear in his dreams when he was little. To his surprise, it was
not her who appeared in his dream, but another creature that he
immediately recognized, even though he had not seen or felt her
before.

'Hyacinthus, you are very lost, aren't you?' her soft voice told him.
Hyacinthus couldn't see her face in detail. He supposed the gods
didn't exactly have one either.

'Aphrodite,' he said. He knew it was her. He didn't need anything
else. 'I don't understand what's happening to me. I don't
understand what's going on with him either.'

'Oh, Hyacinthus, you don't need to call me to know what you feel.
At most I can help you in your way of acting, but you know what
you feel. You know it because it is you, only you, who experiences
it. You humans know that you are in love, but many times, you
play dumb... Why should love be a taboo? It seems that you fear
when you meet a love that escapes your fingers.'

'Is that happening to me?' The deity smiled softly. She was very used to that kind of response. Hyacinthus might be the romantic interest of a god, he might be in love with a deity, but he was still human. Not only was he in love and he did not want to accept it, but he was in love with an immortal being.

'Look, Hyacinthus, love knows no limits, just as there are infinite ways to experience it. True love is that which comes from the soul, false love is that which comes from the body, do you understand? Well, sometimes, what is not grasped by the senses, can be grasped with the soul. Love is not known through the senses, but through our spirit. That is what unites me to you, and to any other animal. All of us have souls. All of us can manage to live through this.' She paused slightly with immense mastery. She gave beauty to every phoneme that came out of her lips. 'Humans think that love is known through the body, and they are so wrong that when they listen to the spirit, something in their mind stops working. That's what happens to you. You try to make a connection between both things, but something tells you no, and you still live in an era where it is customary to truly love. An era in which when you love, you love. Others will come where no one knows how to love.'

'Goddess... Yes, there is something in my head that tells me that I love him, but at the same time, I have something that tells me no,

346

that I simply admire him, idolize him and even have an immense obsession with him. Then I feel I don't, only to later stop and change my mind. I think if he were mortal, everything would be much simpler. I, possibly, would not have this problem that does not even allow me to breathe normally. He wouldn't be trapped between a golden arrow and a dark wall. But of all beings, I have had to eclipse myself in one that will never know the death of a body, since he does not even have one.'

'Hyacinthus, what you feel is normal. After all, despite not believing firmly in him until you met him, despite even having come to hate him, now you have met him and not because you wanted to, but because he wanted it that way. It was then, when your being realized how tiny you were next to him.'

'In fact, I feel like I am a grain of sand lost on the beaches of the world, and he is everything else.'

'Because by knowing him, prince, you have understood his greatness, his power. Just as other mortals who have had contact with him, me or any other deity understand it, even those that you Hellenes do not know. However, I am not here to talk about Apollo. Nevertheless, if you wish we can discuss him.'

'Do you really know, Aphrodite, what he feels for me?' He asked her with great confidence, since, although she was a very powerful, ancient deity, in a certain way she knew that formalities between them were not necessary. It was as if they did not exist.

'Even if I knew, I couldn't say it.'

Of course, Aphrodite knew well how Apollo felt about Hyacinthus. She had seen him walk across Olympus, his eyes darker than when he appeared before mortals, looking down. It had been a long time since she had seen him like this, because to each verse he sang while playing his lyre, he added a simple word, which was either the name of the prince, or 'mortal.' A word that used to be accompanied by 'soul.' By this, Phoebus did not mean that souls died, because of course, they did not, but that Hyacinthus was a spirit condemned to be tied to mortal bodies. Ergo, a soul, since all this was a spirit trapped in a body. The spirit of Hyacinthus, his essence, was brutally condemned, or perhaps it was a gift, to be bound to a mortal body until he died and descended to Hades, where he would rest, perhaps later drinking from the waters of the river... from oblivion, thus returning to Earth, back to a mortal body.

He was a mortal soul, because his body would die a thousand times, and a thousand times he would forget everything.

Aphrodite, in those moments, had the voice of the Olympian god ringing in her head. She could also picture his beautiful face with dark hair, his hands as they played the lyre perfectly, and the tears that fell with every note.

Hyacinthus did not insist, he simply nodded, as he understood the reasons for the silence of the deity in front of him.

'So, if not for Apollo, let me ask you, what are you doing here?' It was a bold question.

'I come to talk to you about someone. She specifically told me that she wanted to tell you something. Although this is not usually my way of acting, here I am. I usually make people follow my advice, but you see, sometimes the plot even seems so interesting to me that I find myself involved in the matter, as is happening today.' She made a slight pause, without taking his eyes off the young man. Hyacinthus told himself that despite not being able to appreciate Aphrodite's face well, he strongly noticed her aura around him. That was enough. 'Hyacinthus, you not only attract attention among deities, but also among mortals. I don't need to give you examples, because although many things escape humans, you still have eyes in your face, and I think they are eyes that see quite well.'

'Who is she?'

'It won't take you long to find out, but I'm only here to warn you, not tell you. Keep your eyes open. She doesn't know I've come to visit you, but I know that if I don't tell you anything, you won't even notice.'

'Aphrodite,' he said just before she disappeared, 'what do you advise me to do about Apollo?'

The goddess smiled. This made her glow. She looked like a human-shaped diamond. Maybe that's what she truly was, a diamond with the ability to take on any other form.

'Honestly, I'm glad to hear that, I expected it. This is what really made me come. Just trust yourself. Listen to your heart and be aware of what your soul says. Read the actions of Phoebus, read between his verses, read his face, read the sun itself. You simply have to read to know, so you will be able to understand anything. If you don't feel him next to you, which is probably what worries you, don't fret. If he deems it best, he'll come back. Not even we gods can change the fate that the Moiras have woven.'

'Thank you, Aphrodite.'

When the thanks left the mortal's lips, the deity had already vanished. It didn't bother him, because he knew she had heard him.

He thought then that perhaps it was time to let himself be carried away by a dream that had little to do with encounters with deities, but he did not even have time to carry out his objective, since a sphere of a strange tone appeared before his eyes in that beautiful esplanade.

'Were you calling me?' asked the voice he had heard so many times before.

'Yes, I was,' he told her, while trying to walk towards the sphere. It seemed to move away with every step the boy took. 'Can't you stop walking away from me?'

'No. You already saw too much of me that last time, what do you want?'

'You've always helped me,' he whispered, stopping. 'You have always given me the best advice. I don't want to know who you are, I just want to know what you would do.'

'What's going on?'

351

'I'm in love with someone, but something tells me, maybe my own intuition, that it won't end well if I continue to have this feeling inside me, how can I put an end to it? How can I kill this feeling?'

'Hyacinthus,' said the voice, 'love, feelings are not like humans, nor like the fish you catch, nor like the deer that in winter you are forced to hunt, but it is something that does its own thing. There is no way to kill it. The only thing you can do is live it.'

'But love will end up killing me.' He truly did not know how right he was in saying this.

'That's because love is the most horrible and feared of diseases. It does not cause fever, but it is capable of blinding the wisest spirits. And that is even more dangerous.'

'So, what do you recommend?'

'You are going to die in any case, but there is not only death in the body, there is also death in life. If loving will make you die sooner, live a dignified life, face forward. If, on the other hand, loving will make you live a life that does not deserve to be called life, nor to be lived, try to hide the ardour, the flame of your spirit, of your heart.'

She didn't even give Hyacinthus time to express himself, she simply disappeared.

. . .

In the days to come, Hyacinthus would write down what Aphrodite said on a scroll, as he was completely sure that it had been real, but he doubted the veracity of the second meeting. This one had turned out to be much blurrier than any other. Despite everything, he wrote down the nuances of the conversation he remembered, which were simply the sensations felt, since the words had faded. He wouldn't remember them again.

So, he would look out every morning this time. He would observe how the sun rose, and later he would dedicate himself to saving his experiences on parchment, sometimes even letting himself be guided by his own feelings. They dragged him to a very distant shore, where he could finally be next to the one he was already beginning to miss. In his dreams, he was often with him; these were not encounters, but simple dreams. In them, he always told him to take his heart, his blood, his body, his soul, his mind, his thoughts, his emotions, his experiences... To take all of them, because what did he want them for if he wasn't there? He once told him, after Hyacinthus confessed his fears, that he would always be there. In those moments, the prince tried to look for him, since it was only his presence that made him immortal.

Hyacinthus would be lying if he said he didn't find him, because he did: He found him every dawn, when the sun rose. Also, in every note he heard being played. In the arrows of the bows that some had, apart from in the verses that he himself composed.

There was one day, in fact, when he remembered the god a lot and for a moment, he thought he was very close, because he saw a group of cows full of harmony, a beauty impossible to accept. It reminded him of the cattle that Apollo used to keep, before the messenger, Hermes, stole them.

Yet again, he told himself that they were normal cows. However, when he was about to turn his horse around to return home, a young man who was walking among the cattle, whom he had not seen, stopped him.

The words that came out of his mouth were so far-fetched and strange that they surprised the boy too much:

'Wait!' he called. Hyacinthus, hearing him, stopped his horse, soon leading it towards him.

'What do you want?' he asked. The prince found it difficult to maintain eye contact with the shepherd.

His skin was somewhat tanned, although not too much. Of course, that of the one with the royal blood was much darker. His eyes were clear and looked very intelligent. They had a mischievous nuance, or perhaps, it was simply the light of eternal youth.

'Even the cows notice your sadness.' The formality immediately faded from his speech. 'Cheer up your face, prince, you seem to have died in life!'

'What?'

'You heard what I said.'

'How do you know my identity?' The boy smiled mischievously although, despite everything, he seemed kind.

'I know many things, since I travel from north to south, from east to west and from top to bottom. Basically, from wherever to wherever I want.'

'That's fine.' It was the only thing he could think of to say in the face of such energy, an anthropomorphic explosive bomb.

'Do you know who is also fine? The one you ask so much about. He is fine, although worried about your melancholy.'

Hyacinthus clenched his jaw tightly, not sure what he meant. Maybe he knew it, but he didn't want to admit it to himself.

The young man, who was none other than Hermes, continued to keep his lively eyes on the prince. In these, Hyacinthus, saw images that he would soon remember.

The god, suddenly, without saying anything at all, vanished. The cows also disappeared.

Hyacinthus would wake up several hours later under a beautiful tree. His back rested on the trunk, and his horse grazed peacefully. For a moment, he would firmly believe the veracity of the facts. Then, he wished that the horse could respond and tell him that it had happened. Next to him lay a travel blanket. Then, he remembered the herald and told himself that if that was not a clue that told him that it was true, it would not exist.

He immediately got back on the horse and galloped towards Tamyris's house, where he usually went when he either needed a friend to listen to him, or simply needed to talk to someone.

That day the citadel was full of passersby. It seemed as if everyone had agreed on being there. As was common, he felt people's gazes on him as soon as he arrived, but he ignored them completely.

He left his horse tied near the door of the Aedo' home, and knocking on it, waited for him to open it.

It was his slave, the same one who had worked for his family for so many years, who did. They shared a couple of words, but immediately, Hyacinthus went to join the aedo, who, to his surprise, was dressed in his best clothes.

'Hyacinthus?' he asked, because he would recognize it everywhere, even if he was blind. He knew who he was, possibly because of the way he walked.

'Yes, Tamyris.' He responded, approaching him. He realized that his voice had sounded deeper than usual. He took a seat next to the former musician. He took him by the hand gently. Hyacinthus was surprised to feel his grip as if he had always known where to find it.

'There is something that worries you.' He stated it plainly. His voice did not hesitate, nor did it temper. He knew perfectly well what was happening.

357

The prince nodded, not realizing that he couldn't see it.

'I'm afraid so. I don't know if I've done anything wrong, but I'm terribly worried, Tamyris. Several gods have visited me in a few days, and they all talk to me about very similar things.'

'You are not worried about the gods, because their visits are blessings, what makes you bitter, my little prince, is that he is not the one who visits you.'

Hyacinthus swallowed hard. In Tamyris's voice everything had a denotation that clarified the obsession with Phoebus that had invaded him.

'I worry that I'm obsessed with him. Call him when I don't want to call him. I know that if he doesn't come closer it's because he has something better to do, or even for my own safety. But even so, I am unable not to recall him every moment. It's like a thorn that I can never completely remove.'

'Don't worry. It's not obsession; rather, love is what you feel. It is not necessary to have eyes that can see to be able to appreciate how your gaze shines now that you talk about him. I don't have to be you to know that your heart skips a beat when other people's lips pronounce the name of Apollo.'

'Tamyris, you know well that I trust you a lot. You seem quite wise to me, and I need your words. I need you to show me the path I have to follow.'

'I can't teach you anything, the only thing I can do is guide you and I'm not going to do it, because I know that you can guide yourself. The gods have not visited me, they have visited you. That is the difference. If they have done it, it is not because of the beauty of your body, a body that the deities do not care about; if they have done it, it is because of the beauty you have inside you. It is worth remembering that beauty is found in the soul of the being, in its essence. Your spirit is beautiful, that's why they came to visit you. You are better than you can imagine. You can find the way for yourself. However, if you want to talk, I will be happy to listen to you.'

'If it is true that your words, possibly, are endowed with the greatest truths, but at the same time I am incapable of realizing it, even when there is something in my head, like a little sparrow with a high-pitched voice that assures me that you are right. You always listen to me. To me and to everyone. Simply for that, the gods should look at you.'

'There are many creatures in this world that should be closely examined by the gods. However, it doesn't happen. We can never know the reason for this.' He paused slightly. 'Who visited you?'

'Aphrodite in dreams, I didn't even call her. She came out of her own accord.'

'Anyone else?'

'It just happened to me.' He then took out the travel blanket that he had found next to him while he was resting under the crown of that immense tree. 'This appeared next to me,' he said, putting it in his hands. 'It's a travel blanket, a cape, whatever you want to call it. And the thing is, I suddenly woke up under an unknown tree, next to this gift and my horse, which was grazing peacefully. At first, before seeing the blanket, I thought it had been a dream, even though I would never take a nap so far from my house; but when I saw this, I assumed that everything I had experienced previously had been true.'

The blind man looked over the entire fabric of the clothing with his hands.

'What did you experience?'

'It is an ominous memory that every time I think about, it gets further away. I would venture to say that the protagonist of these does not want me to think too much about it.'

'Then just say what you remember. Although you think it may be a product of your imagination, sometimes it is not the case.'

'I remember a set of animals in golden tones. They looked like cows, or maybe bulls, they could also be oxen. There were many, but they were all very similar. I didn't realize that there was a human being among these animals, or someone with this shape, so I turned my horse around, preparing to get out of there. However, a jovial voice stopped me. It was very singsong. Not like Apollo's, which is very musical, endowed with a harmony that I have never found in anyone before, but this one, rather, jumped around. It was a young man. I remember he had curly hair, a light colour, if I remember correctly. He was endowed with perfect curls, as if someone had drawn them on a canvas, or sculpted them in marble. He started talking to me. Don't ask me what, because I honestly don't remember. However, there is only one phrase I can cherish at this moment, appreciate it. I can even hear him: *The one you love so much is fine, although worried about your nostalgia.*'

'When I woke up, I thought for a moment that maybe it was Hermes.'

'You were probably right. What did Aphrodite tell you? Do you remember it?' Hyacinthus nodded.

'I remember my meeting with her better than with him. She was telling me about another person, who apparently pines for me. I only know about them that they are a mortal. But that didn't matter to me when she told me and still doesn't. I had so much emotion stuck in my mind towards Apollo, that I ended up asking the goddess of love what I could do.'

'Do you remember what she said?'

'I have it written on a piece of parchment in my room. I haven't read it since the day I wrote it. However, it is true that it is difficult for me to remember it, because it gradually becomes blurrier. She said something about following my soul, my heart... Yes, I remember she said something about that.'

'Then, listen to her words. She is the oldest of the Olympians. She is very wise, as well as knowing about love. Don't lose her advice.'

'But the thing is, I can't follow my heart, nor my soul, if I no longer have them. Understand me, Tamyris, once I met Apollo, I gave him everything I am. Like that. He has my soul, he has my heart, how can I follow him if I don't see him? How can I follow him if that is what I want most, yet he is not here to be followed? I am even thinking about joining a priestly order, but I don't know if my father would accept my proposal.'

'Does he know that Phoebus was actually Apollo?'

'Yes, now he does. Although I suppose, like everyone else, he always suspected it. A mortal like him could not exist.'

'That's true.'

'What can I do?'

'I have also felt Apollo, I have also spoken with him,' he replied. 'The only thing you can do is wait for him, because he knows what is best for you. He will send you the instructions in some way so that you understand it. If he wants you to join a priestly order, he will let you know. Be sure of it. If, on the other hand, this is not his wish, he will not notify you of anything.'

'And if, perhaps, he has forgotten about me?'

'He hasn't. It is impossible to forget you, Hyacinthus. All of us who have known you know that.'

'I have the constant feeling that he is following in my footsteps. However, I cannot have direct contact with him, not even in a disembodied way.'

'Think that Apollo sees everything, he sees all of us, but surely, he places some more of interest in certain creatures. I'm sure you are among them.'

'It's such a strange thing I feel, Tamyris! So strange it is that even I get lost, me! I used to never feel lost.'

'They say that love turns a fool into a king. Perhaps this will affect you even more since your case is quite peculiar. Not only are you in love, but you are in love with a creature quite different from yourself. Although he can become human, he is still primarily a spirit and, before being a spirit, he is a god.'

Hyacinthus nodded, remaining silent for a few moments. He greatly appreciated those conversations with Tamyris, because sometimes he needed to talk to someone who was a man, who was also close to him and had had at least one conversation with the gods. He knew that the former Aedo couldn't help but pay attention to him, something he deeply admired. Despite everything, when he talked with him, there was always room, room for a question that he then felt the need to ask. It was something that caught his attention.

'What I find curious is you, Tamyris.'

'Why?' he asked, looking at him with those eyes lacking the light of sight, but Hyacinthus knew that he could see, even better than those who had prodigious sight. Many times, blind people saw more than those who were not. Tamyris saw it even when, in theory, he couldn't. He contemplated him through his soul, the prince knew it.

'Because you were in love with me. You liked me in some way, and I don't mean in any kind of friendship manner. You know well what I'm saying.'

'I *am* still in love with you.'

'Why do you help me?'

'Because I'm in love with you.'

'Many people would say that it doesn't make sense.'

'What does it matter what people say if I know the truth? I'm in love with you, Hyacinthus. I won't stop being like this for a long time, if that moment ever comes. I am in love with you,

Hyacinthus, ergo, I seek your happiness. I know that I am not the one you love, you love Phoebus, not me, and I just want joy to invade you every morning, every sunset, for happiness to be with you. If it is Apollo who makes you achieve that happiness, whatever! I will fight so that you can be with him, do you understand my perspective?'

'I do. You don't know how grateful I am to have someone like you so close to me. I wish I had listened to you much sooner.'

'I used to be a cretin.' The man laughed. Hyacinthus soon joined him.

'That's true. You were also very annoying.'

'Nothing new!'

'But anyway, the past is behind us. It no longer exists. It is just a memory, a memory that, possibly, will end up being erased from our minds. It is the now that will remain forever. And now you are one of the wisest mortals I could ever meet. People should remember your name throughout the centuries. It's the least you deserve. People should listen to Tamyris in five thousand years and remember the naive Aedo who challenged the muses, the same one whom they punished, although at the same time they gave him the greatest treasure: wisdom, knowledge.'

'Prince, if I'm honest, I don't know if they will remember me, it's not something that matters to me either, because I'm no one worth remembering. I do not want anyone to study my persona, nor my life, nor my holiest personality. I don't want anyone to try to find out what my thoughts were, how I behaved, or something as simple as what my favourite piece was when playing the zither. I don't even want them to know about my loves, my heartbreaks, my childhood, or my lucky encounter disguised as misfortune with the muses. However, what I do want is to remain alive in the souls and hearts of those I touched until, at least, their bodies die. I am not afraid of not being remembered after thousands of years, when perhaps they will not even remember our gods, I am afraid of not being remembered in this life by the people I hold dear.'

'You will not be forgotten by those people. I, of course, don't think I can forget you. You, who had such an amount of mastery in music. You, now, who play the strings of knowledge, don't you realice, Tamyris, that you are still the Aedo you have always been? The difference is that you have changed instruments, but you continue playing, Tamyris. I listen to it. And if I can hear it, so can the world.'

'Why do your words have such a kind tone? I know well that they will remember you. Perhaps, simply, because you are the romantic interest of a god. Perhaps, simply, until the name of Phoebus disappears from history, until the sun itself goes out, but nevertheless, they will remember you. I believe that the world will read glimpses of your beauty, but they will never be able to recreate reality. Art is still imitation, although artists often don't find that funny, but despite everything, it is. No one could ever trace your beauty. Perhaps Apollo and his muses, but mortal ears would not then be able to truly understand his verses.'

The prince swallowed hard.

'Tamyris, I thank you so much for everything.'

'Don't thank me for anything, because there is nothing to thank me for. I just want you to promise me something.'

'Tell me.'

'Don't lose this feeling, don't stop following Apollo. Talk to him, maybe his voice will answer you.'

And so he did.

He left the aedo's house a little later than usual. He got on his horse and started it into a trot. He was sure that it wouldn't be scared that night.

Under the moon and its warriors, the stars, Hyacinthus turned off the path, heading for a small hill. When he reached the top, he simply spoke out loud:

'Artemis, please,' he asked the moon. 'Send my words to your brother. I know well that you are often the presence that I feel before my bed, in my bedroom, when the nights are long. You are that nature that observes me carefully. I don't know what that means, but I don't care. I would be pleased if you could convey the following words to your brother.'

The breeze rustled around them. It caressed him gently. It felt like the moon was shining even brighter.

'Apollo.' His voice tempered slightly with helplessness. He didn't know if that had really happened, couldn't it have been his head? Why had it been him, precisely him, who had drawn attention to the sun? Sometimes, he believed that everything was the product of childish vanity, although that was not the case. 'Apollo, what we are doing is not fair, do you understand?'

There were a few long moments of silence. Hyacinthus knew that no one would answer him, but when he least expected it, at the moment he was going to ask his horse to leave the place, a voice came to him, surrounding him. It embraced him. It was pure musicality, the harmony that had always characterized the god's way of pronouncing. The prince felt his heart skip a beat. At least he could listen to it one more time.

'Justice turns out to be the mirror where our desires are reflected. What is right in the eyes of a mortal is often not right in the eyes of true justice. In your mortal eyes, it is only fair to be together. For mine, it means not being there because despite loving each other, loving you without fuss would be synonymous with taking your life. Now, that's not fair. Well, who am I to take it away from you?'

'Nobody. You are no one to take it away from me, Apollo,' he said louder than the tone he had used the first time. 'No one, but if I have to die anyway I wish that I could at least enjoy some time with you.' His voice did not caress him. He had vanished when he finished saying his words, but even if he didn't answer, he knew he was there, somehow. Maybe it was invisible, maybe it was on another plane, or he was looking at it from above. He didn't know, but he was sure it was there. 'I love you,' the mortal suddenly whispered. 'I love you. That's the problem. Thank you, thank you very much, once again, Apollo. Thank you very much, why? Simple, you have given me life back when I had never experienced it before with this body. It's the least I can say. Thank you very much, and please do not allow me to get lost, to stray away from

370

this path. Are you aware of the mark you have left? I sound like an ignorant person speaking, but truly, are you aware? I'm sure that's the case, but at the same time, something asks me to express it to you. Will we mortals be persistent by nature? Possibly.'

Those were his last words before asking the animal to gallop to get home.

Having finished all his tasks regarding the creature, he headed to his room. Once there, he felt Apollo's presence again.

He had passed an altar that the servants had for him, and he had had the disturbing sensation that his eyes had followed him. His energies had moved away from the stones until they surrounded him again. There, lying on his bed, he noticed it again. He realized that he would always, in one way or another, be with him. He might not be able to see him, but if he focused, he could feel him. Apollo was everywhere.

He was in the sun, in the Earth, in the notes, in the verses, in the medicines, in every sigh of life taken away by a plague, in every relief of the sick person who recovered; also in his heart. He had given it to him and it was too late to get it back. He had been born to die like all mortals, but, in those moments, he knew that he would die for a love that perhaps he should not have felt; it mattered little to him. He would die, he would die following him. It was what his heart dictated. The one that beat in other people's hands. His name would be written forever in his mind, in his soul. He knew that he might forget him, not there, but when he drank again from the waters of oblivion, but then, one day, he would return. When he was ready, Phoebus would return, announcing the truth, bringing messages full of hope, realities, and light, so that, in this way, he would wake up again. Even if the world turned infinite times, he would be there, he would follow him. Hyacinthus became increasingly aware of his response. The ephebe needed him by his side, and for Apollo to need him. The consequences didn't matter, because life was meaningless without death, and death was nothing more than a life of spirit, instead of body. There was no great enigma, much less concern in that. There shouldn't be, at least. He was right, he shouldn't worry about something so natural. If the Moiras had decided so when weaving their threads, it would happen, even if the righteous Apollo tried to stop it. And Hyacinthus knew well that if Phoebus knew that one hundred percent, he would never have come down from Olympus, not even for a second. At least not in a way that the prince could observe. However, among the shadows, in a non-corporeal form, he continued to feel him, because the energies of the deities are completely different from those of the rest of the beings. Once you feel them, you never forget them.

The young man closed his eyes and felt him very close to him. He did not speak to him, and if he did, the beautiful Hyacinthus could not hear him, much less understand him, but, nevertheless, there he was.

He slept like a dahlia that night. It was neither the lightning nor the sounds of the servants that woke him up that morning, but the voice of his sister, who was calling to him at his side.

'Hyacinthus,' he said. 'Hyacinthus.' The young man soon opened his eyes, somewhat sleepy.

'Polyboea, what's happening?'

'Nothing, I just want to know what you did this time.'

'What are you talking about?'

'You haven't fallen in love with another deity, have you?'

'Not that I know. What happened?'

'Are you sure that not even one of them, to compensate you for Apollo, has given you the opportunity for another person, this time a mortal, to fall in love with you?' He shook his head.

'If you speak of Tamyris, the ancient Aedo, he himself has assured me several times that he has been in love with me for a long time.'

'Don't say something I already know, I'm talking about a girl.' The prince clenched his jaw, remembering Aphrodite's words as if they were a hurricane. 'A friend of our brother's.'

'Yes, I know who she is.' He said, standing up.

'Well, she's been asking about you for a few days now. Our brother told me.'

'Polyboea,' he stopped her in an extraordinarily polite manner, 'although the girl is not ugly, she is not someone that interests me.'

'Don't you even want to give it a chance?'

'I only want one thing.'

'Don't you want to love again?'

'I already love. I have never stopped doing it, but Polyboea,' he said, 'I love the sun, its owner, the one who guides it every morning until dusk falls. I love him, and I'm not going to stop doing it. Maybe I can't see him with my eyes, maybe I can't hug him, or feel him between my fingers, but I know that he looks at

374

me, like he looks at all of us. He looks at me and silently loves me. I love him without fear of losing myself.'

'Yes, you must love him. Maybe I couldn't bear it if the one I love disappeared in such a way. Few humans could, I must add.'

'Few humans could... Your words are true, but I am among those very few humans. I feel him so close to my heart, so close to my soul, that I know he will never be far from me. Even if I thought he might, he never would.'

'But, Hyacinthus, he is incredible, that, I know.' His sister followed him closely, while he began to walk towards the gardens of the residence. 'However, I also know that he won't appear.'

The boy continued walking with a terribly firm step, very confidently.

'Shut up, Polyboea, I'm listening to the sound of the lyres!'

The girl did not refute this, since after staying still for a few seconds, she managed to hear the notes of such an instrument. Although they were normal notes, she would never hear them in the mortal world, in the place where they belonged. They were too perfect, making it seem as if that melody was thundering from the sky itself. From the very sky fell the notes that caused the boy's heart to beat faster than ever.

He ended up running trying to find where that melody was coming from, but he couldn't. The notes came from the sky, from the clouds, from the wind, from the branches of the trees, from the interior of the earth, from the roots of the world. This melody came from the sun itself, which from the dome of the world loved him in silence.

He saw a discus flying in his direction and caught it when he realised that it had been intentionally thrown at him.

It was the girl Polyboea had told him about. It looked as if everything had been organized, even though Hyacinthus knew well that it had only been a coincidence of life.

The girl approached him very happily. She had dark hair, brown eyes, with a tinge of full happiness. He wondered then if it wasn't among Polyboea's plans for him to go out to that same area to meet her.

He didn't know how that had happened, but she was now standing before him. Her gaze could not hold the prince's, not even for a few seconds. The girl was not ugly, but she was certainly not

Apollo, and Hyacinthus only had eyes for the god, since he had already taken his heart.

'Thank you,' she said when the young man returned the disk. I've been told that you always catch the discus, would you like to practice a little with me?' The king's son clenched his jaw slightly, since the words had come out of the young woman's mouth as if she had been practicing them some time before. Maybe that's how it had been.

He felt the urge to reject her. Although the discus entertained him, it was not among his biggest hobbies. Especially because even when he managed to catch it in the air, he could never make two throws that were more or less straight.

He was about to reject the invitation, always in an extremely cordial manner of course, but suddenly, he heard the lyre again that he had tried to follow. He knew somehow that accepting it was the only way to get close to Apollo once again.

'Okay.' He responded after long seconds.

'Perfect.' Her smile was resplendent. She was very happy that the boy had agreed, so much so that Hyacinthus was very surprised.

They walked together to the esplanade he had gone to with Apollo several times before, when he appeared in human form. He found himself smiling at the memories, at his strength, at the very sun that was above them.

The girl threw the discus at him. He caught it. He never missed, but at the same time, he thought of Phoebus.

Phoebus, Apollo, the one with the golden curls, the one known as the one who hurts from afar. He had never harmed Hyacinthus, but he had won his heart, his soul, his everything, in less than the crow of a rooster. The endless years he would have spent trying to find a love worth having had vanished. He had skipped them thanks to the fact that Apollo had laid his eyes on such a fragile human.

The wind was blowing slightly, but it was not something that worried him. The trees seemed to agree to maintain silence; the birds, for their part, chirped from time to time. It seemed like they were welcoming someone, a stage, death, a path... Who knew! But it was not the weather, nor the creatures, nor even the intense heat he received from the sun that caused him to need to take off his clothes. He would have done it if that girl hadn't been with him. He had already used his imaginative libido enough to also undress in front of her. It was a voice, a voice and an essence behind his back, that told him how he should throw the discus so that it would move straighter. His mind brought back the memory of the days spent with Apollo, when he tried to teach him the correct technique to use the bow. It was exactly the same. There was his voice, there was his spirit guiding him again so that he would not err. Thus, he was at his side, invisibly until he more or less approached his objective.

Happy to have got so close, Hyacinthus looked over his shoulder at a somewhat distant gap in the trees. There he found a man in a crimson toga. His hair fell over his shoulders, but unfortunately, he couldn't appreciate anything else. However, he knew perfectly well who it was. Apollo was looking at him, he was helping him, he was still there. His smile, along with his clothes, his long hair was the only thing he had managed to perceive before he vanished.

He caught the discus when the young woman threw it to him. He left it on the ground.

'Excuse me,' he shouted at her so she could hear him. 'I have to go. I must follow Phoebus. He told me I could do it, and I can. Excuse me.'

After that he ran towards the area where he had seen him. His spirit guided him like never before. He could figure out exactly where he had gone. Their divine walks lifted the flora and made the fauna sing.

The flutes of nature could be heard, and next to them a very strong lyre that made Hyacinthus free himself from all his fears. What did death matter? What did the dangers matter if he had him next to him even for five more seconds?

He had taken everything. He had to get it back. The only way to do it was to see him again. He knew he would make it. He had him before him, even though he couldn't see him yet.

He would find him.

XVII

His heart was beating strongly. He ran between the trees, feeling like they were just the peak of what they really were, because there, in those seconds, he was perfectly capable of capturing, of appreciating the way in which their roots, which were nothing more than extensions of those bodies composed of wood, travelled through the bowels of the earth, unmistakable amulet of the goddess Gaia.

He listened to the confused voice of that girl, whose name he was never able to remember. He heard her very far away, but he didn't care. He was looking for the fragrance, the essence left by a god who, if he wanted to hide, would do so without even asking.

Nothing more mattered than those musical notes, the voices of the muses, the rays of the sun, the arrows that brought pestilence, and the gentle healing potions. Nothing mattered more than the voice that, in distant Delphi, the fortune teller heard in her temple.

It was nothing relevant except for some wise words that sometimes merged with the dawn. Those accompanied by lyres, which formed eternal verses, those that Hyacinthus looked for every day when he opened his eyes. There was no room in his attention for anything else other than that.

And they could have told him that this would not be the fairest or most logical solution, knowing the destiny that was going to precede him, but it didn't matter, what did it matter if he had him? If he could follow him? What did it matter? It was in his hand, it fell through his fingers, like a cloth that accidentally falls from the top of the abyss. The one you have just a few centimetres away. You know you can reach, but you have to be quick, act without thinking. The same had to be done with the gods. They were so volatile. They left fast, faster even than they came, but Hyacinthus couldn't let him go. He was his love. The lover he needed. He was his light, the key to saving his immense agony. The walls, the houses, the cities could fall, Athens, Lesbos, Sparta could fall, Hellas could be flooded under the waters, but it mattered little. It was worth the risk. It was worth the possibility of falling if in this way he would find again that soul whom, without realizing it, he had always loved.

Perhaps, one day many years ago he would have hated the sunlight, he would have cursed the solar chariot, but that was no longer the case. He loved him now even when he burned, because he remembered him.

He ran along those paths full of trunks, and he thought that not even a storm toppling the trees, nor the nymphs, nor Pan, nor the oceanic girls could stop him, neither a perfectly launched arrow, nor a spear that would be impossible to dodge, nor a lightning bolt that split the trees in two. It didn't matter, he would make it. He would be able to reach the voice, reach the lyre, reach the light, the truth, the joy. He would achieve what he was after if he believed in it.

A believing fierce heart that walks through the world, raising the tides, making the mountains become plains, moving the sky and changing its location. That was his heart, which burned, burned like the flames of the fire that devastated the entire world. All because of an essence, an entity that would always love him. He knew it well. There was no death in life. After this one? More life, more joys, more misfortunes. But above all, there was more Apollo, even through death.

There was more Apollo, because this one was immutable, immovable. There was more Apollo wherever he went. There was more Apollo, because he lived in too many things. He had the growing feeling that he would live forever, that he would wrap himself in his body, in his notes and never forget. He would never leave him, he would always return to him. One way or another, the ephebe always would. Maybe through scriptures, art or people's gossip. Yes, Phoebus's voice would fade away, hidden by that of a new god, but there would be a dawn after that long, dark night. An early morning where his voice would resonate, and his name would return to the soul of Hyacinthus. Without knowing anything, he would understand in a certain way that he loved him, and he would wait, because Phoebus would look for him. He would end up finding him to sing to him again. Apollo, that was all that mattered. Apollo existed throughout the world, even in Hades. Even in Tartarus, he would venture to say, there was the essence of that formidable god. It was, therefore, the light of the pagan soul, the greatest misfortune of those who have lost their way.

The sky was wearing a different colour that morning. The Earth seemed expectant, waiting for a word, for an act filled with unconditional love that had never been seen before.

The birds were silent, as if they knew that they could no longer provide chorus to notes that were too perfect to be real. And, in a certain way, they were not.

The bear that Hyacinthus saw in the distance looked at him wisely. He sang softly to him that if he loved him so much, he should run. He also found a little pigeon. One who had a very sweet look. Full of tenderness. The creature stopped the young man in the middle of the road. They looked into each other's eyes, and the prince knew it was Aphrodite.

Her voice rang in his mind:

Follow him. Follow Apollo. Follow him if you wish. The Moiras have already woven the future. It is foolish to delay it, because it will come. Run and look for the one you love, who undoubtedly loves you too. And be grateful. Thousands of humans talk to me every day hoping for advice about loves that have no foundation; instead, here you are, following a true love. Follow it, don't stop until you find it. Do not lose it.

Hyacinthus smiled and nodded, not delaying a second, continuing to run.

He felt his feet touching the slightly wet earth because of the soft rain that morning. His eyes observed the entire panorama, feeling it closer than ever. The branches embraced him, the animals encouraged him, the spirits sang to him, and the nymphs celebrated. He felt it, just as he knew that far away, on the tops of the mountains, there was a young woman who was watching him surrounded by her hunters. She looked at him with a relaxed expression, which was strange for her. She confirmed that his brother was crazy, but she inadvertently admired the beauty such a person could contain.

He knew it well, and he smiled. It was the only thing he could do. Run, while smiling like a fool because he was close. He felt it.

385

He could appreciate in those moments how the flowers danced to the rhythm of a lyre that, although distant, was getting closer and closer. He felt the energies of the world, just like Apollo had taught him. He ran with the confidence of the most balanced and fastest horses. He ran like he had never done before. There was no stopping even to get some air, because in those moments, he didn't care about losing the very rhythm of his breathing. If he had Apollo in front of him, he could die right there. It didn't matter, as long as he, at least, felt him once more.

'Run, run,' he said to himself. 'Run, Hyacinthus, run. Run as fast as you can. Reach him.'

Reach him. Be guided by the lyre that his hands play. You know the way. The voices of his instinct told him. He knew it. Apollo was so close. He ran, but even when he was tired he did not stop, since he knew that Apollo would do exactly the same as him. Of course the god would.

All the myths, all the stories that portrayed him as a monster were completely false. Hyacinthus knew it. They were manipulated, because that was certainly not the god they knew. His Apollo, his Phoebus, would never do harm unless the creature deserved it. His Apollo was the biggest-hearted being he would ever meet, the wisest being he would ever meet. He told himself for a few moments that perhaps he idolized him, but he was wrong: He didn't idolize him, he never had. Hyacinthus truly knew Apollo, better than anyone. Sometimes stories are altered, and those starring gods were no exception.

Suddenly, a silhouette slipped into the middle of his path, blocking his way, silencing his words. A silhouette whose energy propelled him backwards, even though that was the path he should follow.

'Please step aside.' He asked, sincerely. He had great suspicions about the identity of that spirit that detained him.

'Are you sure you know what you want, Hyacinthus?' The voice again. The one that had visited him so many times throughout his childhood.

'I'm sure,' he replied. 'The Moiras have already woven the fate. I can't do anything, if I delay it, it might even be worse.'

'What do you feel for him? Is it strong enough for you to give his life to him?'

'Without him, I die,' he responded. 'I die without him. I am dead without him and to die alive, I prefer to die truly.'

'Is it really that strong?'

'It is so strong that I would die again and again. It's so strong I would kill the people I love the most. I would kill to be with him, because he completes me. And his love makes me immortal, therefore, I know that I will not die. I do not fear death, because I know that even in death, Apollo continues to exist. Apollo exists beyond the known reality.' His eyes shone as he said those words, ergo everyone present, who were not few, knew that he was telling the truth. 'Apollo will continue even when I am gone. He will continue even when these trees are derived by human hands. When buildings are built on these lands. Apollo will continue even when death caresses this house of ours. Apollo exists in Hades, also in Tartarus, in Olympus and on earth. I only need something to live, and it is Apollo because he is my personal water, so even if I die, if there is a possibility that I can feel him in some way, then I will live.'

The silhouette said nothing. It seemed like it had gone silent. It just vanished, leaving the path free, an unpaved one, which Hyacinthus understood as the path to the soul.

He did not stop to think, to wonder, as he had done other times, about the true identity of that voice. He simply stuck to what he had been doing for the last few minutes: running.

The trees seemed to push him; the nymphs encouraged him. The hunting dogs howled in the distance, the animals brought him positive messages, full of calm, and the sun just watched, warming with elegant air.

From time to time, Hyacinthus looked at the sun and then smiled at it. The sun loved him, and this was the main impetus for moving forward. It made him remember the god he had loved so much, whom he would love so much.

Then, without hardly realizing it, he heard the sound of the lyre much closer, just a few meters away. He stopped, so he could follow the music.

Among the weeds, there was a place with vegetation too beautiful to be real. The trees grew extremely strong and tall in that area. The musical notes surrounded every creature that was nearby, enveloping them, caressing them, healing them.

The birds were nearby, perched on the branches of the wooden giants. Some snake was crawling on the ground. Beings who, upon seeing Hyacinthus, stopped for a few seconds, then did not take long to follow its path. A wolf approached the prince, brushing its body against him. He touched its fur, a caress that the animal deeply appreciated. He felt watched. Thus, he saw some crows whose dark eyes devoured him, although they did not possess any evil, or at least, it was not apparent. Next to these, one could see some very intelligent falcons. A mouse whispered stories to a lizard. It was not that Hyacinthus heard its voice, but he had that growing sensation.

But it wasn't the creatures or the plants that mattered, but rather the being that he would find if he decided to look up.

There he was, leaning his back against a log, with his eyes closed, a man who played the most golden lyre the world would ever see. A lyre bathed in a glow worthy of the sun's rays. Although Hyacinthus knew well that, despite appearing to be a human, he had little of this. He was a spirit, a deity.

His happiness was such that the smile that formed on his face was the truest that would be seen on the face of the Earth for a long time.

He walked quietly towards the god, who seemed to be completely oblivious to everything.

He played the lyre as if it were the last time he would do so. He caressed its strings, so softly that it was barely noticeable, giving the impression that he didn't even pluck them. His hair this time was considerably darker than what Hyacinthus was used to, although it was not completely black. His skin, however, remained the same, slightly tanned, as if the sea and the sun had agreed to hit him. His face was still the same, just like his body, or at least extremely similar.

When Hyacinthus was a few meters away from him, Apollo opened his eyes. The blue had almost completely disappeared, finding a light golden tone intertwined with that beautiful aqua tone, so reminiscent of the prince of the Aegean. He left the lyre resting on the trunk and walked towards him.

Hyacinthus felt a pulse inside him, a lurch in his heart, followed by another, how long before this ended? Never. That was the correct answer.

His arms embraced him, enveloping him. Anyone would have imagined a kiss, would have even begged for it. Hyacinthus didn't think like that. Apollo was a god, and his way of loving was somewhat different from that of mortals: when the gods loved, they did it truly. You could feel this in their energies, even in their words, in the way they smiled and looked, but they did not usually kiss. They didn't need to do it to show that they loved.

His body, his energies surrounding him were what he had been looking for all that time; he finally found them. He buried his face in the essence of the god. He smelled the god's fragrance, slightly like a fire that burns but does not bother, mixed with the essence of those natural lands. That was Apollo, more nature than people usually thought.

Phoebus soon caressed his face with his hands, slightly raising his lover's face.

'Didn't you say it was unfair?' asked the prince, taking a bit of a risk, but confident at the same time. He looked into Apollo's eyes, immersing himself in them.

'It still is,' he responded with that musicality in his words. 'However, it was more unfair to let you die while alive.'

Hyacinthus caressed his lover's hands with his own hands. He needed that kind of feeling for as long as he had left.

'The Moiras had already woven my fate, there is little you can do to avoid it.'

'If I could change it, I would, but not even I know your fate.'

'Maybe we worry for no reason.'

'Maybe.' Although he could see in his voice that Apollo was not entirely convinced. 'You know that if misfortune ever happens, if I could, I would pay to get into that boat with you. I would pay to go to Hades with you. If that means losing my immortality, so be it, but I'd be with you.'

Hyacinthus nodded. Of course, the young prince knew it.

He remained silent for a few long seconds, but it was so comfortable that Apollo was surprised when he spoke:

'Thank you.'

'Why should you thank me?' His voice sounded very soft, very calm. The prince was surprised to realize how much he longed for that.

'For everything you have shown me, everything you have taught me, the immense world you have opened to me, I have to thank you infinitely for all that and more.'

'Hyacinthus, you already knew those lessons, that world you told me about. I have only made you stop and observe it, simply that. And it is something that any being who knows the importance of life should do.'

Hyacinthus remained silent again, but he did not take long to say something:

'One day, a young woman with a philosophical air, who was also quite beautiful, suggested that I meditate on a specific phrase. I don't remember it perfectly, but it was something like this.' Apollo raised his eyebrow, interested. He knew that if he searched through what he had seen and heard, he would find that moment, but he didn't have that need. He was aware that the prince would narrate it as he knew how to. *'Creating gods was the biggest mistake of humans or, on the contrary, creating man was the biggest mistake of the gods.* Now I think about it, knowing that the gods are completely real, much more than us, much more than the ground we walk on... I also have this feeling that the human species is slowly destroying this place we inhabit, and one day they will destroy it completely.'

'What do you think, beautiful Hyacinthus?' he asked, looking into his eyes, continuing to caress the prince's face with the same softness that he had previously blessed the lyre with.

They were very close, but neither made any attempt to move away. They were fine like that. It seemed that no one could keep them away, not even the most horrendous of misfortunes.

'Why did you allow human life?'

'Why wouldn't we allow it?'

394

'I honestly think that allowing humans to live was the biggest mistake of the gods, of the world and of nature itself.'

'I beg to differ. The biggest mistake was separating ourselves from them. The biggest mistake was not letting them evolve but giving them the option to do evil. The human who does good, who is good, is the most marvellous creature that most marvels; he who does evil is the most destructive,' Apollo declared with his well-known wisdom. 'The biggest mistake was making you remember that we existed, while we forgot you.'

Hyacinthus looked into his eyes with a question in his mind. A question that did not need to be asked, because he knew well what the answer was. He also knew in those moments that Phoebus knew what was on his mind, but nevertheless, he did not ask him to say it. The vast majority of the time, being a god, he turned out to be more human than all the individuals of this species combined.

The prince admired his words, his way of pronouncing them, rich in harmony and melody. He did not sing, but any singer would have envied a voice like that, which even chatting and whispering accompanied the invisible instruments. There was so much wisdom, so much knowledge, so much richness in what he said that, at times, Hyacinthus was pleasantly surprised. He was aware of who he was talking to, but that kind of knowledge had no place in his mind.

'Apollo,' he whispered then.

'Tell me,' he said softly.

'I've missed you all this time. I have tried to search for you in every little thing. Without realizing it, I have found you in a certain way, thus managing to achieve a happiness that I thought was impossible...' He paused slightly. 'You once told me that happiness...'

'Happiness can be found even in the simplest and smallest things. It's true, I told you.'

'Yes, and the meaning of that phrase is also true. I found you in so many things, thus also finding a joy that was perfectly palpable. You were in my dreams, but also in heaven, in the flutes, in the lyres played by some aedo, and even in the grace of the horses being led by some expert charioteer. You were also hidden in the wood of the bow arrows behind my door. You were in all those places. And that's without mentioning where I found you best, in my heart, wrapped in my veins, my own skin.'

Apollo smiled with a sweetness that no mortal could ever achieve. Every movement, every act that he performed, every word spoken by his lips, was endowed with the magnificence of a creature of such a dynasty.

'You see it now because I have shown it to you.' Hyacinthus nodded.

'For that I thank you.'

'I know, but you don't have to because it was there all the time. All the time hovering around you, Hyacinthus, at your side, following you. All the time the world was kneeling before you, and you didn't see it, but you could have, even without me. I watched you while I thought that you were an extremely peculiar mortal, but there was something inside me that told me that you would know perfectly everything that you questioned if you stopped to think about it. You didn't need my essence, because I have always been there even without you realizing it. Both me and anyone else. Both me and my sister, my father, or even deities so far away that they will be completely unknown to you. All of you can appreciate our essence if you set your mind to it. You just have to trust and be sure that you will achieve it. The animals...' he said while directing a small glance at the creatures that were observing him in silence. The prince noticed that everyone was looking at Phoebus with the eyes of a lover. They seemed to be captivated by his presence. '...they don't think so much before they act, before they feel something. Ergo, they tend to grasp everything much more easily, even naturally. There are no imaginary obstacles in their minds that keep them from us, or from any other energy or essence. However, humans, who are so restless, so intellectual, are not capable of acting without meditating, without thinking carefully, sometimes without realizing what will happen. That deprives you of many things. If you cannot act without first thinking, much less are you able to feel without thinking. You build your own walls that deprive you of enjoying the views of the immense world that you have before your eyes, because thinking that the world is only what the eye can see is the most hypocritical thing anyone can believe. You can't see the whole world, not even a region, by standing in one place, much less can one know the earth without having learned the main lesson: know yourself, and then you will truly know.'

'And, sometimes, what is not captured by the senses, can be captured by the soul,' said the mortal, remembering Aphrodite's words.

Apollo nodded in agreement.

'Once humans know themselves, the mystery will not exist. Not even the gods will be one. You won't even need us, since at the end of the day, each and every one of us is divine, even those who are mortal, because they have a spirit, the key to divinity.'

'I don't think we will ever stop needing you, even if it is simply to guide us.' Then, Phoebus moved closer. An act that surprised the young man a little. The god's forehead pressed against his. He felt his breathing very close. He closed his eyes without even thinking about it. He had to forget the thought, the flow of his mind, thus focusing on the feeling.

'That's what we do,' he whispered very quietly. 'Do you want to know a secret, Hyacinthus? The gods do not need to be prayed to, we do not need sacrifices. What's more, in most cases we reject them. We don't need people who murder others for not believing in the same thing. We gods are of no use other than to guide, as long as someone wants advice.'

'Aren't you protectors of the cosmos, too?'

'Also, but with respect to humans, we only serve to guide you. You don't need to pray to us. There is no need for you to sacrifice beings who deserve life. Sometimes we are more pleased with a deep conversation.'

'Don't you get angry when we don't pray to you?'

'Of course not. If anything, we get angry when an injustice is carried out. On many occasions, we are not even angry. We simply do something because we know that it is what fate has desired. Most of the misfortunes carried out by gods have an explanation that goes beyond what is told. Someday I will be the cause of the death of a great hero. People will think various things. The truth will be far away and at the same time, close to what the gossip will say.'

'How can you stand it when people say such things?'

'Does the fact that a majority says something immediately make it true?'

'No.'

'There you have your answer. The developed soul will only care about the truth, not what the majority thinks is true.'

'What if it doesn't know?'

'The soul will look for it.'

'And if it does know?'

'They may call him vain, but he won't care, because he will know that what he says is true. Do you remember about the boxes?'

'Yeah.'

'Do you remember the case of the muses?' Hyacinthus nodded his head.

'I called them unjust for having committed such ardour against Tamyris, but now even he is eternally grateful.'

'Sometimes you need an excuse to give a gift that, at first, will seem like a curse. What do you think now?'

'That was the best solution. Tamyris is more authentic than ever. He has reached a level of knowledge that he would never have acquired if he had kept his gifts for music, and his eyesight. I suppose they knew it from the beginning.' He then looked into the god's eyes. 'Did they?' He nodded.

'Yes, they knew it. They were aware that at first it would be difficult, but that later he would be grateful. It is true that he humiliated them in a certain way, but they had admired him for his work, his makings, and they rewarded him with the excuse of punishing him.'

'I no longer consider it as much a punishment as a blessing. I venture to say that Tamyris sees it that way too.'

'Yes, they know it. Me too.' Then, Apollo brushed a curly lock away from his lover's face. 'Why did you come to think that I no longer loved you?'

Hyacinthus was not surprised to hear him say that as he had thought about it all that time. It was a fear that invaded him many times.

'I had that fear deeply etched inside me. However, there was always something that told me that was not the case. I didn't want to lose you, I didn't want to let you go. I just wanted to follow you.'

'What do you want now?'

'Follow you. Follow you wherever you go, I don't want to get away from you. I want to follow you to Olympus, to Delos, to Delphi, to Hades or to Tartarus itself. Wherever I go, it has to be with you.'

'Wherever, but at your side,' he whispered.

Hyacinthus nodded.

'Yes, anywhere, but with you.' He caressed his cheek again, while he locked his eyes on the other's. The depth with which Apollo looked was reminiscent of his antiquity. Hyacinthus then thought that, contrary to what was said, Phoebus must not have been born on any island in the Mediterranean but on some island in a different dimension, on a higher, very ancient plane, much more archaic than the land on which he travelled. If perhaps the cosmos, with everything that this word began to encompass for Hyacinthus, had a beginning day, that was when Phoebus was born, or at least that was the impression it gave.

At that time, the planet was relatively young, the trees too, and so were the sand and the mud. However, Apollo had the same archaic shine that his gaze would possess today. A brightness that revealed that he saw, heard, knew everything that was happening in the cosmos. Every tiny conversation, every act of terror, and every word of love. He saw everything, he was aware of everything, ergo, he knew absolutely everything.

Any secret was in danger before the powerful gaze of Phoebus that hurts from afar.

'Will I ever forget you, Apollo?' Since he'd opened the box of fears, why didn't he let all of them surround the god? He knew even without Hyacinthus saying anything.

403

Apollo then smiled. His smile illuminated that afternoon, in which the sunlight was gradually fading. The animals were still nearby, watching him, the Earth seemed to rotate around him, as it did with the star that heated it. The trees made their roots go towards him. The clouds had vanished, silence filled the horizon, waiting very cautiously for his words.

His voice came out of his lips like a perfectly calm melody. It seemed accompanied by all the harmony in the world, or perhaps he was harmony itself.

'That depends on what you consider forgetting, Hyacinthus,' he said, looking at him out of the corner of his eye. 'What is forgotten is usually remembered. Memories become ominous, then fade later, but, somehow, they always return.'

'If I forget, make me remember. Please make me remember. Don't let me get lost.'

The young man's eyes were bathed in tears. Apollo knew it without having to look at him, but even though it hurt, he stared at him.

'There will always be a part of your being that will remember me, prince. A part of your soul that will embrace these moments forever, eternally. Even if you think you don't remember it, you will remember it.'

'Could I live without remembering you? How could I live without knowing that you exist? I wouldn't mind if my life wasn't infinite, but I need to remember you. It's the only way to truly live.'

'You could really live without me, you know that, right?'

'I suppose, but now I am not able to imagine a decent life in that way.'

'Maybe you can't imagine it now, but if you had to live it you would, but don't worry, I would be watching you, listening to you, waiting for the right moment to return to you. So, I would help you remember. However, I want you to know that even when you forget me, I will be here.' He paused slightly when he saw the first tear sliding down the beautiful boy's cheeks. Apollo pushed it away from his face. 'Don't cry, Hyacinthus. Don't cry, because I'm here, and I'm not going to leave you, not again.'

Hyacinthus buried his face in his lover's chest. Phoebus hugged him tightly.

He felt the energy of the sun surrounding him. Hyacinthus hugged him, understanding that he loved him, not just Apollo but everything he represented, everything he was.

'You hear that,' he whispered a few minutes later, breaking the silence with his voice rich in harmonies.

In the distance he could see the last birdsong, the crackling of some insect, and the piercing song of a wolf that howled ahead of the moon.

'Yes,' he whispered softly. 'The energies of the world.'

'The energies of the world that will always be here,' Phoebus continued. 'Everything you feel, everything you hear will always be here, Hyacinthus. If they remind you of me, I will always be with you. You said that in every little thing you found me. So, you don't need to worry. If you have to remember me, you will. In time, you will achieve it. You can do it, just like you were able to find me. You could find me again, again and again.'

'I hope I don't have to find you,' he said, separating himself a little from the god. He looked at him, curious about what he had just said. If so, it would mean that you have found me before.'

'Don't worry about that, one way or another if our paths separate and have to cross again, they will. But that is an uncertain future that may not even happen, ergo, we do not have to worry.'

'Can you stay with me tonight, in this present?' the mortal risked asking.

'I was waiting for you to propose it.'

. . .

Night had already fallen.

The light of the moon and stars illuminated them from afar. There were two men lying near a bonfire.

The god and the mortal, as it would be said some time later. In this way the nymphs addressed them, gossiping and talking among themselves, telling what they had seen.

One was quite young. His skin was tanned, possibly due to the sun's rays. His hair was night itself, with graceful ringlets that gave the impression of never ending. His lips were slightly full, and he simply smiled. He looked at the other with various feelings that few humans could adequately describe. He was very close to the god. He had his face resting on the other one's body. His voice, from time to time, could be heard commenting on something the other was saying, since they had already dismissed philosophy, along with its profound themes, thus entering a symphony where the only thing that mattered was a present that tasted like eternity.

The second looked like the sun. It was true that his hair had taken on a slightly darker tone than on other occasions, when he was under the light of day. However, he continued to retain that essence that enveloped him entirely. An essence full of warmth, musicality, healing and wisdom. If a hunter returning home a little late had passed nearby and seen him, he would not have approached him because he would have immediately realized that Apollo was anything but human. His features were not human. Too sweet, too perfect, so much so that not even the most beautiful of men could match him.

The flames of the improvised bonfire that they had made to keep Hyacinthus in a pleasant environment danced under their voices as they told each other everything they wanted. Everything they felt, everything they loved. Sometimes they planned, other times they just breathed, feeling the other one's heart. But it had to be said that above all, the sound of the fire revived the bonds of tenderness. His words ended up becoming much more romantic. Their voices revealed a deep feeling. Apollo's gaze was immediately filled with the love he had tried so well to avoid; Hyacinthus's life was invaded by the joy of being able to be with the one who gave him life. Because he knew that, once separated from Apollo, he would not tolerate anything. But Apollo existed in so many things that it was almost impossible to get away from him, even when one wanted to.

The verses and notes that came out of the lyre, those that both tried to sing, ended up extinguishing so that both souls could merge before fate turned romance into tragedy.

Epilogue

Hyacinthus

The last days of my life were, without a doubt, the most wonderful that any mortal had ever experienced.

I always had the constant feeling that Thanatos was watching me. I wouldn't exaggerate when I said that every night, when I lay in my bedroom, I felt his cold gaze on me. I felt, in the same way, his aura radiating immense strength. A strength very similar to that of the other deities I had dealt with, but, at the same time, it was different. It was endowed with a dark hue, but it was not scary, it rather gave the impression of welcoming me to a place that I would visit thousands of times, if I had not visited it before, apart from possessing a little bit of tenderness, If I truly could define such a feeling with an adjective like that, which is so inappropriate for the situation. However, that was the way I experienced it. Sometimes, feelings were not linked to any logic.

When I noticed that deity so close, that which was nothing more than a ticket to Hades, I felt the sun behind my body, and all the fear that could invade me vanished, like the darkness did when it gave way to a new day.

I spent time with Apollo. Every morning, every afternoon, every night, every minute, every moment. He was with me even when he lacked corporeal form. He was there, he talked to me, and I answered him. Sometimes we philosophized, other times he sang to me or perhaps, we simply remained silent, letting our thoughts scream what we felt every time we encountered one another.

Gradually, I began to accept how lucky I had been. I didn't know why people spoke so badly about him, but I didn't care. Rumours spread that I was inventing the god's visit. I also didn't care, because I knew the truth. I found no hatred in my being, nor hardship. I looked back at the misfortunes I had had to endure, and they no longer seemed so miserable to me. They were the only way for me to get to where I was.

Then, when I doubted, there he was. He looked at me, spoke a few words to me, we passed the time, forgetting about the world around us, because when Apollo and I were together there was nothing else but us. There was nothing else, apart from the Sun and the mortal.

We used to compose verses when the sun went down. He sat next to me on the floor. I commonly rested my head on his shoulder, while each of us took a quill and a parchment. Letting our imagination fly, we wrote the verses that narrated our story, also the threads that united it, the love we had for each other. That which was so pure, so clear that few other beings would feel it. He used to touch my hair, brushing the curls away from my face, and then read what was created, often accompanied by the music of his beautiful zither. His voice always sounded perfect, a symphony of colours, emotions, and feelings that was completely impossible to describe appropriately. There was nothing to match the beauty that he was, the beauty that he represented, what he created... It was all Phoebus. It was the only thing that did him justice: his own name to describe everything he said, composed, did... Everything was Apollo.

And, as the late hours of the night fell, he said goodbye to his sister, looking out to the sky, while fixing his gaze on the moon. I watched him, very still. I could see his entire body, which was golden, in contrast with the silver lights, and he never hesitated to tell me that if there was something sublime in the universe, it was my soul.

His eyes conveyed unbreakable security to me. His voice sang again, while I tried to sleep curled up against him. I slept in the arms of the sun god, and even so, the world did not deprive me of suffering the torments that stalked my nights.

I saw in his lips, in his being, I felt in his energies, that he feared more for me. People would describe him as a narcissist, in the past and in the future, but they were so far from the truth... That being was goodness, justice, truth, light. Nothing justified his incredible actions. Nothing but a heart, a soul that could not turn its back on what it truly was. I could see in his eyes that he was afraid of condemning me to misfortune, so I kept repeating to him that there was no misfortune if he was by my side.

When the rays illuminated the surface of the earth, we would go for long walks, or perhaps just ride horses, enjoy nature, or throw the discus.

My hands that morning were asleep, I could tell. My arm had no strength whatsoever, which didn't surprise me either. Despite my increasing weakness caused by an uncomfortable sleep, my legs were still just as fast. Ergo, I did not hesitate at any time to propose it to him. He, with the eyes of heaven, accompanied by that golden hue, agreed. Always with a huge smile on his lips.

The sun was shining as it usually did when Apollo was with me. It seemed like the sphere was transmitting its own emotions. The Earth felt better than ever. The birds did not stop their almost angelic songs. It seemed that they wanted to surprise the god, since they knew who Phoebus was. His hair that day, curly, was bathed in the gold of the world in the early mornings. His gaze, little by little, recovered that golden tone that sometimes crept into his face. His clothes were perfect for such a beautiful body, but they did not last long in contact with his skin.

We took off our chitons.

His soft hands caressed my naked body, bathing it in some oils that my father had obtained relatively recently. After that, it was my turn.

Every part of his being was sculpted, shaped by the golden ratio that dictates what is perfect and what is not. His entire face, his back, his shoulders, his legs were built based on that damned number that was so sought after among intellectuals. They should have seen him. He was the number, but he was not mortal, which made the reason for his perfection understandable.

My hands covered every inch of his body as my soul observed everything. His energies enveloped me, while his voice recited words he had written himself. The verses flew, but I would risk saying that even what was silent, what was stuck in his mind, also flew, because it was sung by the birds that followed him like the sheep follows the shepherd. As the horse follows the rider.

And the humans were hypnotized. That's right, there was nothing that surprised more than a god before the mortal gaze. There he was, a god, smiling at me as he waited for me to throw the bronze discus at him.

My throw wasn't bad, it was actually fairly straight. Apollo advanced towards it, taking it easily in his hands. He seemed to have a magnet for these.

'You've improved a lot.' He yelled at me from a distance.

I smiled, as I always did. I couldn't remove that expression from my face when I was next to him. I was aware that he knew I had heard him, so I didn't say anything.

His throw, however, was perfect. I hardly had to move, because it always went right to my hands. Sometimes he would throw it less close to me, to make me work, but that first one was terribly perfect.

I also grabbed it with ease, a simplicity that did not seem possible at first glance.

My fingers were positioned just right, and with a slight twist of my wrist, the puck flew toward Phoebus again.

I noticed that the sun looked like a mirage, giving the impression that this was the one I was playing with and not the one in the sky. Somehow, my instincts weren't deceiving me.

The first throws passed like this, until the one arrived that would mark the fate that the Moiras had woven:

Apollo threw the discus with force, but a wind made it unable to advance as much as other times, so launching into a race, I headed towards the object made of pure forged bronze.

As I was about to jump to catch it, a wind blew intensely crept into my thoughts, which dishevelled my messy hair even more. It was a wind that did not bring me a good omen. I knew it right away, as soon as I felt it.

It brought me a clear message from which I could not escape, even knowing it because, having jumped for the discus, it fell prematurely, slipping between my hands due to the shock, to the impact caused by the images that had suddenly been unleashed in my mind.

I saw how the discus hurt me before it happened, but when I woke up from that revery, it was happening.

Among the red rivers that flowed from my head, accompanied by the intense pain, the ringing that flooded my ears, I managed to see a shining figure in the distance that was running towards me as if his life depended on it. Maybe it did, because I had always said that I would die without Apollo, but what would happen to him if he didn't have me? What if I died? What would happen to him, being immortal? I didn't want to know. I didn't answer my own questions either. The little flow of my thoughts, the little life I had left, was focused on him.

I felt him close, he murmured, trying to heal me, but even he understood that it was already too late.

I had not fled like Daphne. I hadn't rejected him like she had. I had loved him and would die accordingly.

I heard his cries. I could faintly feel his golden tears falling on my skin. They felt very far away. My eyes closed, hugging the *Ker* who was there. Soon I would find myself on the boat that would take me to my next stop, where the gods existed, but not the early morning sun.

Suddenly, as if it were a gift, I felt him behind my back. His strength called me. It was cold at first, then, as if the sun's rays embraced me. But I had already died, and nothing remained in me except a sigh accompanied by a memory of a life that had already passed.

Despite a little sigh for some whispers of songs at dawn accompanied by lyres that narrated the love that hosted me, the love that tried to heal me. Zephyrus took my breath away, Zephyrus changed the direction of the discus. This spilled my blood on the floor, but my heart would continue beating next to that of Phoebus, Apollo, which hurts from afar. So, I knew that Zephyrus had never loved me like Apollo had.

And in my universe, the one that was parallel, I would run in slow motion with Apollo. In such a place the lyres would never go out. His voice would not break. My blood would not be spilled. His tears would not flow. In that tiny universe we would be eternal. Both gods, both forever, infinite. He and I; me and him being as we always were. If I had to repeat history, I would do it again and again, because yes, love led me to death, but I knew true love, which I could not have found with any mortal.

I would die anyway, but I died having been by his side. Seeing his eyes, saying goodbye to the world with the beauty of his being.

Apollo, let me believe. Allow us to be, even when it hurts.

And, Hyacinthus having died in the arms of the god who had loved him so much, Apollo would follow his mortal soul to the end of eternity.

To Apollo

My god is not the Apollo that contemporaries paint. My Phoebus is the Apollo who once asked Heraclitus to write the key to balance in the universe, the god in which Plato placed so much importance: 'Know yourself and you will know the universe and the gods', showing us that the path only exists through the 'I Am.' The one who said that 'I can't force you to love me, just as you can't force me to stop.'

Apollo, the real one, is the one who tells me every day: 'You can do it, don't give up.' Apollo, true Apollo, is the one who knows that my words are not capable of describing even half of what he means for the cosmos, and for my soul, and still I try, because I want to do it, and I shouldn't give up.

Apollo, Phoebus, who hurts from afar, I write this introduction allowing the reader to enter the enormous, yet little corner of my soul, where your memories with me await, where the feelings discovered thanks to you escape. I open myself to the reader, and with me I open the door to your true identity.

You are not the narcissist that modern stories describe, nor am I Hyacinthus, the one with the purple gaze; you know well that I am a pulse that captures what the senses do not; how well you know who I really am. Well, you, Apollo, know every name I have ever had, every body, every goal... It is you, the one I saw for the first time when I came to this world. The sun shining in the most beautiful sky I could have ever imagined seeing. It was you, that voice that guided me in the darkest moments, and I praise you now that I am conscious again as I have always done when awake.

'When the war starts, I will be the best warrior.' I promised you.

You told me not to make promises I couldn't keep. Promises that perhaps would fade, taking me with them to the deepest hole of Tartarus where those souls who swore badly by Styx await. However, that is what I have been trying to do since the day I lived in this body from which I write to you; I realized that you were neither an illusion nor a dream, that you were far from fiction, becoming the most real being that I had known.

I realized that I could see you when I woke up, that I could hear your voice guiding me while accompanied by the notes of the zither. That you watched me from those stands, watching how my body threw poorly and caught well. And how you whispered in my ear songs of a thousand hopes while I was wounded, sick in bed from my premature death.

Sing to me, Muse, tell me perhaps, how can I write with words what my lips do not dare pronounce? Sing, Muse, my emotions dedicated to Phoebus in beautiful melodies. Sing, Muse, and remember that I am not Hyacinthus with the purple gaze, nor Daphne with the golden hair, but I am a spirit trapped in a time and in a body that little represents it; I am a spirit who dedicates the hours surprisingly granted to him, to my gods and their melodies.

Apollo, you who have saved me infinite times, I sing to you here tied to these four walls of bones and skin. I sing to you, looking into your eyes bathed in the gold of the rising sun. I sing to you as Homer before me did. I sing to you, and I follow you.

A thousand obstacles will be placed in my path, a thousand and one times I will overcome them, to follow your already laid out path. I am like Sappho, with a sweet relationship of union with Aphrodite.

Because today more than ever, with this body of mine, I walk alongside the most ancient deities.

I

We fall from above, and we fall without mattresses to collect our misfortune, but as long as the world continues, we have hope. I look at the ruins of the past and smile, because I know that one day millennia ago people remembered you. They loved you like you love them.

I hear you in the birds that sing your ballads, in the words, in the verses, in the arts and in the sciences, because these remind me of your friends, the magnificent muses, who accompany you full of clay flowers. And I sing to you from below thinking about whether one day you will stop listening to me. If one day, perhaps, you were lost in a different gaze, forgetting about those who sang to you even unconsciously, we would continue loving you, singing to you, trying to improve the world as you ask us to do. We, who are nothing more than souls in bodies, follow your advice, advice from the rising sun, from the invincible sun.

I know that you continue dancing, despite the sacrifices not received. I know that you still run in the woods from time to time with your beautiful sister. I know that you are still up high, playing the lyre, while you look at the mortal world, with a smile plastered on your beautiful face. One which is gifted in a thousand ways. I know that you continue shooting arrows, helping nature to spread pandemics, and when they come out of the laboratories, you are the one who illuminates other people's minds.

I know that you continue to heal those who caress your soul a little, as you healed me on several occasions. Tell me perhaps if I deserved your care... I didn't deserve any of it, because I am not perfect, and I cannot compare myself to a god. Least of all to you, even if people do so. I'm not perfect. I disobey you but, knowingly, you came to alleviate my torment. If you were as unfair as they say, would you do that? No, because humanity has dirtied your name. They don't know what it meant. They do not understand what you meant, and what you continue to mean to the souls of those who know you.

Oh, how could I tell you! I feel your presence in every moment of my life, if we are just luggage, you must be the car in which I find myself, because you are wisdom, light, truth, peace. Because you are everything a good person would look for, how can they not understand your meaning? Let them go back to the past and discover the greatness that you brought to Earth, let them go back to the past! Or that they listen to the universe that sings your name in chorus, without ceasing for even a second.

I could sing to you anything, my dear god. If only you could create the correct word, I would sing to you along with the universe during every second of my existence.

If only I knew how to express how perfect you are, I would. If only I could express to the mortals that your name, Apollo, does not designate atrocity or narcissism, but light and goodness.

If I could express how perfect you are, how magnificent the other gods are, I would sing and tell mortals that your names deserve different denotations that do justice to the beings who bear them.

II

Tell me, God, if I have lost my way on the moonless nights in which we were one. Tell me, God, if I have lost my way in the world of the lost. Tell me perhaps, dear Phoebus.

III

Trapped in my dreamy heart, you are buried among whispers. You let me discover the world you once presented to me, but you follow me in silence. You observe my soul endowed with sad stars, from the firmament. You hear my laughter, which from time to time escapes from lips belonging to various bodies. You hear my voice with different tones. My hair, a different colour every time, touching the sky. You also hear my cries, and you find yourself watching me waiting for the right moment. You see that I know your name, painted as a purely fictitious character in the place where, first Christianity, then science, predominates. You see that I know your name and that, from the first moment, despite hating the culture that surrounds it, I feel that there is something that escapes in a simple five letters, other times seven, that define a being that I once knew, but than now lies in the most hidden and dark place of my mind. A trunk that threatens to open, never to do so.

You feel the desperation sink me; the strength, lift me up. You listen to the threats, waiting for me to rise up like you taught me to do. That's how I always ended up doing it, with platinum, red or black hair. You wait for the restlessness to leave me, giving way to patience and wisdom. You stay close, but silent. You are silent because you wait for a moment, a moment that seems eternal to my unconscious.

You examine my guardians, those who are always with me. You know them, they know you too, could someone not know you?

You, who illuminate everyone with your songs and your immense wisdom. You, who are magnificence in its purest form; perfection embodied in a spirit that has not known bodily prison, but that, nevertheless, has suffered confusion, the oblivion of the beings it loved. You, Phoebus, who shine in the sky, accompanying the radiant Helios.

But, even examining them, you remain silent all the time. How long can a very wise soul that knows no time or limitations wait? An eternity, one, thousands, infinite lives... All bodies would die a thousand times, and you would continue waiting, oh! What is eighty mortal lives to you? A sigh. A sigh as it is for us on the higher planes.

But, Apollo, the time always comes. You taught me that and I should never forget it. There always comes a time when you deem it right. Then, you enter my life, ours, the Hellenes, the damned pagans, like the first ray of sunlight in a darkness that had lasted too long and that we did not even know. Like the first note of the beautiful zither, like the first song in all of history, in all of eternity... Like the first time we finally saw life.

What have I done, Phoebus, to deserve such a splendid opportunity that I don't even know how to take advantage of? What have I done, Phoebus, to deserve the best thing that has happened to me in too long?

A war, perhaps that is what I have done. A war inside my soul that woke me up quickly, trying to make me remember, but I still don't know when your gaze started fixating on me. Maybe it is new, from nowadays, from these times of pure science; or perhaps it is from that time in the year 500 of the time of heresy where I saw myself observing a temple, next to the beautiful Aegean. Or perhaps, in the life of the square and the man who was talking. Or maybe, the games I witnessed... Maybe it's from 2500 BC, when my arm was intertwined with another's... That is if all these are not, perhaps, moments of the same life, lost in Ancient Greece, in the year 3000 BC.

I sing to you, Phoebus, no matter where you follow me from, or why. I sing to you, Phoebus, Apollo, because I do not know any being like you, because all the gods are magnificent, but they are all different. What I find in you is not the motherhood that I find in Hera, it is not the strength that is in her, it is not the skill of Hele, or anything like that, it's something different from everyone else, just as they tell me something different from what you sing to me.

I sing to you, Apollo, for your lessons and your presence in my life. I sing to you, Apollo, even when I have erred a thousand times under your presence. Because I am a mortal above all, and I don't know how to be myself all the time, since the misfortune that I have to face, that I have to suffer, also weighs on me.

IV

The eternal rays sneak through my window. The slits on the blinds can do little against the decision of a star that is more than just that.

We revolve around them and get lost, but we never stop to think if they have an owner. If there is a spirit that, like the dryads tied to trees, is tied to them. Maybe there is more than one. I don't care, but there they are, the eternal rays, all the same.

They always caress my face without wanting to be discovered. Their timid touch makes me leave the cradle rocked by Morpheus, and Hypnos allows me to leave the world of dreams.

They illuminate the interior of my room, which is more like the cave that Plato described.

In front of my gaze, the shadows of reality; behind me, the truth. However, even if I want to, I cannot reach the world of ideas without an invitation. That's where the rays come in, getting rid of the blindfolds that cover and stain my eyes. My previously blinded sight can finally see.

The memories of the past, the stories that I had always been told, were intertwined with my reality: they were all real and I was deceived.

His voice served as my guide; his hands, as unconditional support; his energies were the strength I lacked, and murmuring to me incessantly made me move forward, against the host of my fears, and the nightmares of those who surround me. Against my prejudice, and the disappointment in humans that soon flood my body, taking its full control, snatching it from my own fingers. There he was then, taking the reins, and giving them back to me. Whispering to me in turn, not to waste time in lost battles, to fight in those that are destined to be won or to teach me a lesson, but above all, to live.

I shouldn't waste my life, now that I had managed to live one. He would not allow me to suffer from sad melancholies that he could not fix.

With my heart well kept between his fingers, he looked into my eyes, showing me through them the realities unknown to me.

I immersed myself in two balls of fire, which were caressed by medicine, the arts and a thousand other things that I did not even understand, but if something surrounded my being, it was the light that such a deity gave off.

A light rich in melodies, that sang and sang, filling my being with divine hope.

A light that, like fire, advanced through my inner being, like the cunning Greek warriors who defeated the invincible city. And I, then, whispered thanks that escaped not only from my lips, but from my fingers, from my complexion, from my own soul.

With my heart safely between his fingers, my life began.

And this radiance resumed, alongside the many other lives in which, whether awake or not, I had walked alongside the gods.

At his side, with his hand, Phoebus guided me through all the stars, through every corner of the cosmos, making me aware of so many things that I would swear I would get lost if I didn't have him at my side at every moment.

In front of the mirror in which I once looked at myself, the mirror of the sun, I recited the same winged words that my lips had uttered in ancient times:

'Take my body, which no longer belongs to me, since it is not part of me, nor part of the world. It is part of contemporary society to which I resign myself.'

'Take my heart, which only beats now for one reason.'

'Take my soul, what good is a soul that only follows you? What good is a lost soul who only says one word! A word that is your name over and over again! Name forgotten in time.'

'What good is my life if I can't dedicate it to one of the most perfect creatures?'

'What is the point of living if it is not for you and with you? Oh, *meus carus deus*, who saved me from the gloom! I carry you in my soul, the one whose existence is dedicated to you; because I have lost a thousand important things, and dear to my spirit, by not deviating from the most archaic and true path along which my feet have ever guided me. The path that parted from archaic Greece, saying goodbye to your lips, your eyes, your faces of a thousand different shapes, your fantastic deity essence, your enormous energy, which makes me feel reduced to what humans truly are: a grain of sand in the beach of the world. Thus, taking away my being, the common human ego that only serves to blind and harass other creatures.'

'From your presence, I walked away from that Greece that I remember so poorly, between ominous memories that from time to time, make a presence in my mind, passing through France, Ireland, Scotland, Norway and now, Spain. Because I look at you from so far away, and I observe the path that I have always travelled with the same objective. Without being aware of it, I was looking for you and I *am* looking for you. Without being aware of it, I heard something beautiful in the name that thousands cited to me: *Apollo, Phoebus, a Greek god, a fictitious being*. They called him *fictitious* and it seemed like an insult to me, but I didn't give it importance, how could I know that even silently and unknowingly, I was singing to you from the deepest and most hidden part of my soul? It would never have occurred to me that I loved you even without remembering you. Even now it's hard for me to admit it:

'My heart beats for you. If I don't die it is because of you, and when I do, I will move the entire earth to get to where you are, so I can sing something to you that reaches your soul, as a way of gratitude for everything that has happened in my past lives.

'Because you gave me a new opportunity to live, because what runs through my veins has never been blood. It has always been ink composed of emotions. Now it is an ink that only art knows how to use, and art is you, Apollo. Art is you.'

V

I can't stop mumbling it. I can't stop thinking about it. It is a feeling that consumes me on nights when the moon is not in the sky. It is a turn to my heart when the eternal rays appear, taking me out of the darkest shadows that I have ever had the misfortune to find.

It's a voice. A heavenly voice that sneaks through my disordered thoughts, pushing me to a time that I barely remember. It has remained stuck in my mind, and my memories from then do not return, nor do they think about doing so. But what I do feel are the emotions experienced, because I notice these in my heart, and my eyes that act as mirrors where my soul is protected away from the limits, from bodies and from times, being.

And you are in front of my soul, before my eyes, looking at me with a light of a thousand stars, whispering to me incessantly that I can do well. And I answer you in silence, that I couldn't do anything without having your breath nearby. And you, creature of unknown limitations, cross the threshold of thought, telling me how perfect I am despite any defect, but I am only perfect when I remember you.

When I remember you on the eternal altars, in beautiful Greece and in beautiful Lemuria, surrounded by ancient times. Refilled with past joys, sacrifices and wars fought. When I remember you by my side, I wake up.

I am not perfect, but if I can be, it is with you among my memories. I no longer fear losing myself; I now fear losing you. Because now I am afraid to forget you as I have done on several occasions. However, I always dare to return to you, because of a murmur in my soul or due to your voice, which, endowed with a thousand colours, speaks to me.

If I work it is for eleven souls, because if I have to please someone, it is eleven souls: mine, yours and your muses.

Mine since it is me, and I am the only being that will not move away and whom I will not forget because I exist; yours, for being art and magnificence in its purest state, for being light, sun, a future that I have seen from an early age; and your muses, for being harmony. I am a spirit that only serves two things: himself and the art that is composed of the harmony of the universe. Ergo, if you are art and your muses are harmony, I am yours without knowing it. But you do not desire slaves nor followers. You want lovers. Lovers like my soul that prays every day, every hour, every second to a single force: art, writing, things that transport me to the place where I belong. Because with a pen and your verses, dear Phoebus, and the inspiration of your muses, I write words that reach the soul and transport you to other worlds. And they transport us to our past, the one in which they sang to you from day to nightfall, and from dusk to dawn.

Because Eos, the one with the pink fingers, split Uranus, and from that moment, humans sang to you and to your entire blessed caste. Because I am a pagan child, trapped in a little body that grows and grows, without asking him for permission. Because I am a child of the 2500 in the era of heresy who sings for your verses, because I am that little boy who is in front of your temple, thinking about whether to abandon everything to join you; because I am that young man who looks at you from a distance, who hears your call and cannot reject it. A little boy with blue lights who hears your name and feels love in his soul, and a very light turn of his poor little heart that beats and beats for no apparent reason, but which truly wants to join your guard.

I was once a young boy looking at your temple, battered by the winds, and surrounded by the Aegean, there in distant Delos, the land of your birth. The same one that gave a great gift to the beautiful Leto. I am still that young man who, after hearing your call in another's body, stands in front of the ruins of an ancient temple, believing that, with his fingers touching the stone, he will be able to travel in time.

I am a young man with curly hair, who looks at you from afar, and has always loved you, but without knowing it.

I am a young man who awakens again, asking you to never stop being eternal.

I am a young man who awakens again, wishing that the human world hears your verses once more.

VI

I hear you in every note, in every step, in every tree, in the plants, in art and in the sun. I hear you in the scrolls I read. Also in my dreams, on the paths I frequent, when I lie lost, sleepy. In the past of my body, in my soul and its eternal home.

I listen to you when I'm in danger. You take care of me, you watch over me, and I, without wanting it, love you.

I love you without wanting it, turning my devotion into feeling, because life is a dream; the memories, the past of the heart. Without wanting it, I love you.

If I dare to get lost, I find a hyacinth that shows me the way home. I look up then, and right there I see the laurel of glorious victory. Your eyes in my mind, fresh as if they were in front of me again.

Your face shines, your smile immense. I love you without wanting it. I love you without knowing it.

I know that the path will be the right one, because you look at me from Olympus, from your chariot and its golden horses.

VII

<u>Romance to Phoebus</u>

The mysteries of yesterday,

they ignore our world,

secrets are lost

between the waters of the river.

So I look at the sky,

between the birds and the beak,

where you hide safely,

between a thousand and one sighs.

Hidden from the mortal eye,

in the prison of the eternal

you look from the firmament,

the root of memory.

In your golden chariot you see

suffering rise,

among the melancholies

of the beautiful thought.

Our dark and fragile

feeling halts,

as what we know,

without believing it, we forget it.

Caught in the breezes

from the darkest sky

where you reign hidden,

with the face between stars

and a heart of times.

But I look at the sky,

among the cross of shadows,

and I sing to you as before:

Where are you, dear Phoebus,

you with the most beautiful face,

and very long hair?

Where are you, dear Phoebus?

I look for you in the shadows,

blinded, and I can't find you!

In: *Tamen nunc ego te amo*

In the cold breezes I find you

in the music notes,

and the chords well played

on the bow and arrows,

in the cure of the sick

and in the faith of the healer,

among the skilful manuscript

and in the beautiful liquid ink,

that engraves on the parchment

between cloud and *Sol Invictus*

sun and arduous vile hell.

In the bronze discus,

captured by a young man.

Amongst art and dreams,

between the real and the eternal

between all this and all that

in the city of verse,

it is the place where lives

Your eternal teacher soul.

I wait for you on Earth,

in ashes consumed

now my blood is ink;

my eyes, clear stars.

I wait for you hopefully,

with my Helen heart,

gnawed by steel.

The Moiras weave fates

and I sing with a sad voice,

will the world realize

that without Timbreo we die?

Will the world realize

that what's Olympic is true?

Let the winds be silent!

They drag petty verses,

let the winds be silent!

The green hues

full of vile lamentation

may souls divulge then,

the glory of the times.

I know well that you are there,

hidden from the mortal human,

singing when I'm silent,

laughing if I smile,

dancing if I dance,

healing me if I get sick,

guiding if I die,

saving me if I fall.

And there I have your soul

very close to my verses.

Amongst infinite words,

I find your presence.

Us facing the fire

of the strange, imposed fate.

Our yesteryear as a weapon,

we know that we will live

always united by

the glory of the times.

Nunc I sing to you in the name of

knowledge lived in the eternal

Apollo, Phoebus of the light,

I write for you only

from the ancient temple,

and from the modern altar.

My self with Helen skin,

and the one of Hispanic origin

dedicate his hands to you.

And my cold heart,

dedicates its heartbeat to you,

who hurts from afar

dear eternal god.

Notes from the Romance to Phoebus:

Nunc: Latin for "now."

Tamen nunc ego te amo: From the latin "however, I love you now", alluding to the hatred of anything Hellenic the writer used to have.

Acknowledgements

I thank my ancient languages teacher, Lorena, for showing us the beauty of that period. I must admit, I hadn't thought about thanking you, but right now, the voices of the Olympians have asked me to do so. So, thank you, Lorena, for inspiring us and fighting to keep the flame of the past alive.

I thank the muses for inspiring me in the narrative of a life that was already lived.

I also thank the true Hyacinthus for fighting for his dreams, for following his heart, even when logic imposed the opposite. You are an example for my spirit, you already know that.

I thank the true Tamyris who has walked by my side for too long: you're the most important mirror of my existence. Thank you for sharing your lives with me.

I mainly thank the real Phoebus, the one who appeared in my life, showing me how much light there was in the universe. The one who, without even following his advice, continued to enlighten me. I was once told that my writing seemed kissed by a god, by the god of the arts. I know they were not my words, but yours. They are always yours, even if I take the credit.

Finally, I thank the reader for having come this far, and I take the opportunity to tell them that, in reality, life is simpler than it seems, that we are worth it even if we are told otherwise, that we deserve to be in harmony with the cosmos, and that hate is a destructive force that all of us can banish, if we risk embracing love. I do not believe, but actually know, that this lesson can be channelled through this work.

To eradicate hate and give way to what is golden, we just need to love, love each other, know each other. We just have to understand that the key to happiness is not found outside of us. It is not found in something foreign, but rather it lies within us:

'Know yourself and you will know the universe and the gods.'

Special Acknowdlegements (English Edition)

Special thanks to my translation team, Ybernia SC, without them this could not have been possible. In case you wanna work with a professional publisher, this one is your best option.

Thanks to my beta readers, who read a weaker version of this manuscript, and to my ARCs: Lou, Jennifer Günther, Michael Dunlop, Bentini Matilde, Sara Pereira, and all the others who have preferred to remain anonymous. Without you, this would not be possible.

And a huge thanks to a fellow writer, Nerea Díaz Martos, for helping us fixing our issues with the cover. Without her, our book would not have been possible.

For those who were waiting for it to come out earlier, thanks for your comprehension. My apologies.

Letter to the reader

Many thanks to the readers for the support provided in the Spanish edition of the work. I hope this edition is much more to your liking.

I wanted to take advantage of this new edition to tell you that new books are coming soon, very similar to the one you just read. While Hyacinthus's story has ended, there are some characters we can still dive deeper into. Stay tuned to my social networks to find out!

Once again, it has been a dream to see how readers have embraced Hyacinthus online. You are the best!

Lastly, take a break from time to time. The world is becoming a little darker than it used to be, but I have faith that we have enough power to restore peace to this beautiful place. Trust yourselves. You are enough. You are perfect. Stay calm when you see that things are getting complicated. Breathe. Sometimes we just need to keep breathing. The sun will always welcome us to a new day. Trust and take the risk to live, to truly live. Be who you truly are, and if you need anything, you know that my private messages are always open.

Liam.

Instagram: @l.alarconmiguel

Tik Tok: @l.alarcon

About the Author

Liam Alarcón Miguel (L.Alarcón Miguel) is a Spanish writer who began writing professionally at the age of eight.

At the age of nine, he had already written his literary debut *Rhindanos El Retorno de la Oscuridad* (The Return of Darkness). He currently has over thirty completed works.

At present, he holds a degree in parapsychology from the University of Edinburgh (one of his great passions). He graduated from humanities (Ancient Greek and Latin included) where he started to love the ancient Greece world. After some time trying to learn about new cultures, he immerses himself in history and politics while his eyes look to a future in which the focus of his life is his books.

Made in United States
Orlando, FL
10 June 2025

61994944R00268